THE DOCTOR'S CONFESSION

OTHER BOOKS BY ELIZABETH SEIFERT

THE DOCTOR'S CONFESSION

By Elizabeth Seifert

DODD, MEAD & COMPANY

NEW YORK

Library of Congress Catalog Card Number: 68-31334

Printed in the United States of America
by Vail-Ballou Press, Inc., Binghamton, N.Y.

For
Ruth and Will Fleming

THE DOCTOR'S CONFESSION

ONE

"If i had a larger house," thought Phoebe, "would there be only a larger mess? Or could I organize things better?" One of her "lists" in hand, she stood in the middle of the living room and turned to survey the "mess" which she already had—two foot lockers, open, half-packed; the sleeping bags, rolled—

"Linda," she called, "did you put your pajamas in the sleeping bag?"

Linda answered something unintelligible from the bathroom at the end of the hall. But her mother, from long training, understood what the girl had said. "Don't open the rolls again," she said automatically.

She went to the kitchen and picked up her coffee cup. The telephone rang and she answered it, smiling at both girls who appeared in the hall doorway. Linda was half-dressed. Mary had only that minute tumbled out of bed, her yellow hair a bird's nest. Phoebe waved her cup at them. It was one of the mothers. . . .

She listened, she talked, she listened again. "I think we'll make it, Jane," she said with more confidence in her tone than she felt in her mind. "I believe it is normal to be in this sort of a whirl twenty-four hours before takeoff. Yes, call me again—but not until after five. What? Oh, yes, I have to work. Poor Dr. Sam couldn't possibly get along without me for more than half a week."

She hung up, set her coffee cup down, and picked up the list. "She forgot to get Jenny's t-shirts," she told the girls.

"Oh, my gosh!" cried Linda, professing to fall back against the door.

"I told her Penney's had lots of shirts," said Phoebe. "Now, let's see." She lifted her voice. "Mary, you should be dressed and eating your breakfast. Yes, you do too want some. Now, you girls listen."

She went into the short hallway where she could see Mary in the bedroom which she shared with her sister, and also keep an eye on Linda, who wanted to turn on the TV set, and would turn it on the minute Phoebe left the house.

"Josie will be here, of course, and will do the washing. Linda, you can iron the blouses. And do them well, or they will have to be done again. Don't put a thing into the trunks—or take anything out, for Pete's sake!—until I get home. We'll finish up tonight."

She sighed, gave herself a little shake, and went into her bedroom. It was a hot day, and she had a million jobs to do—small and not so small. The girls' things must be packed—six weeks in camp meant a *lot* of gear! She must scramble together some things of her own for her four-day trip. After work, she would finish the packing, set the house in order—Josie would not be coming while the girls were away. Phoebe could save that expense! And certainly take care of herself.

She smoothed her thick, taffy-golden hair and put on lipstick. The girls were talking like magpies—yackety-yack—but of course this excitement was part of the fun of going to camp.

The telephone rang again, the clock's hands raced around the dial, Mary and Linda quarreled fiercely, Phoebe said, "*Stop it!*" sharply, and the girls stopped.

Josie came in through the garage, and she was grumpy. That figured. She always was grumpy when, under pressure, things got hectic. Phoebe ignored her. She said she must start for the hospital. Did Josie understand? Mrs. Flowers had left a schedule on the board as usual. Sandwiches for lunch, and milk shakes. Would Josie please change the beds, then wash up everything in the hamper, as well as the sheets? Linda was going to iron the girls' blouses.

"But you might do my green chambray. Please?" said Phoebe, halfway through the door into the garage. "I have to run."

"Yes, ma'am," said Josie, putting two slices of bread into

the toaster. Phoebe could only guess how much time Josie took to eat her breakfast—toast and two Cokes.

It didn't matter, just so she got things done. Maid-sitters were not easily come by and, grumpy or not, Josie was dependable.

"The girls gonna be gone six weeks?" she asked.

"That's right. But I'll be home on Tuesday sometime. You said you wanted the six weeks off."

"Yes, ma'am, I do. I'm gonna see my sister in Cleveland, and git my own house cleaned up, and do some canning."

"All right, then," said Phoebe, getting into the car. " 'Bye, girls," she called. "Be good." She started the engine.

She must go to the bank that noon for money. Traveler's checks—would twenty-five in her own cash be enough? There would be the five girls to feed lunch, dinner, breakfast, snacks—one night at the motel. The other parents were paying, of course. In fact, for driving the girls up, they would pay the entire cost, except for the wear and tear on the car . . . and on Phoebe.

Well, she'd make the trip fun, and not worry. The drive to Wisconsin would be a real adventure. Going up might be rough with five chattering girls . . . Coming home alone, Phoebe could take her time and enjoy the break.

She pulled into the parking space behind the hospital, picked up her purse and her list, locked the car door as she got out, and then she walked across the lot, a slender young woman in a red skirt and a red and white striped blouse. She had nice legs, and the sun struck sparks from her yellow hair.

"Hot!" said Phoebe, coming into the hospital lobby. She pulled her card and waved through the glass window at the kitchen personnel. The porter watched her appreciatively as she pushed through into the corridor and went toward the desk to pick up Dr. Green's mail. Dr. Green had the best secretary in the hospital. Miz Flowers was nice-looking, and a *nice* person! Some man was going to marry her, sure, and then—who knew . . . ?

Phoebe picked up the doctor's mail. For her, there was only one doctor, the surgeon of this small, excellent hospital. She arranged the stack—magazines, large envelopes on the bottom, smaller journals and letters next, on top she judiciously placed the boxes of pharmaceutical samples. Picking up the edifice, she held the whole thing secure with her pretty round chin.

Down along the corridor, through the heavy glass doors, and finally into Dr. Green's waiting room—her phone was ringing.

Not ringing. The phones in the doctors' offices were geared with musical chimes. Four notes for Dr. Sam— Phoebe spilled the mail across her desk and leaned over to take the phone.

"Dr. Green's office. Oh, *Woody!* I've just come in! No, I am not late! Let me look at the schedule . . . Yes, he's operating. You should keep your own list. Of course he'll want the plates."

Even as she talked, Dr. Green's secretary slid into the desk chair, and her free hand began to sort the mail. Some

5

things Dr. Sam would want to see, some—

Within five minutes, Phoebe was hard at work, her eye on the clock. By the schedule, the doctor would be in o.r. until ten or so—he had no appointments until eleven. Between, he would either dictate or call her to make rounds with him. . . .

She handled the mail, she carried to the inner office the items which her experience told her would interest the surgeon and require his attention. She straightened things there to his known liking. Returning, she answered the telephone, made appointments, answered a question—she set out the forms waiting to be filled out. Insurance, Medicare—there were always forms, always paper work. Her typewriter rattled busily; the doctor's day schedule began to fill, and the next day's—

Did Dr. Sam remember that she would be gone for four days? She must get her substitute in here for an hour or so—

Two walk-in patients showed up. One elected to wait, the other got an appointment for the afternoon. Phoebe again bent over her typewriter. She must *not* leave unfinished business for the other girl; she was beginning to listen for Dr. Sam's buzzer when she heard Sharon, the internist's secretary, greet Charles Reid.

Phoebe stifled a groan. Not today! She just did not have time! Why did he have to drop in? Well, maybe then he wouldn't come to the house tonight. Phoebe certainly would not have time for him then!

It wasn't that Charles was not a nice guy. He was! And

ordinarily Phoebe was glad to have such a nice guy interested in her. Phoebe liked Charles and had considered the man as a "possibility." That was the only word she had let herself use.

It was pleasant to have a friend like Charles, to be asked to a dance at the country club, to be taken to a concert at the university—but anything further—Phoebe, with two daughters and a job, had little time for anything more and, to be honest, no interest or time for anything approaching serious man-girl stuff.

She let herself glance up at Charles and flip a hand at him. He immediately came down to her end of the counter.

"Hi!" he said warmly. "How are you?"

"Busy," she answered, still typing.

He stood there, looking at her. She made a mistake, and she frowned. "I really *am* busy, Chuck," she said, reaching for her eraser, rolling the paper up, flipping the first page forward. "Go 'way, will you, please?"

He stood there.

The error corrected, Phoebe sighed deeply. "I'm sorry," she said, "but if you had a lick of sense, you'd know . . ." Then she smiled ruefully. "I'll start over," she offered. "I really am sorry." And she had just heard the sounds which indicated that Dr. Green had come into his private office. "But you know I am getting ready to take the girls to camp tomorrow. I don't want to leave things undone here. And at home—" She lifted her shoulders. "Besides," she said, in a desperate effort to justify her brusqueness, "I am

7

dreadfully upset today, because last night I had a most disturbing telephone call from my mother."

She heard Sharon's indrawn breath of sympathy. Charles Reid nodded. Everyone who knew Phoebe knew about her mother.

Even Dr. Green, who had overheard her conversation with "that newspaper fella," mentioned the call when Phoebe came in with her book and memos.

"What's the trouble with your mother now, Phoebe?" he asked.

Phobe smiled at him. "Now, how do you know . . . ?"

Dr. Green nodded and leaned back in his desk chair. He was a large man, bald and scrubbed-looking. "I heard you say something . . ."

"Talking too loud again, hummm?" asked Phoebe. "I'm sorry."

"I went into the passageway for a box of Wipes. That swinging door is open, top and bottom. What did she want this time, dear?"

For three years, Dr. Sam Green had been Phoebe's boss, mentor, and father-confessor. She did a good job as his secretary, and he appreciated her efficiency, her discretion, her friendly personality in his office. He had become genuinely interested in the young woman and in her problems as a pretty widow with two growing children, one of them slightly handicapped with a spinal condition.

One of Phoebe's problems, and a big one, the doctor thought, was her mother—a thin, ginger-haired woman in her fifties, Sam Green would judge, who alternated

8

between absurd claims upon her daughter and a declared independence from all claims that might be made upon the mother and grandmother. The time when Phoebe had bronchial pneumonia at Christmas—would the old bag come and stay with the kids? Or take them to her home? She would not. Friends had had to fill in.

"What did she want?" he asked again.

Phoebe sighed. "The same old thing," she said. "It was only that I was so busy, and to have her break in—"

"What did she want?" the doctor repeated sternly.

"Nothing specific. She was whining—and I know that sounds dreadful, but it is what she does. She has managed to make a mess of her own life, and now she whines about the results. Last night she even brought up the fact that her husband, my father, had left her. As if I weren't aware that he had. And do you know, doctor?" She leaned forward in her chair, her eyes dark and earnest. "There are times when I can understand *why* he walked out. But that was more than twenty-five years ago! Why hasn't she made a new life for herself? Why doesn't she do it now? She isn't old. Fifty-one, or two, I think. She must have friends. . . ."

"And she works, doesn't she?"

"Oh, yes, she has a job. A good one. It should be interesting, too. And I am sure she meets all sorts of interesting people. But, aside from that, she does have a family! In spite of all she says. She has two children—though of course we're scarcely children any longer. Richard is thirty; I'm two years older."

"And your brother is out of the country."

9

"Oh, yes. He's an engineer, and does things over in the Persian Gulf. Kuwait, Saudi Arabia—he moves around. He's doing quite well, I think. But instead of being proud of him, as she could be, Mother complains that he doesn't write. Just as she complains that I don't call her or come to the city. And we don't, I guess. Not often."

For a half minute, Phoebe sat, her head down, her pencil doodling on the top sheet of her tablet. "You see," she said then, glancing up at the doctor, "from the earliest I can remember, Dick and I have been on our own. We fixed our own breakfasts, went off to school, came home and did our homework, alone. We each worked our way, Dick through college, me through business school. I can quote you any number of discourses Mother made on that subject. We were individuals, she always said. We must work out our own problems. And we did! Entirely. She was not interested when I married. . . ."

"Didn't she like the man?"

"It wasn't a question of liking or not liking. She just didn't care."

"But again you did all right."

Phoebe smiled a little. "Yes. Except that when my young husband died, I realized that I shouldn't have had the children. But of course I did have them. When they were born, Mother began saying that I would find out how ungrateful one's children could be."

"Have they been?"

Phoebe leaned across the corner of the desk. "Ungrateful for what?" she asked. "For life? For the love I've given them, and enjoyed giving? For the fact that they have no father? Do you know, the way she acted when David was killed, I felt Mother was glad. And even disappointed that he left enough insurance to provide some security for the girls."

"And you."

"If that is needed, yes. But I hope to use the money to give them a good education, without the strain I knew. I can earn enough for the three of us to live comfortably. And we enjoy each other, we share interests. . . ."

"Like this camping expedition." The doctor was smiling.

"I've talked a lot about that, haven't I? And Mother's call was about that. I'd sent her a card, telling her that I was taking them up to camp and would be out of touch for a few days. And last night she called, saying that she thought, instead of going off to some camp in the woods, I should bring the girls to the city to see her, or she would come up here. Which she can do, of course, and I told her so. Not that she will come. She just went on and on about what we owed her."

"Do you owe her anything?"

Phoebe stole a glance at her wrist watch. Dr. Sam didn't have time to be so kind to her. "I suppose we do," she conceded. "But nothing that she would really want. Our presence bores her. I told her that she could come to see us at any time. And then, of course, I urged her to snap out of this mood, ιo get rid of the blues."

"Do you know why she has blues? I mean, could she need money?"

"Oh, no," Phoebe said readily. "She has a very good job. And my father provided for her, to some extent. Not enough, probably, but she has had the house, and I feel sure there was some kind of settlement. Not that Mother has ever talked about it, or about him, other than by inference. I suppose we do owe her something for the fact that she clothed, fed, and sheltered us, though I feel obliged to do that for my girls. Her situation and mine have been enough parallel that I am pretty sure money is not a problem with my mother. But she does have this kink in her character: she wants, or thinks it is possible, to live intimately within another's personality. When we were just little children, I remember her asking us what we dreamed about, how we felt when we sang in church, how food tasted on our tongues. And she would listen to our answers in a way . . . It was as if she tried to *feel* the things we felt. As if she wanted to crawl into our skins, and *be* us. And when she could not, she was hurt, and she would say that we were not good to her. But I decided that she was wrong, not us. She couldn't live our lives. No one can do that. I can't with Linda, or with Mary."

She broke off and laughed a little. "That Linda!" she said, shaking her head. "Just *try* to live her life! Oh, the girls. They have long, confiding talks with me which are surprising and wonderful. I believe we love each other. I hope so. Respect for one another's individual rights could be a large part of that love, too. But we are, each of us, individuals!"

"Was that your mother's trouble with your father? Her

probing into his personality?"

"I don't know, Dr. Green. It could have been. I was too young to remember him at all, and the things she says concerning him—judging from the way she talks about other people—I don't believe the picture is a true one."

"Where is he now?"

"I don't know. He could be dead, I suppose."

A telephone call interrupted, but, finished with that, the doctor returned to Phoebe's problem. He was a kind man, and interested in people. "Is your mother lonely?" he asked his secretary.

Phoebe considered this. "She need not be," she said thoughtfully. "She works in a big department store. She is called a coordinator. She deals with several departments, you see. Furniture, housewares, linens—I don't know too much about it. Except that she sees a lot of people, and she must have some friends connected with her work. Then, of course, she lives in a big city. She's lived there all her life, and her own family lives there. I mean, she has a couple of brothers, and sister. Of course—" Phoebe's shoulders lifted—"she doesn't get along with them either."

"Do you know these people? They'd be your uncles and your aunt. There might be cousins—"

"There are. But, no, I don't know them. I remember, one Christmas, we were invited—I took the telephone call. But Mother wouldn't let us go. She didn't say why. She just said, 'Of course we can't go there.'

"Still, I do have a few memories. There is one cousin,

Dick's age—Patrick. And Mother's sister, my aunt, always brought us a basket of Christmas cookies. They were delicious, but we didn' dare say so before Mother. She'd go into such a—such a *tantrum*, it was, really. And once I remember a man coming to our front door. He was very nicely dressed and wore a Homburg hat. I remember . . . But Mother had seen him through the glass of the door, or the window, or something, and she wouldn't answer his ring. She made Dick and me be very quiet, not even move. And of course he went away. It was a Sunday afternoon in the fall, with the sunlight very bright through the tree branches. I am sure that man was an uncle, and I still can see him silhouetted against the frosted glass of the door pane. His hat, his broad shoulders—he was tall. . . ."

Dr. Green picked up one of the papers on his desk and held it in his clean-scrubbed hand. "Could she come here and live with you and the girls?" he asked. "She'd not be lonely then, and she could help you care for the girls and for the house when you are away. . . ."

"No!" Phoebe's tone was sharp and definite. She heard the sharpness. But— Of course Dr. Sam did not know her mother, her notions, and moods. . . .

"No," she said again, and just as firmly.

Dr. Sam regarded her for another few seconds, then he bent his attention to his mail, to his reports. Phoebe's pencil flew across the page.

Finished with his dictation, she called his attention to his appointment list. He glanced up at her. "You are going to be away for the week end, I believe?"

She had told him that she would be; she had asked his approval before making any such plans . . .

"I'll be back Tuesday sometime," she said quietly. "One of the girls from the front office is going to help out here."

"They never know where anything is," the doctor complained, but good-naturedly. "Four days, eh?"

"Yes. I am driving my two girls and three others to this camp in Wisconsin. Jenny Martin, and Donna and Betty Winters."

"The little Martin girl is deaf, isn't she?"

"She has a hearing problem. But my Mary has her back to cope with. This camp takes such girls, though it is not one especially for handicapped children."

"Oh, Mary isn't that handicapped!"

"I know she isn't. But, still—"

"You want her watched."

"That's it. This camp takes allergies and such things into consideration, too."

"I see. And Mary wants to go? Even though she should not attempt long hikes—things like that?"

"Oh, yes, she wants to go. She told me last night that she was glad I was not sheltering her!"

The doctor laughed. "That should have been a reward."

"It was," Phoebe assured him.

TWO

THE WEATHER for the whole week end had been hot, and Monday offered no promise of relief. Hot weather made things difficult in a hospital. Even with air conditioning, the weather affected the patients and the personnel. The dietitian revised her menus, the doctors came in dressed casually. An office girl came to work in a slit-sided shift over brief shorts. Dr. Green said someone should speak to her. . . .

Outpatients called to break appointments, "I'll come in when it's cooler." On the other hand, there were more patients to handle. Old people "felt" the heat and suffered collapse. The need to cool one's body put an extra load on the heart. Children were hurt at the swimming pools—there was a case of food poisoning after a Sunday picnic.

"Summer is no time for vacations," grumbled one of the doctors, noting Phoebe Flowers' absence.

Phoebe's neat little green house was strangely quiet and deserted-looking. There was no bicycle in the driveway, no clogs on the front stoop, no excited chatter of little girls from the backyard. Inside, all was unbelievably tidy—beds made, no bottle caps or drinking straws on the counter by the sink, no radio, no TV—only the telephone ringing and ringing again.

At the hospital, the telephone rang, too. The strange girl in Dr. Green's office became a little wild-eyed. "I didn't know he'd be *this* busy!" she told Sharon.

"Oh, it's Monday morning. People begin the week by making appointments, and patients dismissed at the end of last week call in to check on things like a loose bandage or a cramp. . . ."

"That last one wanted to know if she could *wash!*"

Sharon laughed. "Doctors used to send home letters with their patients. I don't know why they've stopped doing that. Did you tell your patient she could wash?"

"I'm waiting to ask Dr. Green. I have two long-distance calls for him. There was a long-distance for Phoebe, too, earlier this morning. I said she was on vacation."

"She'll be back at work on Wednesday."

"I hope!"

By eleven, Dr. Green was out of surgery, and when next the phone rang the strange girl could, with relief, switch the call directly to him.

"My God, it's the police!" she whispered to Sharon.

"Hang up," said Sharon calmly. "Surgeons are always

getting calls from the police."

Which was true, but not calls such as Sam Green took that hot Monday morning. He barked into the phone, he said "Yes!" He listened. "Say that again!" he said sharply. It couldn't be. . . .

But it was. The voice in his ear was the firm, authoritative one of a Sergeant Floyd Jones of the homicide division of the St. Louis Police Department. He was, in his line of duty, seeking to locate one Mrs. David Flowers. Could Dr. Green help him?

But—*homicide?* Echoes of *Dragnet* interfered with the doctor's clear thinking. What had Phoebe . . . ?

"Well, I don't know," said the doctor. He didn't know. Phoebe was out on the highway somewhere—and he didn't know, either, if he wanted to tell this man, without knowing why. . . .

"Just why do you need to locate my secretary?" he asked crisply.

"Well, sir, it seems that Mrs. Flowers' mother—we think she must be her mother—died of a sudden and violent illness sometime last night."

Dr. Green frowned.

"We found Mrs. Flowers' name and the telephone number of your hospital in Mrs. Edwards' purse."

Edwards. Yes. Just a day or so ago, Phoebe had mentioned her mother's name. Julia Edwards. But—

Dr. Sam rubbed his free hand back over his bald head. He was perspiring.

The police sergeant went on to give details, and the listening doctor, shocked and unbelieving, still thought about the things which Phoebe had told him on Friday. Her mother was a whining, possessive woman—not in money difficulties—not lonely—but whining, complaining. . . .

She must have been ill. And Phoebe—*Dear God!* Poor Phoebe!

He told the policeman where Phoebe was, in a general sense. He would see what he could get together in the way of information—car license number, her itinerary. He would call back.

He got up from the desk feeling as if he'd been bludgeoned. He wished Phoebe need not be hurt by this thing. But, of course— He stuck his head around the swinging door and called to Sharon. "Will you come in here a moment, please?" he asked, as if he were regularly in the habit of asking Dr. Branch's secretary to come into his office.

She was surprised, but she rose at once, shaking her head at the supply girl.

"I've had a message for Phoebe," Dr. Green told her at once. "Her mother has died in St. Louis. I got an impression of suicide, though the word was not used. The police are trying to locate Phoebe. I thought you might know where—"

Sharon frowned. "Oh, dear. I can't even remember the name of the camp—it was in Wisconsin, but she would have started home—she was going to drive through

Illinois—I tell you! Charles Reid might know. He's Phoebe's boy friend. Or he'd like to be."

"Oh, yes. He works for the newspaper?"

"That's right. In the advertising department. Oh, Dr. Green, this will be terrible for Phoebe. Could it wait until she gets back?"

"The police don't like delays. . . ."

"No, I suppose not. But that poor girl, driving alone—I'll get Mr. Reid for you."

She did get him, and the dark-haired, personable young man came immediately to the hospital. Dr. Green was favorably impressed. Phoebe could quite reasonably . . .

He told Mr. Reid of the message which he had had. "I thought perhaps you would know—"

"We went over the road map together. I know the route she planned to take. But she didn't make reservations to stay at any particular place. We can get her car license number. Look!" He stood up. "Maybe I could start out, meet her— This thing's going to be a shock!"

"Sit down," said Dr. Green. "It will be a shock. But I don't think trying to meet her is a good idea. She's still in Wisconsin probably. You'd miss her. I'd say the thing would be to get her license number and alert the highway police. . . ."

Charles nodded. "Yes," he agreed. "That is the best way, and the quickest. I just thought if someone could be with her—"

"This will be a shock, though I don't believe she and her mother were close."

"Oh, they weren't. But maybe in that case— I'll get the license number and notify the police—"

"Get it and tell me. We'll let the city police send out the stop order."

When Phoebe thought about it afterward, and when she told a few people about it, being stopped by the state police was a startling thing to have happen to her. Afterward, she still could not believe it had happened. When she first heard the siren . . .

There she was, tooling along, thinking that she really should stop at the next restaurant. She had promised Chuck that she would stop every two hours—but getting off the freeway and back on it again always took so much doing. And she wasn't hungry. But—yes, she would watch for a place.

She heard the siren. In the mirror, she saw the police car coming up behind her. She saw the flasher going, but she did not dream it could be for her. She was driving in her own lane, five miles below limit. She— But there was the car and the trooper, pulling up alongside, gesturing to her to stop.

She lowered her window; the trooper did the same.

"Mrs. Flowers?" he asked.

"Yes . . ."

"Will you follow me to the next turnout?"

Well—of course she would follow him. What else did a person do? But *why?* She knew that she had done nothing illegal. Had someone identified her car mistakenly? No.

The man knew her name. Well, licenses— *The girls!* Something had happened at the camp! The girls—Mary, probably—left behind so happily last night— Phoebe felt her hands go wet; she leaned over the steering wheel in an effort to be calm. Oh, it could not be the girls!

She was in such a panic that she almost missed the signal given her by the police car in front of her. She jerked the wheel too far, straightened it, came to a stop—too close to the patrol car, but the man did not frown. She was out on the ground before he was.

"What's happened?" she demanded tensely.

"I—" the young man said. "There was a stop order for your car. An urgent message." He took out a notebook. "You are to call this number. A Dr. Green."

Her house had burned down! Or the camp had called home. . . . "Don't you know what it's *about?*" she asked tensely.

"No, ma'am, I don't. But I'll take you to the nearest telephone."

It wouldn't be far. Yards ahead of them was a cluster of buildings, a filling station—

Never once did Phoebe think of her mother! Afterward, she would feel guilty about that. The girls, her home—but never her mother.

The trooper stayed with her; he even supplied the coin and told the operator that this was a police call; he gave the number, then handed the telephone to the badly shaken woman.

The hospital answered, then Dr. Sam himself—he had

been waiting. Phoebe could lean against the strength in that slow, deep voice.

"Where are you?" he asked. "Is somebody with you?"

She told where she was, she told about the policeman in the wide-brimmed hat, she cried, "What's happened?"

Then he told her concisely, quietly.

And all Phoebe said was, "I can't go to St. Louis."

He was patient with her. "You must go, dear." And he repeated what he had told her. "You mother has died. Everything is waiting for you to get there. You're halfway already. I'd not try to make it tonight, but you should get there by around noon tomorrow."

"But, doctor . . ."

No grief, no expression of shock or sorrow—that would come later. Not then. Then, in that telephone booth outside a yellow stucco filling station, Phoebe argued with Dr. Sam about, of all things, clothes! "I can't go into the city! I'm here with a cotton suit and a small bag of dirty clothes. Oh, Dr. Sam, I was so afraid something had happened to the girls!"

"Well, it didn't. But something has happened to your mother, Phoebe. Do you understand me? She is dead, and you must get to the city and attend to things. If you don't think you could drive, get a plane or a train—the police will help you—"

"Oh, I can drive," she said brusquely. "It's just—"

"Forget about your clothes. I mean, you can buy anything you might need. I can have Sharon go to your house, pack some things and send them to you."

Yes. Sharon would and could do that if necessary. "I suppose I'd better go," she said wearily.

"Of course you had better go!" He would let Charles Reid take the bag to her. That young man would jump at the chance!

"If you'd tell me where to locate your brother . . ." Dr. Sam said to Phoebe.

"Oh, I'll send word to him. But he's halfway around the world, doctor. I'll let him know, but there's no need for him to come. When did—when did my mother die?"

She asked a few more questions, beginning, though still remotely, to grasp what had happened. A violent death meant—

Dr. Sam answered her as best he could, adding that she should call her uncle; he, too, had phoned the hospital.

Her *uncle!* "Which uncle?" she asked Dr. Sam.

"A Mr. Robert—hold on a minute—it's Robert Lewis. His phone number—"

"I'll call him after I get to the city. I'll go straight to Mother's house, I suppose." Though why should her Uncle Robert be called? He hadn't been interested in his sister when she was alive!

Phoebe told Dr. Sam the address and the telephone number of her mother's house. "I'll go there," she said, "and attend to things. The funeral—things like that. But I'll be back with you soon. This won't take more than a day or two."

Telephone in hand, Dr. Sam sat behind his wide desk and

shook his head. *He* would call Mr. Robert Lewis. The man had sounded capable, dignified, and pleasant. And Phoebe was due to learn a great many things in the next few days, even, maybe, that she loved her mother. She would need someone capable and pleasant.

"You are to stay as long as you are needed," the doctor said firmly. "The girls are at camp, and safely so—for six weeks, Sharon tells me."

"But you need me, too."

"Nonsense! You girls think we can't get along at all without you. But we can. Now you had better get on your way, Phoebe. Keep in touch with me. And call your uncle; your mother's family will want to help you."

Phoebe made no comment to this. She hung up the telephone; she thanked the policeman. Briefly, she told him what had happened. Yes, of course she could drive. Yes, she would stop somewhere for the night.

It was five o'clock when she went back to her car. She would drive for an hour or two, eat dinner, go to bed—

These things she did. Feeling tired and drained, but with her mind beginning to function, she did all those things. Not wanting to eat, she did eat. At the motel, she decided to take an aspirin or two when she was ready for bed. She would need to sleep more than she needed to think.

For an hour, though numbly, she lay thinking about her mother. Memories passed through her mind. Her mother washing her red hair, her mother reading in her bedroom on Christmas morning. Three days ago, her mother's voice on the telephone. "Why can't you come here, Phoebe?"

But finally she slept, and so deeply that it was later than she had planned when she awoke. In a flurry she rose, took a quick shower, debated the need for breakfast. Yes, she had better . . . and she should get gas.

Having attended to these matters, she again found herself driving along the endless freeway, a road map on the seat beside her. She wished she could make notes of things as she thought of them. Suddenly there seemed to be a dozen things for her to do. She would memorize the list—notes to the girls, a dark and decent dress for herself, a hat—

With still more than an hour to go, she stopped at a promising place for lunch. She ordered a sandwich and a glass of milk.

Yesterday at this time, she would not have said that, so soon after knowing that her mother was dead, she would miss the woman. She had thought, in the years of school and work and marriage, a home, children, and work again, that she had become a stranger to Julia Edwards, and Julia . . .

She had last heard her mother's voice four days ago. Julia had telephoned her, two nights before Phoebe must start for Wisconsin. "I am not well, Phoebe," she had said. "And you must know that a woman my age . . . I need you, Phoebe. More than you have ever realized."

Well—if there had been a need . . . If Phoebe could have done something for her mother . . . Evidently she had not been well. And Phoebe should have listened to her.

Maybe she could not have gone to her, what with needing to take the girls to camp—those arrangements were too fully made, the money paid out—there were the children to consider—but, still, if anything might have prevented . . .

Back in the car, ready to drive away, she saw a Western Union sign. Richard! She had forgotten to send that cable.

She went into the small shop-like building and told the man behind the counter what she wanted. Yes, he said, and pushed a form toward her. Phoebe wrote, she scratched out, she wrote again. Finally she achieved what would have to do.

"Mother dead. No need to come. Will attend to everything. Phoebe."

The man read it over, his impersonal, nasal voice making it sound as it probably would sound, or read, to Richard. Bald, unfeeling . . . But it would have to do.

She got back to the car and started off, the words of the cable in her ears. *Will attend to everything. Will attend to—*

What things "everything" would include, and whether she would attend to those things— Phoebe could feel her confidence drain away.

The city began to rise about her, the horizon hazy, the tall buildings silhouetted. The weather was still hot, the lawns looked burned, and the trees drooped. Which uncle was it who had called? Oh, yes, Uncle Robert. A lawyer,

27

Phoebe thought. One uncle was a doctor, and the other—

Of course she could have gone to the undertaker's. . . . Though which one? She might buy a newspaper and find out. Phoebe laughed a little grimly. To find out where her own mother was? But Phoebe did not know. She did not know where her mother had died. At home? In a hospital? And what was meant by the term "violent death"?

The Heights, where her mother lived, was a section known in the city as a "quiet neighborhood." It was an old one, with the houses, most of them, old, large, and respectable. Beginning in the eighties, Phoebe remembered being told, the houses had been built over a period of thirty years, high-ceilinged to carry off the heat of just such a day as this one, and ornately trimmed. Streets, trees, shrubbery —all were well maintained. Today a young woman in shorts and a pink overblouse walked a Dachshund along the parking area. Phoebe did not know her, of course.

Her mother's home would be empty. These days, no "crepe" or funeral spray would be hung beside the front door to signify a death. Phoebe had no key—her mother used to hide one in the bird bath. . . . She drove slowly along the street, past a square stucco house with dark green shutters, a pink brick house with limestone window trim and a shiny green tile roof, a turreted house, coming eventually to her own childhood home, also turreted. It was built of buff-colored brick, with bay windows, porches and balustrades; the railing at the front steps was of bronze, anchored in lead to the stone. Carefully, Phoebe turned her car into the drive; the lawn was neatly cut, the shrubbery trimmed. Many of the window shades were drawn. But her mother had been using only a small part of the large home.

Phoebe got out of the station wagon, realizing that she was tired from all the driving; she glanced at her suitcase, but took only her purse with her when she turned toward the house and stopped short in surprise. Coming out of the house was an attractive, middle-aged woman wearing a print dress. She was smiling a little. She came to the top of the steps.

"You are Phoebe?" she asked in a clear and pleasant voice. "I am your Aunt Dorothy. Come in, my dear."

THREE

ON THURSDAY, Phoebe Flowers sat at the desk in the sitting room of her mother's house and stared at the small portrait of a naval-type gentleman which hung on the wall. It had always hung there—her "always"—and she had no idea who the man might have been. There was a glass lamp on the desk, a bowl of flowers, and a telephone. The wood of the desk was red, rubbed to a fine glow, but it needed dusting. Phoebe got up, went into the kitchen, found a cloth, came back, and dusted the desk, the lamp and the telephone. Then she sat down again, ready to confess that she was tired and drained of all strength and will. Dispiritedly, she dialed the area code and the hospital number; she glanced at the clock. Dr. Sam should be in his office.

He was.

His big voice boomed in her ears, and she closed her eyes in a longing for the office and home. If only now she could be sitting across the corner of the desk from Dr. Sam, watching his fingers tent together as he talked to her.

"This is Phoebe, Dr. Green," she said in a small voice.

"Well, hello, Phoebe! How are you, my dear?"

"I—oh, I'm all right."

"Humph!" said the doctor, and Phoebe smiled.

"I called," she said quickly—she knew his time was valuable—"to tell you that I have decided I must stay here for a little time longer. I had thought I would be coming back—sooner."

"Well, of course you must stay," he told her. "As long as is necessary. Now tell me, really, how you are."

Phoebe sighed, and her hand brushed her hair back from her cheek. "Well," she said, "I don't know how I *really* am. I guess you would have to say that I am confused."

The doctor made a sound of commiseration. "There must have been many things to do," he agreed.

"Yes, there have been. And so many things to learn, to find out about, doctor. I had no idea! When David died, things went simply, and in order. But here—there have been delays. The coroner required an autopsy. I don't think, sometimes, that we'll ever be through with it all." Panic trembled in her voice.

"Do you need any of us?" asked the doctor calmly and kindly.

"Oh, no . . ."

"Mr. Reid told me he would go to the city . . ."

Phoebe nodded. Dr. Green was matchmaking for her again, and that could be a part of his kindness. "I don't think so," said Phoebe quickly. "Not just now, at any rate. But if you see him, you could thank him for the flowers he sent. They are roses—I have them in a bowl on the coffee table in here." Along with a stack of her mother's books and an unopened magazine. Her mother's sweater still hung over the arm of a chair. Really, if Phoebe was going to stay in this house, she should clean it up a little.

Dr. Green was saying for her not to worry about him or the hospital, but to keep in touch—

She said that she would, and she put the telephone back on its rest. She should have thanked him for the flowers which the hospital had sent to the funeral home. Well, she would. She thought of the funeral home and the people who had been there last night—people she had never seen before, and would never see again. Had those people really known her mother? Had she known them? There notably had been one man—he had introduced himself to her as "Julia's close friend." Had he been? He was a very thin man, with the brown skin of his face stretched tightly across the bones. His eyes were deep-set, burning, dark. His mouth—he talked all the time, in an urgent way. His clothing was rather too much in the way of elegance—his gray silk suit, the handkerchief in the pocket, his white shirt cuffs and the jeweled links showed below the sleeves of the coat. Oh, there was something about the man that Phoebe did not like! He had offered to do a dozen things for

32

her, but she felt he was too anxious to take over. Perhaps she was unfair, but just then she was waiting, watching— she had only thanked Mr. Rotan and told him that, yes, she would call on him.

But why should she ever need to?

She began to move about the room straightening things. The books would need to be returned to the library. She shook out her mother's sweater and folded it. She would put it on the stairs to take up to her mother's room.

This morning there had been a Requiem Eucharist service at the church which her mother had been attending. Phoebe, in her new blue suit and small veiled hat, had gone, in a daze, down to the front pew and had tried to follow the service. Had she done her part in it? She hoped so. There had been about fifty people in the church. Her mother's family all had been there. Aunt Dorothy, the two uncles, an aunt, and some cousins—even now Phoebe's mind could not identify each one. There had been a clergyman among the family group at the church, and later at the cemetery. Except for Aunt Dorothy, who certainly had been kind, Phoebe had made no real effort to identify these people. She had let them talk to her; she had said, "Thank you." But among them all, she had felt alone, as her mother, alive, had been alone. . . .

There were neighbors, too, at the church. One or two of these Phoebe did know. Not well. She had been away for a long time. Various people from the store came and spoke to her. They were strangers. The things they said about Julia—her mother, indeed, could have been a "fine" woman, a "wonderful" one. Phoebe had not known her either.

She had gone through the motions of doing what had to be done. Someone said she was being very brave.

She was not. This was an unpleasant task set for her to do. But how could Phoebe be brave, how could she grieve for a woman she did not know? Whom she had never known?

After the burial, Phoebe had asked to be allowed to come back to the house. Sitting beside her Uncle Howard, she had asked in a small, clear voice what was meant by the term "violent death." Had her mother been murdered?

Her uncle was shocked. "No!" he said loudly. "Oh, *no*, Phoebe!"

"But—"

"Yes. The term. Well, she died unattended. Unexpectedly. The coroner required . . ."

"Yes." Phoebe knew about that rule. And she said no more. She really did not want to be told that her mother had committed suicide.

Having reached the house, again assuring her uncle that she would be all right alone, carefully she had changed out of her new suit, and she had called Dr. Green. Now, quickly, she must get about disposing of her mother's affairs. Uncle Bob, the lawyer-uncle, was going to help her, tell her what must be done—and do a great deal of it for her. But Phoebe herself would need to go through the house. . . .

The bell of the side door rang, and Phoebe welcomed the

interruption. She did not want to think about cleaning this big house.

Standing in the shadows of the porch, she found a young woman who lived next door, Phoebe thought. She was a smiling, rather pretty woman, somewhere near Phoebe's age. In her hand was a covered plate which smelled heavenly of hot pastry, cinnamon, and sugar.

"I made this coffee cake," the visitor said. "I wondered if you had eaten any lunch . . ."

Phoebe stepped back to admit her caller. "It's very kind of you," she said shyly, leading the way to the garden room.

The neighbor looked around appreciatively. "I've never been in here," she said. "Mrs. Edwards was away so much. She didn't have time to neighbor, and I didn't know whether you'd want to neighbor either, but I thought—"

Phoebe took the covered plate. "I have some fresh coffee made," she said. "Will you share this with me?"

"I'd love to," said the young woman. "My name is Melba Spires, by the way."

Phoebe smiled at her. "Sit down," she said. "I'll get the coffee."

Melba Spires, she thought, was a pleasant, friendly person. Back home she would welcome and be nice to such a person. Whatever her mother's attitude, she could do the same here.

Quickly she arranged a tray and returned to the garden room. Melba stood where she had left her, staring up at the chandelier.

"I don't think my mother has washed those prisms recently," said Phoebe, filling the cups.

"It must be a chore."

"It is. I used to do it when I was a little girl."

"You live away from here, don't you?"

"Yes, and I work, so I haven't come home often. I'm a widow, you know, with two children. Girls."

"Then you do have your hands full."

Phoebe smiled faintly. "Your coffee cake is delicious," she said.

Mrs. Spires said again that she hadn't known if Phoebe would want to neighbor. "But I thought, what the heck? I'd do the right thing. Most of us here in the Heights *are* friendly."

Phoebe wondered just how unneighborly her mother had been. . . .

Her visitor answered her question. "Well, you see," she explained, "your mother worked."

"Yes," Phoebe agreed, "she did."

"Are you going to stay here?"

"Oh, I don't think so," said Phoebe quickly. Then she smiled a little. "But if I did—if I do—I'd have to work, too. As I said, I'm a widow. My husband was killed several years ago."

"Oh, that's tough. What sort of work do you do?"

Phoebe told her. Over a second cup of coffee and the coffee cake, they chatted in the friendliest fashion. Melba asked about the girls and Phoebe told her. Mary was twelve, she said. Linda, ten and a half. Mary was a little crippled—the doctors thought she must have had a mild case of polio as a baby. Now she was bothered with a weakness of her spine. "We are afraid of curvature, of course. I'm going to take her to a specialist this next year."

"Oh, I would. Linda . . . Is she all right?"

Phoebe laughed. "If she were any more so, I couldn't take it."

"You look too young to have children that old."

"I'm not. Mary was born when I was twenty."

"How have you managed working with two small children?"

"I live in a small town. I have what is called a maid-sitter. I don't know if this is done in other places. But I have Josie, who isn't really good, but she is reliable. She cleans the house, irons—and is in the house to look after the girls when I am not at home."

Melba had one boy, now sixteen. "Of course sitting is no problem for me any longer, but we do have a woman here who serves as block mother. She earns her living that way. She lives in that house with a stick-out round bay window, and she has an invalid mother. She takes care of children in the neighborhood who have to be left alone—like yours—after school, or if they have a cold and must be home for a day or so. She'll even care for them overnight."

"It sounds like a wonderful arrangement," said Phoebe warmly. "If her charges are reasonable."

"They are. And the whole thing works out well. Mrs. Haines earns some money, and the children are safe."

37

Mrs. Spires left, and Phoebe went into the big, dark kitchen to wash the plates, cups, and silver which the two women had used. Idly, not actively curious, she wandered through the rooms of the house, remembering them as they had been in her childhood, which was easy because nothing seemed to have been changed. This was an old house, and a handsome one. The furniture was made of fine woods, the carpets, the parquet floors, the stair rail—all spoke of wealth and taste, both perhaps departed.

This had been the family home of Phoebe's father. There were portraits, not marked, and she tried to remember the few things that her mother had said about the people who were depicted, but soon decided that she could not trust her memory. Her mother, really, had spoken seldom about her father or his family.

This big house, which still was fine, and had been very fine indeed when first built, was a part of Armand Heights, a neighborhood of fine homes. Close to the downtown business district, it should, by all sociological laws, have become a place of decay, a slum. Instead, the hundred homes formed a bastion of standards established and maintained.

In Armand Heights there was a covenant, a pact. One family only could occupy the one house permitted on each "lot." Rooms were not to be rented, not given over to various relatives of the established families. Anyone suspected of encroaching on the pact's rules could be, and was, hauled into court. Families as such were clearly defined. Phoebe thought eating breakfast together was one of the test points.

There were no racial restrictions in the covenant; the aim was only for peace, quiet, and residential elegance. Cash customers who bought into the Heights and were objectionable—noisy or untidy—were persuaded to change their ways. Barring that, ostracism usually brought on their departure. Phoebe remembered her mother talking about such measures, sometimes admiringly, sometimes wryly. Phoebe herself had decided that a solid front and constant vigilance had maintained the Heights from the encroachments of modernity. To remain a resident of the Heights, one went along with the rules. Julia wanted to stay in the big house, so she did the things required of her. The lawn was groomed, the shrubbery trimmed, the sidewalks swept, the big windows washed regularly, and the paint renewed. Inside the house—

Her interest livening, Phoebe wandered from room to room. The library-garden room, with its immense chandelier and its carpet of gros-point squares. The sitting room where the fireplace needed cleaning. The cluttered, dark living room; the dining room, large and handsome with scenic wallpaper and mahogany.

The house as Phoebe looked at it that day was both beautiful and hideous. And the message given to the young woman was of other women, other inhabitants than Julia Edwards. Julia had bought none of the various bits of bric-a-brac. Except for her sweater over a chair arm, she seemed to have added nothing of herself to the house. Nothing had changed essentially since Phoebe's childhood.

The draperies, the setting of the furniture, were all as she remembered them, and were as they had been, probably, since Julia had first come to the house as a bride. Had she actually never changed anything, even to replace a cushion or a set of window draperies? To Phoebe's touch, some of the hangings were fragile, even though protected by the closed blinds.

But there *must* have been renewal and change! Her mother had lived in this house for thirty-four years! She had come there as a bride. It was her husband's family home. Had that girl, Julia Lewis, been happy here? And the bridegroom—William—Bill Edwards—what of him? Raised in this house with all its associations, he still had walked out of it, turned his back on it, and on his wife and children. How could a man do such a thing?

Phoebe could not remember her father. Just the things which Julia had said about him, usually angry, sarcastic— bitter. He had walked out. He had given up his wife and his two small children—and his profession. But why? What had he exchanged for his home and family?

In this house, in a position of responsibility, Phoebe asked questions which had previously only been vaguely in her mind. Was her father now dead? Or alive somewhere? What was he doing? Did anyone know? Perhaps she should, perhaps she would, ask sometime. Someone.

She continued her tour. The whole hourse—twelve roms, she counted—was stuffed with furniture, bric-a-brac, cupboards, cabinets and bookshelves, dishes, books, papers, clothing. In the vaulted basement there were stacks of newspapers. Upstairs there were brown envelopes of old checks and old bills—silk scarves—gloves—even unopened Christmas gifts. "To grandmother, from Linda."

Between the kitchen and dining room, the cupboards of the high butler's pantry were crowded with dishes and silver. Curiously, Phoebe reached up and took down a gold-rimmed plate and found herself being showered with money.

Startled, she cried out a little, and looked down at the green bills scattered on the tiled floor. Feeling odd, she stooped to pick up the money; she stacked it neatly on the side of the soapstone sink. Her mother . . . ? She found a towel in a drawer and tied it around her waist for an apron. She mounted the small stepladder and began to move other dishes, working down to the cabinets under the counter. Curiosity and wonder driving her, she moved every dish and wrapped silver pitcher, teapot, footed vegetable dish—and she found more money. Her hands became grimy with the dust.

She went into the garden room to get a small wooden box which she remembered seeing on a table there. She put the money into it and stood both dismayed and thoughtful. Would she need to go through every shelf and drawer in this big house? Idly she opened the nearest drawer. There was no money there. But when she took down some books, money fell out from between the pages.

Oh, dear, oh, *dear!* How would she ever clear out this—this squirrel's nest! But of course it must be cleared out, and with money evidently scattered about, Phoebe

41

would have to be the one to do it. She counted what she had already found. It amounted to over two hundred dollars. Phoebe sighed. Who had hidden the money?

Her mother? Yes, certainly. But—*why?* Her mother was a business woman. Why had she done so unbusinesslike a thing as to—

Security. Phoebe knew the answer, or could guess it, because her knowledge of her mother—which she had thought to be exact—gave her the answer. The Julia Edwards whom her daughter knew had had one aim in life—and one fear. Both had had to do with security. Perhaps she had a bank account. But that would not be enough. Banks could fail—so Julia would hide a little money here. She would always have it in case she needed a dollar or two. And if one cache of money was good, another offered double security. Yes, there was the answer.

But how, how, *how* would Phoebe go over this house, and—? The task would be a staggering one and would take weeks—months even. And she wanted to go home soon to the familiarity of her small house, to her nine-to-four job at the hospital, to her friends.

She would go, too, of course, just as soon as she found a way to dispose of this house and its contents. She laughed a little hysterically, there in the garden room, dust swirling in the bands of sunshine which poured in through the long windows. The task before her was taking on the aspect of a monster, an octopus, always producing another waving arm of difficulty, of stricture, upon Phoebe's independence, strangling her emotionally—

She should not panic. The more she had to accomplish, the less good panic would do. That day, when the trooper had stopped her on the road and told her that her mother was dead, she had felt panic, but she had managed to do the things required of her, one thing at a time. She had driven here to the city. She had attended the funeral services for her mother, inwardly shaking, outwardly calm.

She had handled that awful Eugene Rotan. A lawyer, he said. He said, too, that he had been Julia's friend. Phoebe had never heard his name, and she immediately decided that she did not like the man. But she had managed to answer him when he spoke to her and, she hoped, had concealed her feelings. She would, she had agreed, call upon him if she needed to do so, but she had not ventured to look forward at all, nor to decide what she would do about him.

She had met the members of her mother's family in much the same way. One member at a time, one thing at a time. Aunt Dorothy's being in the house when she arrived, meeting Uncle Robert at the undertaker's, riding to the church with Uncle Howard. She had seen them, talked to them, and not allowed herself to decide anything about them, whether she would accept her mother's opinion of them or form her own judgment.

It was a large family, the adult members of it evidently prominent in the city. The newspaper articles about Julia's death, the things said to Phoebe at the funeral home and at the services told her of the importance of the Lewis

43

family—a situation which her mother had never mentioned. In fact, she had seldom spoken of her two brothers and her sister.

But there they were, *here* they were, for Phoebe to "handle"—or not—as she decided. Meanwhile she had not agreed to stay with any of them, not even for the first few nights. They knew she was standing aloof, and perhaps they knew, too, that she was not going to accept her mother's ideas without examination. Up to this minute, that was as far as Phoebe had gone.

She went into the downstairs lavatory and washed her hands and her face. Then she got an apple from the kitchen; her Cousin Patrick had brought a basket of fruit. She sat down in a corner of the fringed, green velvet couch in the garden room to eat the apple and to think about the "family," to attempt to sort them out.

There was, first and oldest, Uncle Howard—Dr. Howard Lewis, a surgeon, Phoebe thought. He was a slender man, well-dressed, with a tight, self-restrained face—not handsome exactly, but certainly distinguished-looking. Patrick was his son, a young man about Phoebe's age, and also "Dr. Lewis." He was handsome, tall, brown-skinned, with a small, neat mustache. There seemed to be no women in that family unit—so Uncle Howard could be ticketed as a widower and Patrick a bachelor. Was that right? It would do.

Next there was Uncle Robert Lewis, a brother younger than Julia. He, too, had a neatness of feature and of dress which seemed to characterize the whole clan. His hair was beginning to thin, and he wore half-lens, Ben Franklin glasses, and he was ready to be a kind and friendly. He was an attorney and well-blessed with a family of his own. His wife was "Aunt Katherine," a somewhat plump—pleasingly plump—woman with pretty dark hair and a friendly manner. Phoebe would be glad to like Aunt Katherine.

The third older man was a priest of the Episcopal church. He was Aunt Dorothy's husband, a very tall, Ichabod Crane sort of man. Quite kind—he had not conducted Julia's funeral service.

Aunt Dorothy was a sweet woman, shorter than her sister Julia had been, younger, and much prettier. She was ready to be as kind as Phoebe, as anyone, would let her be.

The children of the family—the young people, rather—were attractive, well-mannered, and exactly the sort of young folk Phoebe would like her girls to know. Would Linda and Mary stack up with them? Phoebe thought so. There was, in fact, a boy, Kirk, about their age. And Joanne, his older sister, would be about fifteen. She was a nice, freckle-faced girl—Phoebe liked her. And the older son in Uncle Bob's family was really handsome, with a shock of red-brown hair and a ruggedness to his chiseled face. He was Danny, still in college, but married. Phoebe had not met his wife.

So that made—how many? Phoebe's fingers counted the tally. Nine beside herself and the girls, all ready to help Phoebe.

But they were being careful, too. They watched her and

let her make the decisions. An offer from them was that only, for her to accept or reject. They would not push in.

And why should they? Why shouldn't they wait and see about Phoebe? If she should turn out to be like Julia . . .

Yes! And if the Lewises should prove to be what Julia had always declared *them* to be . . .

Were they that way?

Could Phoebe judge, even now? They had been kind, but had their kindness to her been more than that conventional show of good manners? Phoebe could put a little thought to that question.

Take Uncle Howard, called "Uncle Doc," even by the other adults. He had driven Phoebe to the church and to the cemetery. "Bill, your father," he had said to her, "was my friend." He had, Phoebe remembered, spoken of her mother as "poor Julia"—in a forgiving way, as if he wanted Phoebe to pity the dead.

Well, she did—in a way. That her mother had died alone. That Phoebe had not been the daughter her mother, probably, had needed.

She gave herself a little shake. She was going to move forward, she should remember, not back.

So she would go forward to think about Uncle Bob, the attorney. Not one, she judged, in the same class with the Rotan fellow. Her uncle seemed to be a kind person, with a dry wit. His children were loving to one another, his wife Katherine was a very nice person, or Phoebe was no judge.

This family was ready to be friendly and—yes!—kind. Evidently Julia had not kept in touch with them.

"There was no will?" Uncle Bob asked Phoebe.

"I don't know . . ." said Phoebe.

"There should be . . ." he said in a worried tone. "Everyone should leave a will."

But Phoebe's mother had not been "everyone." Had she possibly made a will through Rotan? Was Phoebe going to have to ask him? Wouldn't he already have produced it? As she thought these things, her Uncle Bob had been watching her keenly. He patted her shoulder. "But don't worry, my dear," he had said. "I'll help you, Phoebe, if you need help and want it."

Phoebe had made no answer beyond a faint "thank you." She knew that she would need help, and that, really, she wanted it. But her mother had hated Uncle Bob, and there must have been some reason.

Now she finished her apple and leaned forward to put the core into an ash tray. Then, she thought, there was Aunt Dorothy, who was a sweet and pretty little woman. Did those very qualities offend Julia? They could have. Hers was a bitter, resentful spirit, ingrown, and carpingly critical.

Her younger sister was a friendly soul, and energetic. She had wanted to help Phoebe, and had managed to do many things for the girl. She had volubly expressed her opinion of the big, dark basement—she had gone down there after her niece had said she must wash out some things. "We should mark a trail down here," Aunt

47

Dorothy had said. "Are you going to risk using that washing machine? It should be in a museum."

Phoebe's instinct was to like Aunt Dorothy. And her clergyman husband, too. The tall, thin man had a rare sense of humor, she had discovered. She had heard him rallying even dignified Uncle Howard. Evidently he did this often, because Aunt Katherine had protested. "Are you needling Uncle Doc again, Cecil?" she had asked.

Uncle Howard had not seemed to mind. Phoebe had seen him put his hand on the clerical shoulder as he walked away with his tall brother-in-law.

This Reverend Cecil Paule had not functioned at her mother's funeral mass, nor at the committal service. He had stood in the circle of family members, responding in unison with them—which seemed an odd situation to Phoebe. It must have seemed odd to her mother's friends and business associates. Had the family, as a whole, thought it odd? Or was there some reason?

Questions, questions, questions!

It seemed incredible that Phoebe should know so few answers. But her mother had never talked much about these brothers or her sister—not even when Phoebe still had lived in this house with Julia and Dick. Not at all, or scarcely ever, when Phoebe had returned to spend a week end here or when, infrequently, her mother had come to visit her and the girls. Those times were not many and had almost dwindled away entirely in later years.

When a sense of duty made Phoebe bring the children to see her mother, Julia had been an indifferent hostess. She

48

would offer Phoebe money. "Take them to the zoo or something." She would be too busy for more than a dinner at some restaurant. "I'll meet you at Hulling's. But I'll have to see some salespeople afterward. You and the girls could go to the movies." One didn't do much family gossiping under such circumstances.

So grandmother, uncles, the Lewis family had only remotely existed. Phoebe had grown up, even as a child, to think of her uncles and her aunt as enemies. To be avoided, if at all possible.

Had they been enemies? Julia's, perhaps. Or was it just her mother's unwillingness to engage in family relationships? And if they had been Julia's enemies, what had they done to create such a situation? Or—and this was more believable—what had Julia done?

Yes, that fitted into the jigsaw puzzle better. Because these people had gone out of their way to be kind to Phoebe, now that Julia was dead. They had, for one thing, not allowed her to stay alone at night in this big house. Aunt Dorothy had stayed the first night, Aunt Katherine another. Her cousin Patrick had offered to sleep this night on the couch in the sitting room. "Not that I would be of any help once I went to sleep," he warned Phoebe.

She had not needed them, but they had done these things. But from tonight she would stay alone. She wanted to, and she would—for the time it would take to go through her mother's things, dispose of the trash and the too-personal items, and make ready to sell the rest.

And, faced with this monumental task, she had better get

49

to work as of this minute!

Upstairs, downstairs, basement and third floor, where would she begin? A slender, big-eyed girl, she turned about, and about again, faced with the enormity of the task ahead of her. She was now in the garden room, and she might as well start right there. The books on the shelves, the cupboard, the window seat . . .

She climbed the ladder to reach the top shelves and looked into the jar in the arched space above them. Taking down book after book, shaking each one, she found to be a monotonous job. She was down to the third shelf when she was rewarded by a note written in her mother's hand.

"I do the best I can," wrote Julia Edwards on the back of an old laundry list, "but I don't seem able to communicate my best intentions."

Phoebe sighed and set the note to one side. The trouble with her mother's efforts to communicate, she reflected, had been Julia's unwillingness to let the other fellow state his position. She had always been that way. "Wear your blue sweater, Phoebe."

"But, Mother, I like my red one with this skirt."

"Don't argue. Do as I say."

Phoebe sighed again and moved to a lower shelf. There were four of these tall book shelves, one in each corner of the room. The books were dusty, the pages yellowed.

It was a laborious task, marked with varied interruptions. A neighbor paid a call, a woman crisp in a monogramed linen dress, with short white gloves sparkling upon her hands. Phoebe, feeling gritty, unhappily talked to her.

Again, she could only say that her plans were indefinite—and they were!

Twice the telephone rang—Aunt Dorothy called to confirm that Phoebe really did want to stay alone. And a real estate agent asked if the house would be for sale.

In between, Phoebe worked, finding some more money. She was putting the box to good use. Had Julia remembered where she hid these oddments of cash? And she found some more notes written by her mother. One note was "to my granddaughter, Mary." Phoebe read it, an odd feeling choking her throat.

Julia, rather obscurely, was advising the girl who must "carry a handicap through her life." Feeling a surge of her old impatience with her mother, Mary's mother crumpled the sheet of paper and would have thrown it into the fireplace. Phoebe had never let Mary feel sorry for herself.

She now looked dubiously at the notes which she had found. If she was going to find messages of that sort all over the house, she would do better to go back to her original plan and let the appraisers come in at once. Then she would sell the house and its contents unexamined.

But of course pride would not let her do that.

Deciding that she was tired of books, Phoebe moved on to the window seat. It was packed with old coats, sweaters, and, down in the bottom, the Parcheesi set with which she and Richard had used to amuse themselves. Curiously, Phoebe shook out a coat she remembered wearing—and in the pocket of it was a hundred-dollar bill. Of all places, of all *things!* What had got into her mother . . . ?

Unwilling to find an answer, if one there was, Phoebe explored all the pockets, and found no more money. She wrote GOOD WILL on a sheet of tablet paper and laid it in the refilled window seat, then thoughtfully closed the lid.

She glanced at the clock. She should clean up and go out for some food—eggs, milk, meat . . . What would she do with the money she had found? What loneliness, fear, and troubled thoughts had caused her mother to hide it? More than she remembered ever feeling while her mother lived, Phoebe now worried about her mother.

This situation was definitely odd. If Phoebe had stayed close to her mother, would she have done such things? Would she have been so lonely, so frightened, so—so disturbed?

Because her hospital experience gave that word special significance, Phoebe sought to discard it. Julia had not wanted anyone to live with her. When her daughter was eighteen, she had told her, "You are on your own now. I gave you life. I owe you nothing." She had told Richard the same thing.

But now that daughter must wonder why. Because her mother had not wanted her children around? Or because she had feared for them . . . ? Neurosis, psychosis, would not seem to be compatible with the job which Julia had held. Phoebe knew her mother to be a bitter introvert, and that probably was the whole of it.

Phoebe took the box of money and the notes upstairs; she would clean up, change, and go on to market. She had a letter to mail to the girls.

At the head of the stairs, Phoebe hesitated. She had not, before this, gone into her mother's bedroom. But now, still worried about her mother, she was deciding that her mother's room was probably where she should search for some answer to her questions.

She looked at her watch—she wouldn't have time to do much if she meant to shop—but she could look around.

The room was in order. It was really a pretty room, with cherry furniture and green-on-white wallpaper; there were green draperies at the windows, a chaise in flowered chintz.

She lifted her head in sudden resolution. This should not take long. Methodically, she began to take things out of the drawers of the chest and of the dresser. She found only clothes. No more money or notes. The cushions on the chaise were cushions only, the dark blue vases on the fireplace mantel were empty.

Phoebe made a mental note to look between the mattress and the box springs—and began to take the clothes out of the closet, which was a deep one. There were a lot of clothes, for all seasons, in zippered bags. Phoebe ran her hands down into the shoe bags, shook out the purses, and found some change, as one expected to, in purses. The hatboxes were innocent of anything but hats. Phoebe regarded the large box on the closet's highest shelf. It was difficult to balance and bring down. But, gasping, Phoebe managed it and brought the thing to the bed. She expected to find furs inside; there was an envelope taped to the lid.

Again with that strange reluctance, Phoebe pulled it free. On the underside was written in her mother's angular hand, "Bury me in these."

Oh, dear; oh, *dear!*

Before Phoebe had arrived, Aunt Dorothy had selected the dark silk dress in which Julia had been buried. "You can change it if you like," she had said. But Phoebe had been glad to have such matters decided for her.

But now, here was this box.

Not wanting to, Phoebe lifted the lid. There were folds of tissue paper, and within them, clothes. Underwear. Pretty underwear, lace-trimmed. Stockings. And a dress. A dress of gray crepe, the bodice beaded, the skirt pleated.

Phoebe gasped, tears stinging her eyes. She had not wept much for her mother, but now she did weep—because the dress was dreadfully out of style. Not for at least ten years had women worn such crepe, such beading, such long, pleated skirts.

For ten years, a dozen years, had her mother been worrying lest she die alone? She had prepared this box that long ago. It must have been after Phoebe and Richard had left home, but not much after. Her mother had seemed to want them to go, to be on their own. . . .

But, still, Julia had been left alone. And worried lest she die alone, as she had died. Feeling as if she were violating a case in some museum, Phoebe lifted the dress from the box and let it fall from the shoulders. Yes, it was long—and heavy. The gray crepe had discolored, as gray sometimes did discolor, turning a strange pink tone. The dress certainly could not have been used. Which did not exactly change the fact that for a dozen years her mother had had a box like this ready for her illness and death.

Why had she done it in the first place, a woman of forty? Had she been ill? No. Phoebe would insist that she had not been. Morose, yes. Depressed, often. Her mother had behaved strangely at times, but she had never said that she was ill.

She had never said, either, that she had a—had a—*shroud* —ready for her burial!

There at the foot of the bed, Phoebe collapsed, the gray crepe fallen into a heap beside her. Phoebe wept with real sorrow and regret. Julia's daughter should have known these things!

Shadows lengthening across the room reminded her of the time. She got to her feet, folded the dress to put it back into the box. Placing the lid, she fingered the envelope. It was sealed, and there would be a note, or even money, inside. She opened it with her forefinger, jaggedly. Yes, there was a sheet of paper . . .

Reading the note, Phoebe backed to the small chair and sat down. This paper—this sheet of notepaper—was—was her mother's *will!* Written in longhand, witnessed and dated— What were such wills called? Something-graph. Phoebe's trembling hand rustled the paper, and she steadied her fingers with her left hand. Her mother— "I leave all I

55

have to Phoebe and Richard, my children," the will read. "Let Phoebe attend to things. She'll like that. Of course they will fight. In which case Eugene Rotan is the one to straighten out legal details."

Eugene . . .

Phoebe looked at the date. The will—this one, at least, had been made only two years ago. So her mother knew that the awful crepe dress was awful and out of style, and—

Phoebe took a deep breath. All the old, familiar anger and exasperation with Julia Edwards returned full force. "Let Phoebe . . ." Julia had written. "Of course they will fight."

Why, Phoebe and Richard did not fight. Not over anything important. As children, yes. Who took a bath first. Who got the largest apple. But—not for years had they disagreed. And Julia knew it! But still she could say—

Curiously, Phoebe turned the piece of folded paper over in her fingers. What should she do now? The witnesses— one name was familiar to Phoebe as being connected with the store. That woman had come to the funeral and sent flowers. The other was probably a similar friend. If this will was valid—*Rotan!* She had not liked the man. She wanted nothing to do with him.

And with Uncle Bob in the family—he had told her to watch for a will. He had offered to help. Could he, even with Rotan mentioned in the will? Didn't the will say that Rotan was Julia's attorney?

Phoebe straightened the paper and unfolded it. Was having been Julia's lawyer the same as being executor? The will read . . .

It read: "Let Phoebe attend to things. She'll like that."

Well, Phoebe did not like it!

In a ten-minute whirlwind of activity, Phoebe put the big box back on the closet shelf, hung the clothes bags away, closed the closet door. It was five o'clock, but she would make an attempt to reach that Rotan character. She flipped the pages of the big directory and picked up the telephone. She more than hoped he would not still be in his office—then she would need to do nothing until the next day, or even the first of the week—

Oh, dear. Mr. Rotan was in. Would Mrs. Flowers hold?

Rotan's voice came—low, suave. Oh, yes, Phoebe! Yes. Yes. He would come right out to the house!

Phoebe set the phone down and took a deep breath. She certainly had hoped—

She went upstairs and washed her face and her hands and arms, smoothed her hair. Her dress looked rumpled, but she didn't care. She—

The doorbell rang and she went downstairs again, not especially hurrying. Eugene Rotan could wait, and he would. He did.

Phoebe led him back to the garden room. In spite of his elegant clothes and his polished shoes, the man looked sick.

And he did seem to be nervous, at least. His eyes darted about, his hands moved restlessly. He spoke rapidly, too loudly, too effusively. He had been waiting, he said, for Phoebe to call on him.

She stepped away from the hand he would have put on her shoulder. "I've been sorting out my mother's things," she told him. "Since you seem to have been taking care of my mother's affairs—"

Rotan laughed nervously. "Oh, Julia did a fine job of taking care of her own affairs," he declared. "But I stand ready with advice, you know."

Phoebe looked up at him gravely. "I have found some money here in the house," she said.

This impressed Mr. Rotan. "Oh?" he asked. "How much?"

"Two or three hundred dollars. Put away in odd places. So she'd have cash on hand, I suppose."

Rotan was breaking off a pink rosebud to put in his buttonhole. "Have you told anyone?" he asked with a show of indifference. But Phoebe did not think he was indifferent.

"I'm telling you," she said bluntly.

The man turned and smiled at her brilliantly. He had a big mouth, and his eyes were—were— "What are you doing with it?" he asked.

Phoebe had left the box upstairs. "Well, actually nothing," she said. "I'm putting it together as I find it." She was collecting the notes, too, but she decided she would not mention them to this man.

Rotan sat down in the green velvet chair and crossed his legs. "You are supposed to take only perishable things out of the house," he said. "And of course money sure is perishable. . . ." He swung one of his shiny, narrow shoes.

Money—perishable— Was that this man's idea of a joke?

"And I found this," said Phoebe, extending the envelope toward him. "Since your name is mentioned . . . I think it is a will."

Even before he read the thing, Rotan showed that he was disturbed. As he read, his mouth drew into a thin slit, his hand clenched. He was angry. But why? Curiously, his response served to calm Phoebe. She felt able to handle things. . . . She crossed the rug and took the will from Rotan's hand.

"Tear it up!" he cried. "It's no good."

Phoebe put the sheet of paper back into the envelope. She believed now that the will was good. "I called you," she said, "because I thought this was a will." She tucked the envelope into the pocket of her dress. "If it isn't, why, I'm sorry I bothered you."

Rotan was recovering his poise. "No bother," he said. "And I'm glad of a chance to get to know you."

Phoebe was not glad. She wished she had not phoned Rotan. She wished she had taken the "will" to her uncle. "I believe," she said aloud, blurting the announcement as Linda would have done, "that I'll take this to my uncle. My mother's brother, as you perhaps know, is an attorney."

Rotan sprang to his feet. He was a lithe man, quick of motion—and he was, again, an angry man.

"Don't you know how Julia felt about her brother?" he demanded. His voice was shrill, almost a scream.

Phoebe fell back, away from the glitter in his eyes.

"That man . . ." cried Eugene Rotan. "You don't know him, do you? Oh, sure, he was holier than thou at the funeral. I saw him. All the family, in their dark suits, and their hats. . . . Stuffed shirts, the whole lot of them. Julia gave them the back of her hand. You know that she did! She wouldn't even let them come into this house! If you have any regard at all for your mother's memory—"

Phoebe said nothing. Now her one wish was to get this man out of the house.

Rotan came toward her. "Look," he said, "give me that note your mother wrote. It isn't a will—she didn't make a will. I told her that she should, but Julia thought that she would live forever. That thing you have is just one of her scribbles. She scribbled all the time, you know. Some of her notes are pretty darn funny, and some you couldn't print. I don't like my name being on one of them. Although your mother was quite a girl, Phoebe . . . And there's no use dragging her through the talk there'll be over this sort of will. Without it, you and your brother will still be the heirs.

"When she was alive, you didn't do much for her, but now you come around, you take over—and I guess you have that much right. But the probate office will do

60

anything you can do. I can see you won't let me help you fix things the way Julia would have wanted them. I saw that when I told you to pocket the money. But you really shouldn't bring your uncle into this. Julia says to let me advise you, and my advice is to burn any notes you find, along with that so-called will. Just burn 'em. Things written on paper can read differently from the way intended. They can make trouble. If you like, I'll help you go through her things, and—"

Phoebe stepped aside, indicating the door. "Thank you for coming, Mr. Rotan," she said. "I only thought I had found a will."

He looked at her pocket. For a minute she thought he would put his hands on her. But he did not. "I'll be back," he said, and left. Phoebe quickly closed the door behind him and locked it. He must have heard her turning the latch, but she didn't care. She was afraid of that man!

She went to the couch and sat down. There must have been something between her mother and this oily lawyer. He looked more like a dancer—he moved like one. And he was a cruel man, Phoebe was sure of that!

She drew the envelope from her pocket and sat looking at it, remembering exactly what was written on the page inside of it, remembering how each letter was formed—

It was a short will—less than fifty words. But Rotan had been afraid of it. Rotan—Phoebe did not trust that man!

Of course, questioned, she would have to admit that she

knew nothing of him. But her instincts told her—and then, her mother had liked him, and her mother's judgment—

Oh, for heaven's sake, that was no way to decide things! Phoebe's knowledge of her mother was based purely on feeling. And feeling was not a substitute for wisdom or judgment.

Rotan's taste in dress was not Phoebe's. But was that any basis for distrust?

All right. On what, then, would she base trust in a man? A man she had met three days ago, and under emotional circumstances. As she had met Rotan. As she had met Uncle Bob. If she were to trust her uncle, did she have a reason for that trust? What reason?

Well, he had been kind to her. Not urgent, not persuasive—just kind. Was that enough?

Distraught, Phoebe stood up and walked the length of the room. She was not thinking sensibly, and she knew it.

Ten minutes ago, Rotan had made fun of her uncle's appearance. Well, certainly it was different from Rotan's— what Mary would call *groovy*—clothes. Uncle Bob's sober charcoal gray, his smooth hair and dark-rimmed half-glasses on the end of his nose— He *looked* the part of a reputable lawyer!

Uncle Bob was a member of a large firm of attorneys. Dr. Green's office had had correspondence with this firm of lawyers . . . and that at least meant the firm was well-established here in the city.

Uncle Bob—Julia had not liked him, as Rotan had said,

and that alone would make Phoebe—inclined—

Oh! she pounded her hands together. Here she was again! Taking her mother's judgment as a counterindication—

She should not do that. But—still—she did want to trust Uncle Bob. He and Aunt Katherine were the precise types she had admired at home, the man a vestryman of the church, the wife a worker in the hospital auxiliary. Their children . . . Respectability. Rotan despised it. Phoebe considered it a goal in life. To be pleasant, dignified . . .

And—she *must* trust someone. It would seem that she had to trust her uncle.

Phoebe brushed her hand across her brow; she had a headache. And no wonder! She couldn't ever remember thinking this hard! She had put in a long, hard day—and—now—

She went upstairs and opened the door of the medicine cabinet above the wash basin. She gasped a little, because the shelves were literally stuffed with bottles, vials—all kinds of medicine, prescriptions and pharmaceuticals. Why, there was even a syringe in a box.

Now, why would her mother have a thing like that? Did she have use for one? Diabetics did, of course. . . . But Julia was not a diabetic, or not so far as Phoebe knew.

Oh, she was not going to start work on another puzzle this evening! She slammed the cabinet door, not finding or taking anything for her headache. Almost in a panic, she ran down the stairs to the telephone.

With it in her hand, the dial tone buzzing in her ear, she scrabbled about to find the card which Uncle Bob had given her. It was his business card, but he had written his home telephone number upon it.

Feeling limp with a strange relief, Phoebe dialed the numbers.

FOUR

UNCLE BOB'S VOICE was casual and friendly. Yes! he said warmly, he would come right in—as if he had been expecting her call. If he had, Phoebe was doubly glad that she had made it. She ran upstairs, changed into the Paisley-printed voile dress which she had bought, brushed her hair, and came down again. She guessed her headache was hunger. She would eat something as soon as Uncle Bob left. There were cans of soup on the shelf. First thing in the morning she would shop. . . .

Uncle Bob did come right in, pulling his green Buick into the drive, running up the steps to the side door like a man in his twenties. Well, he was a lean, well-cared-for man. Tonight he wore a white sport shirt and blue denim slacks. Phoebe had interrupted his grass cutting, he told her. "Always a welcome call."

She smiled at him faintly and led him into the garden room. "I could maybe have told you over the phone . . ." she said.

"Has something happened?" He snapped on a couple of lamps against the gloom.

"I think something has," said Phoebe. "I've started going over things here. You know—drawers, and Mother's clothes."

"Did you find something interesting?"

Phoebe smiled faintly. "Plenty of disturbing things, I guess," she said.

"Look!" said Uncle Bob. "I'll bet you haven't eaten a thing today. You look peaked."

Phoebe's hand went to her cheek. "I did have a headache," she confessed. "And I meant to get some food in. But, yes, I've eaten. An apple—and a neighbor brought some coffee cake. I ate two pieces of that, with coffee."

"Ha!" said Uncle Bob. "Come along. I'll take you home for dinner. It's pot roast. Just what a peaked girl needs. We'll talk out there."

It definitely was a relief to let someone take over and tell Phoebe what to do—someone she liked and, yes, trusted. Phoebe went out to the car and tucked herself into the right-hand seat. For the short drive they talked about the hospital at home, Dr. Sam, and her girls.

Uncle Bob told her that he lived in the near-suburbs. Within a half hour he was slowing to turn into the drive of a home which made Phoebe clasp her hands together with pleasure. Yes! This was right, the low house, buried behind shrubbery—a window gleaming, a red roof and wide chimney. There was ground ivy along the path to the door, and a friendly welcome within.

Katherine came quickly from the kitchen. "Hello, Phoebe," she said warmly. "What sort of salad dressing do you like?"

"Could I help . . . ?" Phoebe asked.

"Oh, no. Talk to your uncle. Joanne and I have everything under control."

Phoebe nodded and followed Uncle Bob into the long, pleasant living room. An old basset hound came and sniffed at her shoe; she fondled his silky ear.

"I found what I think is a will," she told her uncle. "You told me to watch—"

"Oh, good!" said Uncle Bob. "I hope you brought it with you?"

Phoebe picked up her purse. "I did. There are a lot of notes around the house—and I found some money, too. Hidden away in strange places. Even in the pocket of an old coat."

Uncle Bob frowned. "Much money?"

"Well, several hundred dollars, and I've only begun to search. Or, not *search*. I thought I should go over things—the first bills fell down when I took a plate from the shelf in the pantry."

"Where did you find the will?"

"Upstairs in Mother's room. There was a box with an envelope fastened to the lid. This sort-of letter was in it."

"A holograph will!"

Phoebe nodded. "That's the word," she cried. "Mr. Rotan says it's not a good will, but—"

"Rotan!" said Uncle Bob crossly. He looked grim.

"I don't like him very much," said Phoebe apologetically. "But Mother mentioned him—" She drew the envelope from her purse and held it out to Uncle Bob.

"You showed this to Rotan?" he asked Phoebe.

"I'm sorry. I thought, because he was mentioned in it— I don't know about these things, Uncle Bob."

"Did you tell him about the money you've found?"

"Yes. He said I could keep it and say nothing."

Her uncle nodded. "That's Rotan."

"He was angry about the—the will. And he said Mother was odd. I think he meant that she was not entirely responsible. He told me to tear up that and any notes I found."

Uncle Bob nodded again. "He would," he said, his face very grim indeed. Still holding the envelope and the sheet of notepaper, he got up and went out to the telephone in the hall. Aunt Katherine called something to him, and he said for her to wait a minute.

He spoke into the phone crisply, with an authority which Phoebe admired and leaned upon as she would have rested against a large tree trunk.

He identified himself and talked to a police lieutenant. He located Julia's home, he identified Phoebe—and he asked that a special guard be put on the house for a time. Yes, he agreed that it was in a quiet neighborhood. But if

68

word got around that money could be found there—

He thanked the lieutenant and came back to Phoebe. "I think that should take care of any notions Rotan may have," he said.

"Would he . . . ?" asked Phoebe, alarmed.

"I don't know what he would do, my dear. I'm sorry you mentioned the money to him."

"But it must have been there, some of it, for quite a time. Oh, Uncle Bob, *what* am I going to do? There are so many things! That big house—all the stuff in it. Her notes alone confuse me."

"What are they about?"

"I have them in a pile. One said to watch the milkman. I think—Mother thought—he was cheating."

"That would be Julia!" said Uncle Bob. He opened the will again. "The thing to do," he said, "is to make you executor."

"Can you do that?" asked Phoebe. She blushed prettily. "I don't seem to know anything these days!"

"Estate law is a difficult study, my dear child. But, yes, of course we can make you executor."

"You think the will is good?"

"Certainly it is good. I'd know Julia's handwriting anywhere. And probably she has stuff all over the house to use for comparison. Her writing in this 'Let Phoebe attend to things' is enough to make you executor."

"But she mentions Mr. Rotan, too."

"Only as a possible lawyer. You should be able to handle him."

"Not without help, Uncle Bob," said Phoebe earnestly.

"I'm sure I'll need help. Would you . . . ?"

"Of course. Sure. I told you at the beginning—and now we'll make some plans. But first, perhaps I should tell you that it is usual for us Lewises to have a family conference on a crisis such as this."

A family . . .

"And you don't want to be out on the limb alone," said Phoebe gravely.

For a long minute, Uncle Bob gazed at her, taking off his glasses to do it. "You're a smart girl, Phoebe," he said then.

She flushed. "I didn't mean to sound rude."

"You didn't. Only smart."

Well, at home she had thought . . . "I'm not very smart," she said. "Though I've had to be a little that way to get myself through school, you know, and then, after my husband's death, to take care of my girls. . . ."

"We're only beginning to know those things," Uncle Bob told her. "All right, then, we'll have a family conference."

He would call Uncle Howard, she supposed, and Aunt Dorothy.

He went first to the kitchen. Dinner was to be held up, he told his wife, who took the announcement philosophically. "Do I feed the whole gang?" she asked.

"Can you?"

"I'll try. But when you call Dorothy, let me talk to her—she can bring some things."

During the flurry of the telephone calls and resetting the

table, Phoebe found herself sitting in the kitchen with a cup of coffee and crackers and cheese on a plate. "To hold you," Uncle Bob explained.

Young Kirk decided he needed to be held, as well, and joined her.

Aunt Katherine talked to Phoebe about the hospital-volunteer work she did two days a week. "I thought I wanted to be on the wards," she explained, "but I find I like it in Admissions. Of course I am shocked at the young girls—just children—who come in for maternity care. Asking for abortions. And then the drug users, Phoebe! It makes me wonder *how* I can raise a family!"

In a little more than an hour after Phoebe and Uncle Bob had left the house in Armand Heights, the family had gathered and sat down to eat dinner—the pot roast, Aunt Dorothy's sliced ham and her spaghetti—the salad in small cherry wood bowls—a huge bowl of apple sauce, two cakes cut into generous squares . . .

The women saw to it that the family was fed; the men talked about something called MSD. Trying to listen and be helpful, too, Phoebe realized, belatedly, that the initials referred to something called Medical Students' Disease. The subject had been introduced by Uncle Howard; Patrick, his son, said that it was a real item in the hospital complex.

"Didn't you have it?" Uncle Doc asked his son.

"A very bad case," agreed Patrick readily. He turned to Phoebe and explained that MSD referred to the imaginary diseases many of the medical students acquired during their four years of study.

"Don't women students get it, too?" she asked.

Patrick laughed. "I think they do. Why shouldn't they?"

Phoebe shrugged. "I wouldn't know. My medical training consists of knowing how to spell some of the big words and fill out Medicare forms."

"But you must be a genius!" said Patrick.

"All this sounds like a job for the psychiatrists," said Uncle Cecil Paule.

"The psychiatrists do get in on it," Uncle Doc agreed. "Though the imagined diseases run to organic trouble about twice as often as to purely psychiatric manifestations."

"Then, it is a serious problem?" asked Uncle Bob, evidently having decided that the medics were not joking.

"We're told that we should consider it to be serious," his brother said. "That it could be an early sign that the medical student is heading for emotional trouble."

"I think it's good for the guys," said Patrick firmly. "When I decided I had nephritis—that was during my third year—I found myself studying the whole field and remembering what I read."

"Speaking of learning things," said Aunt Katherine. "Did they bring that boy in today, Doc? The one who was shot down at the lake."

Uncle Doc nodded. "They did, Katherine. I saw him this afternoon." He glanced at the others around the table.

"This boy," he explained, "and two others were target shooting at the family's lodge down at the dam this morning. The father and a friend had gone out in the boat, leaving the three teen-agers target shooting. When the father returned, he found the boy—he's twelve—lying on the ground. He didn't think the kid was badly hurt, but on a chance, he wrapped him in a sleeping bag and took him to the hospital at Rolla. An X-ray showed an air rifle pellet had lodged in what is called the 'shadow of the heart.' "

"Are you going to operate?" asked Uncle Bob.

"Not me. I may work along—our problem is perhaps a simple one. We are uncertain whether the pellet is within the heart or lodged outside the heart sac. The latter surgery would be simple. But in case the thing has penetrated the heart muscle or chamber, we'd need the heart-lung machine and a team ready to do open-heart surgery. Just now the boy is in intensive care, and surgery probably will be done during the night."

"Since you're apt to be called," said his son, standing up, "hadn't we better get Phoebe's problems straightened out?"

Phoebe flushed. She had forgotten her "problems" in her interest in the talk.

"We'll take our coffee out to the terrace," said Katherine. "Phoebe, we have an assembly line set-up to get the dishes to the washer in the kitchen. You'd better stand to one side. Later, we'll fit you into the program."

Their assembly line worked most efficiently. Within fifteen minutes the whole family was gathered on the terrace, where the late darkness of summer was beginning to fold in. The children, even young Kirk, were present. These family meetings were evidently often-enough occurrences to make the procedure entirely familiar. Had Julia ever participated? Phoebe shook her head. Not her mother.

Uncle Bob reached for her hand and held it warmly in his as he began to talk. Phoebe thought she might cry. Not since David's death had a man held her hand so, strong, comforting, reassuring.

Her uncle was saying that he had called this meeting because Phoebe seemed to need help and had asked for it. He went on to tell about the will—a holograph—he explained the term to the children. "Unless and until we find something else, I am prepared to admit this will to probate and have Phoebe qualify as executor. That should not be too complicated a process. Unless your brother would contest?" He turned to look at Phoebe.

She shook her head. "Dick will agree to anything we do here, I'm pretty sure."

"We'll need some signatures, of course," murmured Uncle Bob. Then he told about the money which Phoebe had found in the house. Uncle Doc snorted.

Well—it had been foolish of Julia. Phoebe thought so, too.

"Was it a lot?" asked Kirk.

"Several hundred dollars," said his father. "I've had the police set a guard on the house. Once word got around of hidden money— We'll have to identify ourselves, Phoebe, when I take you home."

"She is not going to stay there alone tonight!" said Aunt Katherine and Aunt Dorothy in a single voice.

Phoebe smiled at them in the dark.

"Did you find all of it?" asked Joanne.

"I don't know," said Phoebe. "I haven't gone through the whole house, by any means. That's going to be an enormous task. I did part of the garden room and the closet in Mother's room, some of the pantry. There's so much *stuff!* Books, magazines—boxes and drawers."

"Did you find the bankbook?" asked Uncle Doc.

"No-o," said Phoebe. "Not a bankbook. Her checkbook was in her purse. There is a bankbook, I suppose. . . ."

"I meant a particular bankbook," said Uncle Doc firmly. "Your father kept a joint account with her, you see. And when he died, the amount on deposit automatically became hers, though I never thought Julia . . ."

His voice faded from Phoebe's hearing. Her head was ringing, swimming from all the blows which had been rained upon her. She was numb.

"My *father?*" she asked faintly. "Is he dead?"

For a long minute, no one spoke. Then—"Don't you know?" asked Howard Lewis softly.

Phoebe lifted her chin. "I know only one thing about my father," she said in a clear voice. "That he left my mother."

Again there was silence. Thick, like fog.

"And you knew that we treated her badly, didn't you?" asked Uncle Doc, his tone sharp.

75

In the darkness, Phoebe could feel her cheeks go warm. She clasped her hands tightly together and spoke with some spirit. "I grew up here in the city," she said clearly. "I lived here, all the time, until I was eighteen. I know that I was never in your home, nor can I ever remember your being in ours."

Someone coughed. Someone's foot scraped the flagstones. "How far back do you remember?" Uncle Doc asked quietly. "I mean, what is your earliest memory, Phoebe?"

"I think it must have been of my first day in school. I remember how I hated my long stockings. Other little girls wore anklets, but Mother—" She said no more.

"Yes," said Uncle Doc, as if he were completing her sentence. Then he said, "Your father, Phoebe, left your home when you were three and Richard was one."

Phoebe sat, head down, thinking about all this, making pictures. Finally she looked up at the shadowy people around her. "What happened?" she asked meekly.

But no one spoke; again the silence was a palpable thing. Suddenly, her cousin Patrick stood up. "Tell her!" he said gruffly. "*Talk* to her!"

"There must be a record—a bankbook—of that account," said Uncle Doc. "I have reason to think Julia did not spend—"

"What reason?" asked Uncle Bob.

"She told me so. And the money should be there. Otherwise you might look into the circumstances for its not being there."

Beside her, Uncle Bob made a movement of exasperation or distress. He took a paper out of his shirt pocket and wrote something on it in the dark.

"I didn't find any bankbook," said Phoebe, wanting to help. "But there were notes. The will itself was really only a note. It was pasted on a box of clothes she said she wanted to be used for her burial."

"Oh, my *dear*," breathed Aunt Dorothy.

"It's all right," said Phoebe quickly. "We couldn't have used them. Except for being sad that she thought so much, and for so long, about dying—it's all right. Those clothes must have been in the box for ten years, or longer.

"There were notes almost everywhere. Some were just memos—I make them, too, to remind me to do things."

Uncle Bob crackled his paper, and Phoebe laughed. "That's it. Though some of the things— Oh, she mentioned Mr. Rotan, and a scarf she had given him. I don't like that man much. She wrote about flowers for the church; she said they cost too much. There was a mention of Uncle Howard—she just said *Howard*—he had a new car, and she wrote, 'I'm glad I didn't pay for it.' "

"She was being glad she hadn't paid me any medical bills," Uncle Howard explained dryly.

Phoebe fell silent; she should not have told about that note. She would wait now and let her uncles talk or comment. Or her aunt. Someone turned on a lamp; the light was soft yellow upon the tree overhead and the people seated in a half-circle.

"I think Patrick was right," Aunt Dorothy said firmly.

"We should talk to Phoebe, though of course we can tell her only our side of things."

"Which is fair enough," said Uncle Bob. "Because she knows her own side—or at least Julia's."

Phoebe sighed. "A week ago I thought I did," she confessed. "Now—I know the house in Armand Heights once belonged to my father's family. There are heirlooms —and the house itself must be valuable."

"Not very," said Uncle Bob. "It may be worth thirty-five thousand dollars. It looks like more, of course."

"My mother never told me that it was the family home," said Phoebe unhappily. "A neighbor did. In fact"—the words quickened—"about all I know about my mother and her family affairs was that you didn't like her."

There was another pause, another wait. Phoebe clasped her hands together. "I don't want to sound rude," she said. "I know Mother was difficult."

"And she wrote notes about me," said Uncle Doc wryly.

"Yes, she did, sir," Phoebe agreed. "One said success had gone to your head. That was almost like a compliment."

The successful surgeon shifted in his chair and smiled grimly. "From Julia, yes," he conceded.

Phoebe glanced across at her Aunt Dorothy, and at the clergyman who was her husband.

"Was there a note about me?" he asked astutely.

"Yes," said Phoebe, flushing, "there was. On the back of a wedding invitation."

The clergyman nodded and took out his pipe. "Your

mother's religious conviction," he said slowly, "was that the clergy should be celibate."

Oh, dear. In other words, Julia had decided that these two gentle people were living in sin. The note . . . "Was she crazy?" Phoebe blurted.

"No," said Uncle Bob and Uncle Doc.

"She was unhappy," said Cecil Paule softly. "A most unhappy woman."

Phoebe sat back in her chair, ready to accept the word. "Should I have stayed with her?" she asked, distressed.

"Oh, no." The clergyman was quick, definite in his decision. Uncle Doc agreed with him. So did Uncle Bob.

"Julia," Uncle Doc said, "was always well aware of her difficulties with human relationships."

"Always?" thought Phoebe. She smoothed the soft folds of her dress skirt. "All right," she said briskly in the tone she used to her daughters, "tell me about it."

"Tell you what?" asked her uncle.

"Well—to start—tell me about my father. Then Uncle Bob might go on to explain to me why Mother selected a—a *thing* like Rotan for a friend. Tell me anything I should know—and don't."

Uncle Doc looked uncomfortable—perhaps at her vigor. "This is a big city we live in," he said. "We none of us lived near your mother. We lost touch."

"And she wouldn't talk to you. I know. She wouldn't talk to me, either. But you do—you did—know some of these things."

"Oh, yes," agreed Uncle Doc, and then he said nothing further.

"We'd have to speak only from our side," said Uncle Bob, as Aunt Dorothy had said before.

Phoebe looked appealingly across at Cecil Paule. He smiled at her and unfolded his long legs as if he might stand up, though he did not. His wife laid her hand on his arm, and he smiled down at her. "I think Phoebe can decide for herself," he argued, "about the truth of anything we tell her. Now, my dear," he leaned toward the pretty young woman, "I would suggest that we begin this by your asking us some questions which we can answer. You are unhappy and confused, I know. But the truth is, all of us are embarrassed, too."

Phoebe's big eyes told that she had her doubts on that subject. "All right," she agreed, "I'll begin. . . . And this, I suspect, you can tell me with or without embarrassment. Why were my mother's services not held in your church?"

Uncle Cecil leaned back, looking relieved—as did Aunt Dorothy. "Your mother," the Reverend Paule said, "did not attend, or belong to, my church."

Phoebe nodded. "I know . . ." she agreed.

"You have visited her, haven't you?"

"Not as often as I should, perhaps. But, yes, I have visited her. And she's been in my home."

"And you have two little girls."

Phoebe always brightened at mention of the girls. "Oh, yes," she said. "They are at camp now, in the north. They

are ten and twelve, you see—and I sent them to camp—
I'm trying to do more for them than she—" She broke off
shortly and flushed painfully, then she blurted, "I just
happen to believe that parents *owe* things to their
children!"

"They do," said Uncle Bob gravely, there beside
Phoebe. "They owe their kids a lot."

Phoebe drew a deep breath. "I've had to think about the
fact that my girls have no father. My husband, you know,
died some time ago."

"And do you support the children?" asked Aunt
Katherine.

"Well, there was some money. Insurance, you know.
But I'm saving that for the girls' education or for any
emergency that might come up. It helps, too, with things
like this six weeks in camp."

"Tell us about the work you do," suggested Aunt
Katherine.

"I work in a hospital," said Phoebe shyly. "I am
secretary to the surgeon of the hospital. It is different from
what Uncle Howard and Patrick are used to. Dr. Green is
a good doctor, but the hospital is small and old. I—I am a
secretary, but I talk to the patients, and sometimes I do
things for Dr. Green. You know, a little follow-up on a
case, or an investigation of a patient's ability to pay. It's all
part of doctoring, the way Dr. Green does it."

Dr. Howard Lewis coughed and glanced at his son. "We
probably could use a secretary like you in our hospital
here," he said gruffly.

Phoebe laughed and shook her head. "I'm a secretary," she admitted. "And not too bad at that work. But your big complex, contrasted with our hospital . . . Look. It was once a lovely, yellow brick home, with porches and an attic and—things. It sits among tall hickory trees, with squirrels and nuts—all that sort of home atmosphere. When Dr. Green's father started the hospital, there was no elevator. A surgical patient had to be carried on a stretcher up a wide staircase to the operating room." She looked around the semicircle of interested faces. "We have built a new clinic wing that is as modern as anything you have, and we have brought in five younger men who are modern, too. We even have facilities for deep X-ray treatment."

"Does your Dr. Green still own this?"

"We're a corporation now. He is an owner. And he still is the chief surgeon."

"Does he keep up?"

"Oh, I think so. Medicine has become very complicated, of course, and he is always ready to say when a job is beyond his training and ability."

"A good thing in any doctor," approved Dr. Howard.

"Yes, sir, it is. Of course Dr. Sam is something of a character. He insists on maintaining certain reserves. As a doctor, he gives himself freely. But as a man—he has no social life. His young wife died years ago, and he never remarried. Of course the town talks about him." She paused, then looked up again at the family members. "Now," she said, "tell me about my father."

The family had become so interested in what she had

been telling that they glanced at one another in surprise.

Phoebe rubbed her hands together; suddenly they had turned icy. "I've never," she said faintly, "even seen a picture of him."

Was he tall? Short? Fair? Dark?

The family stared at her, shocked.

Abruptly, Uncle Bob got up and went into the house. He came back with an eight-by-eleven framed picture in his hand. He gave this to Phoebe and turned on the wall light behind her chair.

Phoebe sat looking at the picture, studying it. It was of a young man in his thirties, perhaps. Blond. Smooth-haired, his eyes steady, but with a certain brightness. "Do I look like him?" she asked.

"Yes," said Uncle Doc. "Yes, you do."

Phoebe sighed. "Is that why my mother hated me?"

"Did she hate you?" Uncle Bob asked gently.

"I've thought so. I don't suppose I understood her very well. I did know, of course, that she worked hard—at the store, you know. To support us children and herself. Her hours were long, and she would come home tired. I think she wanted very much for us to grow up able to care for ourselves, should the need come to us. As she had had to handle such a need. I mean, support us when my father left us. He—" She broke off and again looked around at the faces. "*Tell* me!" she cried tensely.

"All right, my dear," said Cecil Paule quietly, calmly. "We'll tell you. In the first place, we should tell you that your father did not leave your mother."

Phoebe leaned toward him, her eyes very bright. "But—" she protested.

"She put him out of the house. And—there are times and circumstances, my dear girl, when being a gentleman is a great handicap to a man."

Phoebe put the flattened palms of her hands to her cheeks and sat shaking her head.

"Your father," said Uncle Cecil, "was a busy doctor."

Yes. Phoebe had known that he was a doctor. And a selfish one. Always putting his profession before his family— Her mother had always laughed at, derided the image of a self-sacrificing physician.

"Your mother," Uncle Cecil was saying, "was always religious. As the term goes. And with that type of intensely religious person, one preoccupied with the emotional aspects of one's faith and experience, sex became a problem to your mother. The time came, quite early in her marriage, when she decided that sex was not a necessary part of life, or even a desirable part. Frigidity, denial, are usually a part of this development.

"And after a time, which was an expected result, too, her frustrated young husband, Bill, committed some minor adultery . . ."

The men in the circle laughed explosively at his term. The ladies smiled but looked a bit shocked as well.

"Yes!" said the clergyman. "And when your mother found out about it, she put him out."

Phoebe could well imagine that scene. Her mother, tense, angry, reproving. She would have dwelt endlessly upon the wrong done to her, and she would afterward have held the wrong in her heart for all her life.

"Did he . . . ?" Phoebe gulped. "Did he leave the city?"

"Oh, no. Not at first. I think he attempted to continue with his profession. But then, after a year or two, he decided that he had better leave."

And Phoebe knew why. Her mother had nagged him, reproached him, whined to him. By telephone, by notes written in the dead of night and sent special delivery the next morning. Phoebe well knew the process. When she had married David . . .

"Bill went into the navy," Cecil Paule was saying. "This was about nineteen-forty, I think."

Uncle Bob grumbled agreement. "Still peacetime," he said, "but—"

"Yes," said Uncle Cecil. "I have been told that before he left he set up a modest trust fund for the maintenance of the home, and he established a joint bank account with Julia, his wife."

"Then the war broke out," said Howard Lewis grimly, "and three years later Bill Edwards was killed in a plane accident."

Phoebe was estimating the years. She would have been nine. Old enough to have such things register. "Did my mother know?" she asked sharply.

"Oh, of course she knew!" Everyone seemed agreed on that.

"But—"

Would these people know? They had not been around. There was of course that shadow of a man on the ground glass door pane—but— *Was* her mother mistreated? By Phoebe's father? By her family? How, if she knew, could she have concealed knowledge that her husband had been killed? How—

Phoebe looked up, almost pleadingly. "I've always thought my mother was overstrict," she said. "To us, as children, you know. I thought she was unable to show emotion. At least, she never did show it. And in not giving us many pleasures, she also denied herself pleasure. She made Dick and me earn any education we got beyond high school, and we both left home to do it. That was hard—but actually it didn't hurt us. The main thing was, she wasn't interested in our getting an education. That did hurt us both."

"You young people seem to have made a good job of your educations," said Uncle Cecil. "Haven't the results been good?"

Phoebe shook her head. "Resentment is a bad thing to feel against one's mother."

"Toward anyone. Yes, it would be."

Phoebe clasped her hands together and sat forward in the chair. "Oh, I *wish!*" she cried. "I wish we could go back, gather up all the years and live them, knowing what we do know now. We'd know each other . . ."

"You couldn't have persuaded Julia to do and feel differently," said Uncle Bob firmly.

Phoebe glanced at him. "You tried?"

"Oh, yes. We all have tried. And you, too, perhaps?"

"Well, not enough. I don't suppose I said any right things to her."

"I wouldn't worry about it," said Aunt Katherine. "You do know us now, and we know you. Bob, if you have any plans—and of course you do—I think you should be discussing them now."

FIVE

PHOEBE STAYED in the city for two weeks—two weeks of hot, July days spent in sorting out the contents of her mother's house, which she dusted and cleaned as she progressed. With the girls busy and reportedly happy in camp, she thought the task should be done immediately and quickly.

After a night or two of going out to Uncle Bob's, she insisted on staying alone in the house. Nothing had happened, nothing would happen. She was used to being alone—or at least the "man of the house." She worked so hard during the day that she was too tired to do anything but sleep at night. The neighbors were friendly and kind. And there was so much to do.

She found more money and more notes. She was appalled at the clothes stowed away in trunks on the third floor. After a day when the contents of the house were appraised, Uncle Bob said she could dispose of these things, should she wish to.

She did wish to. The Salvation Army came with a truck and carried all the clothes away. It took a load from Phoebe's mind to know that the things were gone.

Her mother—often Phoebe was shaken by the insecurity which her explorations told her had possessed Julia Edwards. She had hoarded everything. There were great supplies of food. Canned goods in boxes and on shelves. Sacks of sugar turned as hard as cement. Could Phoebe use any of it? She would ask Patrick how safe it was—or Uncle Doc, if she dared.

Thinking about this, she went up to the second-floor bathroom and swept the contents of the medicine cabinet into a basket, took it out to the kitchen door where it would be picked up by the city trash collector.

The next day, Uncle Doc asked her about medicines. Had Phoebe found any? The family were again eating dinner at Bob's home. This time it was Sunday dinner, at two o'clock, with Cecil promising to go off somewhere immediately for a nap. The roast and vegetables were on a heated tray on the side table. There was a large bowl of salad.

One could eat as much or as little as one wanted, go quickly about his affairs afterward, or linger to talk.

This talk was varied. Someone asked Phoebe what she'd found that week, and she told about the food stores. "I don't know if the stuff's fit to use."

Canned things, with no leaks or breaks, should be.

Then—"What about medicines, drugs?" asked Uncle Doc. "Did she hoard those?"

"Not really," said Phoebe. "There were quite a few things in the medicine cabinet in the bathroom. I dumped the whole mess out! Ice bag—she even had a hypodermic syringe. Why, I'll never know."

Her uncle leaned toward her; everyone else was eating busily. "Are you sure you've thrown it all away?" he asked.

"Oh, yes. I'm sorry if I threw out things you might have found use for, Uncle Doc."

He drew back quickly. "Oh, no," he said. "I think you probably did the right thing."

"I hope so," sighed Phoebe. "I am going to have to go home this week. I've about gone through the whole place—and Uncle Bob says the house can't be sold for nine or ten months. Even then, what will I do with all the stuff I haven't thrown away?" She looked in dismay from one to the other.

"You'll have to divide it between yourself and Dick," said Aunt Katherine. "Unless one of you decides to live in the house. Couldn't you live there and be close to us?"

Phoebe smiled at her gently. By now, she had come to know the family and to like them. She felt a part of the group. She had her duties at these family gatherings, she knew about Uncle Cecil's allergies, and that Uncle Bob preferred apples and cheese to dessert. . . . The cousins had become her friends. Patrick teased her, not always gently, and Danny, Uncle Bob's older son, talked to her as if she were wise and experienced. Danny, at twenty, a student at the University, was married. His young wife was expecting a baby any day—

This was a closely knit family; they liked to do things together. All but Uncle Doc enjoyed a spur-of-the-moment picnic. Likewise, dressed in their proper best, they filled two pews at church on Sunday. Every Sunday. Phoebe's presence among them was taken as a matter of course. "Are you going to stay in the city, Mrs. Flowers?" friends would ask her as she left the church.

"Oh, I don't think . . ."

"That's such a lovely house, and the Heights would make a fine place for you and your daughters to live. I think young girls would love living there."

They would. As Phoebe had progressed through the house, she had often thought how Mary and Linda would enjoy the roominess of the big place. The girls might even attend the private school where Joanne was ready for her last year. She liked what had been done for Joanne, and David's insurance money added to what she would get from her mother might best be spent for the girls' education. She had been planning to do that.

Then, there was the chance that Uncle Doc might be able to do something for Mary's weak spine.

Her Uncle Doc was a distinguished surgeon, and a fine man. He had been not quite so friendly as the other members of the family, and Phoebe had done some thinking about that, trying to decide if his coolness were because he had been "Bill's friend" and resented Julia's treatment of her husband, or it could be only that he was a reserved man, not ready to express his feelings quickly and freely.

"I wish you wouldn't leave," said Aunt Katherine, for at least the tenth time.

"I have a job back home," Phoebe reminded her—again.

"You could have a job here."

The others—Patrick, Aunt Dorothy—they all agreed. Of course there were jobs—a job—for Phoebe here in the city.

They were right, but—"What on earth would Dr. Sam say?" she asked ingenuously.

"What not ask him?" suggested Joanne so sensibly that her elders laughed.

On Friday, Phoebe followed that advice. She drove home, finding at once, to her dismay, that the town, and even her own house, looked strange to her. The key fitted the front door lock, but inside the rooms looked unlived-in, impersonal, not her own.

She drove downtown to pick up her mail, to pay a bill and do a few other errands. At the post office, she ran into Charles Reid.

He whooped aloud at sight of her, loudly called out her name, and would have kissed her there in the busy, crowded place. Well!

Phoebe liked Charles. A time or two she had even wondered if she might not let herself become interested in the man.

But today he was pressing too hard, she thought. Phoebe drew back. Charles felt her do so, and she herself felt the restraint she was putting on her feeling and behavior. And on Charles . . .

She did not want to hurt him, but—things were a bit different.

Oh, dear. Were they? Really?

She planned to go on to the hospital, and she wondered if that, too, would have changed. Or was this a matter of her having changed within these familiar surroundings?

The hospital, she decided, had not changed. Except that she did not pull her card when she went into the lobby, things were exactly as they had always been. The porter pushing his soft broom said, "Hi, Miz Flowers, glad to see you back."

The nurses going off duty, those coming on, all greeted her gladly. And Dr. Bradford, the pediatrician, bustling through, his arms loaded with papers, called out to her, "Phoebe, will you ask Dr. Sam to look at the Hayes X-rays sometime this afternoon? I want his opinion."

"Back on the payroll," murmured one of the nurses.

"Seems as if," said Phoebe, who had said, "Yes, of course," to Dr. Bradford.

She laughed about this with Dr. Sam when he was free and she could go in to see him. "I don't think he knew I'd been gone," she told her old friend.

The big, pink-scrubbed man beamed upon her. "I missed you," he assured her.

"Oh, I'm sorry. But, you see—"

"Suppose you sit down, Phoebe," he told her warmly, "and talk to me about it."

For half an hour, she talked, a pretty, animated young woman in a bright blue dress. When it seemed that she was about finished, he nodded. "Good!" he said. "It would seem, Phoebe, that you have found the roots which you have needed. Could you stay in the city and let those roots nurture you, strengthen you?"

Phoebe frowned a little. She had not mentioned staying. . . .

"I've been offered a job," she told him. "But I feel you have first claim; you have been so very kind to me."

He brushed this away with a sweep of his big hand. "You are a good secretary," he said. "What's the job? Is it a good one?"

"Yes, I think it would be. I'd be personal secretary to the Chief of Medical Services in the University Hospitals."

Dr. Sam whistled. "That *is* a good job!" he decided. "Do you like the man?"

Phoebe laughed. "I've not met him. Uncle Doc—my uncle, Howard Lewis—told me that the position was available. I said I would want to talk to you first."

"And you are talking to me. I am sure you could do the work, Phoebe. But perhaps you should consider this. Do I remember your telling me once that your mother actively disliked this brother? Your uncle, who is a doctor?"

"I probably told you that," Phoebe agreed. "She hated him, and I don't get the impression that he lost any love on her, but I am not going to work for *him!* My boss would be a Dr. Kinnamore. Uncle Howard is a surgeon."

"I know who Howard Lewis is. I know he'd be a big man in the hospital where he's a staff member."

"It's a very large hospital, Dr. Sam. And I suppose, if he could get me this job, Uncle Howard must have influence. I'd remember that, and try extra hard— Then, there's another thing. In these past weeks I've discovered that my mother often was mistaken in her judgment of people. For some reason, she didn't get along with the people in her family, or with those who should have been her friends. I suppose she did better in business. But—well—I think her family didn't argue with her or try to persuade her. They just stepped back and let her do as she chose. I've done that, I know."

"Do you have a sense of guilt, Phoebe? About your mother?"

She sat looking down at her hands. "I'm afraid I do," she confessed. "My mother died a lonely death. Though—" she looked up—"I've found her family to be very nice people. And I'm glad I can like them!"

"Good," said Dr. Sam. "I'm glad for you, Phoebe. I think the reestablishment of yourself in a family could be the best thing that ever happened to you. If you want my advice, and even if you don't, I'd say you should take this job in the city. If things don't work out, you could come back here at any time."

On Sunday, Phoebe telephoned to her Uncle Bob that she had decided to move to the city. Would he tell Uncle

Doc that she was accepting the job—she thought she could get things in order to come on Wednesday? "I—I am glad I'm coming," she added shyly.

"Well, that's fine, Phoebe. Because we're glad, too."

She put the phone down in a fine glow of anticipation. She still had to tell the girls—and do the necessary work to make this house ready. . . .

Her friends were dismayed to hear that she was leaving—and, talking about it, Phoebe found, on her part, a growing reluctance to make the change. It would, really, be easier to stay right where she was. She knew what to expect here, she knew her friends, she knew the town. She gave Charles Reid a dinner date, and he was so nice to her that she came home feeling like an ungrateful woman for leaving him. He looked so forlorn. . . .

And then there was Dr. Sam. He did not look well, she thought. Talking to him that first day, as interested as he had certainly been in her future, there had been moments when he looked tired! She shouldn't walk out and leave him to train a new secretary.

On Tuesday night her friends gave a patio party, which was fun but put her to bed at midnight, weeping at the thought of leaving. It was hard to abandon the little house which she and David had bought. Of course she was not losing it. She knew the people who were to rent it, and she could always come back. . . . Were all moves, all important decisions, so hard to make? Did they all have two sides?

She didn't sleep well, and, the next morning, she was

grateful to have Charles show up to help her pack her personal belongings into the station wagon. "You're awfully good to me, Charles," she told him.

"I'm cutting my own throat," he assured her.

"I may be back," said Phoebe.

"I wouldn't count on it," he said morosely.

SIX

BY THE LATTER part of September, the Flowers family was established in their new home. The girls were immediately content with the change. They accepted their new school, liked and looked well in their uniforms of white blouse, green blazer, gored skirt and knee socks. Nine Armand Heights girls attended the Institute, so the bus picked them up each morning and deposited them by four-thirty each afternoon. The block mother, Mrs. Haines, was glad to welcome two more girls.

"I'm always afraid we'll stop having children," she told Phoebe. Phoebe arranged to pick them up each evening at five-thirty, or six if she had shopping to do.

"They can stay here for the evening or the night," said Mrs. Haines, "when you have a date."

"Oh, mercy, I won't be having dates!" Phoebe assured her.

The girls had settled into the Lewis family circle without a ripple. They were excited about the big old house and explored it thoroughly, then agreed with Phoebe that part of it should be closed off when their mother reminded them, "We three are going to have to keep it clean. The rooms we don't use should be closed, and kept that way. It will save heat and dusting— Oh, all sorts of things."

The third floor would be out. Definitely. What about the basement?

"Just enough for a clothesline and storage."

"There's enough room for that!" the girls giggled.

As for the first floor, Phoebe made the decision. "I think we'll use the sitting room," she said, "and the garden room." Mary sighed with relief. "We'll make a habit of coming and going by the side door, but the front hall must be kept tidy. We won't need the big dining room, unless the family all come for a meal."

"Who's going to wash the windows?" asked Mary. "You said—"

Phoebe explained about the neighborhood yardman system. These same men and boys would wash the windows on the outside. . . .

"Looks like we're all set, then," said Linda pertly.

Phoebe laughed and said she hoped the girl was right. She still felt that she had taken on a big responsibility.

In the same week that the girls started school, she began to work in the big hospital complex, getting lost at first in the maze of corridors, tunnels, walkways, elevators and stairs, and found again.

She decided at once that she could do the work of Dr. Kinnamore's office. Correspondence, reports, forms—she had done all those things for Dr. Sam.

This new doctor, called the Chief—this Dr. Kinnamore —was a youngish man. Younger than Dr. Sam. In his late forties, Phoebe estimated. He was a large man, muscular, his hair beginning to gray and recede from his wide forehead. He had very blue eyes, a large and flexible mouth. He was a hard worker and expected others to want to work hard. He was a pleasant person, kind—and completely intolerant of mistakes—of failure.

Phoebe determined not to make many mistakes. She wondered at those she saw—an intern—a technician—who would risk Dr. Kinnamore's wrath by evading their duties or by employing short cuts. He always found them out, and his wrath was instant, complete.

As a legacy from her working in a small, intimate hospital, she found herself taking too personal an interest in events and in cases. Dr. Kinnamore's office was on one of the medical floors of the Center's tall main building. This was his decision to keep him closely in touch with the pulse of hospital life. Other staff doctors used the office space afforded in the Medical Services tower. With their office in the hospital itself, Phoebe could—and did—step out of the suite, a sheaf of papers in her hand, and run into the distressing experience of a junkie—she learned to use the term later—being brought in. The man was suffering from withdrawal; he was wild, incoherent, noisy. Those who cared for him—a policeman, an orderly, a resident doctor—must, or at least did, use violent means to restrain the young man.

Phoebe was shocked at the whole experience. She appealed to the floor superintendent, she ran to an attending doctor who came out of the elevator. "Do something!" she cried. "They'll hurt that man!"

"He's already hurt himself," said the doctor sternly. "Stand aside, miss. These hopheads can do *anything!*"

Phoebe returned to the door of her office. The young man's shouts and pleas were now somewhat muffled by the closed door of his room. He had been awful, she conceded, but the orderly had been entirely too rough. What were they doing to that poor man inside?

A young nurse told Phoebe what ailed the "poor man." "These cases are worse than crazy, you know."

"He's sick, or he wouldn't be here."

"He's sick all right," the nurse agreed. "And he'll be taken care of."

"Are you sure of that?"

"I'm sure. We get lots of hopheads."

"And beat them all?"

"When indicated, I guess we do," agreed the nurse, walking away.

Phoebe stood shaking her head, undecided whether to be sick, or to find Dr. Kinnamore and tell him, or—

"Is something wrong, Phoebe?"

She jumped. People just didn't call her Phoebe around

here—but this was her Uncle Howard. Forgetting the reserves she had about this man, she turned to him with passionate relief. "Oh, yes!" she cried. And she told him excitedly, pleading with him.

Her uncle listened to her, then he took her elbow in his hand and directed her back to Dr. Kinnamore's office. He opened the door and indicated that she was to go inside. She did, and he followed her, closing the door behind him. "I suppose Dr. Kinnamore is not here?" he said coldly.

"No. He—"

"Why were you out in the hall?"

Phoebe looked at the papers in her hand. "I was taking these notices to be duplicated and posted."

"Is there some urgency about doing that?"

Phoebe flushed. "I thought it would be quicker to take them myself. And I wanted to be sure . . ."

"Very commendable. You were looking after Dr. Kinnamore's interests."

"Yes, sir," said Phoebe meekly. "But—"

"Then, passing through the corridor of a large and busy hospital, you let yourself become involved in a case that was being admitted."

"But, Uncle Howard . . ."

"I think, here in the hospital, you had better call me Dr. Lewis."

"Yes, sir. I—"

She still was agitated. Her gray-blue eyes were wide, even her smooth yellow hair trembled. She gestured with her empty hand.

"When you took employment here, Phoebe," said her uncle, "were your duties defined to you?"

"Yes, sir." Now she began to look confused.

"Were those duties secretarial, or were you asked to perform certain medical duties?" His voice tinkled with chips of ice.

"Oh, Uncle Doc . . ." she cried.

"Obviously you saw a distressing thing this morning. To my certain knowledge, you will see other distressing things, Phoebe. We all do, working in this place which exists because of the distresses of life. But we, all of us, are trained to do certain, defined things. Some appear to be directly connected with the relief of distress, actually all things done here contribute. You do, when you type notices and see that they get promptly posted on the correct bulletin boards. May I suggest that you accept your defined position in this medical center, and consider that word, *promptly?*"

He didn't need to be so nasty! Phoebe told herself, as again she hurried down the hospital corridor. Even if he was right, he did not need to speak so coldly, so—severely. She had had every right to be upset.

On Saturday, Phoebe drove the girls to the church for junior choir practice, and imposed on their relationship to go into the rectory for a cup of coffee with Aunt Dorothy. Her Uncle Cecil was there, too, and he welcomed her gladly. She could, he said, help him carry in wood for the fireplace.

His wife told him to behave himself, and poured Phoebe a cup of coffee. The gray and white cat rubbed his back against her ankle, and she told these friendly people that Uncle Howard was a very crusty man.

"Oh, he is!" agreed Cecil Paule. "He crackles when he walks."

Phoebe smiled very faintly.

"Has something happened, dear?" asked Aunt Dorothy.

She told them briefly of what had happened on Thursday, and of Uncle Doc's lecture.

"He was trying to protect you, Phoebe," said the clergyman.

"I felt he was trying to protect his nice, shiny hospital. He didn't want me pulling a scene. Does Patrick live with him?"

She saw the glance exchanged between husband and wife.

"He has a room in his father's apartment, yes," said Aunt Dorothy.

"I think Uncle Doc talks to him. Pat was warm and friendly when I first came here, but now he acts—well—suspicious."

"At the hospital, you mean. Your relationship would be—well—modified there."

"Oh, I know that! There I call them both 'Dr. Lewis,' as prim and proper! But Pat—the other day I wanted to get some antiseptic to have at home—I wondered if I could get drugs at the hospital pharmacy, and I asked Pat. But, my goodness, the questions he asked me!"

"Oh, dear," sighed Aunt Dorothy.

"I only wanted a small bottle of Merthiolate, and some hartshorn to use for honey cookies. You'd have thought I was starting a business in illicit drugs. Or bootleg alcohol, maybe." She laughed a little, because of course she was joking.

"He asked me if I'd been making friends, and if the girls fitted well into the school— Oh, I don't know. He just seemed to be suspicious of us."

"Phoebe," said Cecil Paule firmly. She looked up at him. "Have you ever considered what the family has felt, to have you come here, and then decide to live among us?"

She flushed. "I thought you wanted me to do that. You asked me . . ."

"We did ask you. We wanted you to come. But, still, my dear, can't you imagine our side? Or Patrick's side? He thinks you will be, at least, loyal to your mother. And she was not friendly with any of us."

"I know . . ." Phoebe did wish she could escape the shadow of her mother. Perhaps she had made a mistake coming here where people had known her. The neighbors, the family— Of course they expected Phoebe, or even the girls, to be like Julia. At least to have accepted her judgment of things.

Uncle Cecil was watching her. He was a very wise person, Phoebe had decided. Compassionate, understanding —and wise. "Some day," he said now, "you are going to have to think through the situation concerning your mother, Phoebe, learn what the facts were, learn to face them. You will need to discard emotion and dwell with the results of your thinking—"

Phoebe's eyes were steady. "Isn't that the same thing Uncle Doc told me to do about the junkie at the hospital?" she asked.

"Yes, I suppose it is. You are a bright girl to see the analogy."

She shook her head impatiently. "I'm not *bright* at all," she cried. "I just wish my mother and the rest of you could have had a different relationship!"

He shook his head. "Then I am afraid you are not ready to begin your task, Phoebe."

She sighed. She still wished . . .

She wondered if she could talk to these patient, kind people about Jesse Holland. If he *had* known Julia. . . .

She didn't speak of him that morning, but, driving home again, she thought about Jesse.

Young Dr. Holland was a man to give a girl plenty to think about. He was a resident doctor at the hospital. A resident in urology, and so directly under Dr. Kinnamore —a dark man, slender, volatile—*brash*. That was the word Phoebe would use for Jesse.

He had claimed Phoebe's interest—at least her attention —on the first day he came into Dr. Kinnamore's office, saw Phoebe, and frankly announced to all concerned that he had fallen—but *hard!* but *flat!* for Mrs. Flowers.

He told everyone that. Phoebe herself. The floor nurses.

Even Dr. Kinnamore, who laughed and said he was relieved to know that Dr. Holland had such good taste.

It became a running joke on the floor, Holland's infatuation. Phoebe passed the whole thing off as being just one of those things, a gag, until the day when Jesse bought her a milk shake at the cafeteria and told her that he had known her mother.

Instantly she became acutely conscious of Jesse. Did he know Julia? How had he known her?

It was hard to get answers to those questions. Jesse was hard to pin down. The girls called him kooky, and Phoebe was inclined to agree with them. Certainly he was—different. Even odd. Sometimes she thought she didn't like him. He was too bold, too aggressive.

He could be—brash. Just as certainly he could be taken by strange, silent, brooding moods; he was subject to strange impulses. He had immediately claimed friendship with Phoebe and often would come to the house. At the end of a day, she would find him in the station wagon, ready to go home with her, pick up the girls, and eat supper. "You'll have to earn your keep," she assured him.

Or he would show up on Sunday afternoon, ready to suggest an excursion to the park. The river? The zoo?

"I have work to do."

"All right. I'll help."

And he did help. Sure, he would carry the girls' foot

lockers up to the third floor. He did carry them, Phoebe going with him to see if there were things to bring down. She had not yet gone thoroughly through things up on the third floor.

The day was a warm one, and Phoebe opened one of the windows in the gable to air out the place. "Don't let me forget to close it again, Jesse," she said.

Jesse went over to the window and stood looking out at the tree branches and down at the lawn. "You know, Phoebe?" he said, not turning. "I could fly as well as any bird. I could, this minute, dive out of this window and glide down and across to the street."

She started to laugh and say something—then she looked sharply at the dark young man in his white shirt and bright blue knit jacket. And she thought that he might try to do it—to fly.

Fear that he would began to crowd her throat. What should she say? Or do? The wrong word, the wrong move . . .

It was a relief when he turned away from the window and followed her down the stairs to sprawl in a deep chair in the sitting room.

Phoebe let him alone. She went back to the third floor and closed the window, pushing the foot lockers into a corner.

Those moods of Jesse's could frighten her. After that afternoon's experience she told herself not to "bother" with such a man.

But he was good company. He could think of "fun"

things to do. One evening he took Phoebe to a very good Italian restaurant. On a Sunday afternoon he took her and the girls for a trip on the small excursion steamer on the river.

At the hospital, it was nice to see his friendly face, to have him wave to her from the far end of the corridor, or bring his lunch tray over to the table where she sat in the cafeteria, and always tell her tidbits of hospital gossip. If she stopped "bothering" with Jesse, she would miss him, even after so short a time.

He loved to come to the big house, and seemed fascinated by it. She must admit that he could be a great help when he was there; he was tall, and reaching down the soup tureen from a high shelf, or bringing up some preserves from the basement shelves did save Phoebe steps and effort.

He said she should "make some sense" out of the food supplies in the basement, and spent nearly all of a week end rearranging boxes and helping her catalogue what was usable down there. It was on that Sunday afternoon that she came down the basement stairs after answering the telephone and saw Jesse find some of her mother's squirreled-away money in one of the cartons; he quickly pocketed the bills—there seemed to be three, and Phoebe had no idea of their value. Julia had hidden dollars as casually as she did the hundreds and twenties.

Phoebe thought she would ask Jesse about his find, but she did not at once, and even after a half-hour it became awkward to do it. So she guessed she would not mention it at all. She would just not let the man come around any more.

She did say to him then that they would have to finish the food cataloguing at a later time. "The girls and I can do it, you know. And just now I'll have to put you out because I must clean up. We are going to my uncle's for a family cookout."

He left reluctantly, even offering to go along.

"I'm glad you got rid of him," said Linda when she, Mary, and Phoebe were driving out to Uncle Bob's.

"He was helping us," Phoebe reminded the child.

"He acts as if he lived in our house," muttered Mary. Phoebe chose not to hear her.

Except for the brief, and temporary, threat of Jesse Holland, the girls did seem happy in their move to the city. They loved the big house, every inch of it. From the third floor to the vaulted basement, they explored, admired, and cherished the place. They liked their school, and almost immediately began to chatter French.

"They already have outclassed me," Phoebe confessed ruefully.

"You'll get used to that," Uncle Bob assured her.

The girls enjoyed their newly enlarged family, especially the cousins. They were ecstatic when it was arranged for Joanne and Kirk to stay with them while Uncle Bob and Aunt Katherine attended a Bar Association meeting. Joanne could ride the same school bus, Phoebe would take Kirk to his school, Aunt Dorothy would pick him up.

The girls flew about the house making things ready for their visitors. Kirk, they decided, would occupy the room that Mary had been using.

"And where will you go?" asked Phoebe.

"Oh, we have that all planned," the girls told her. "We are going to use Mary's room as a permanent guest room."

Phoebe's eyebrows went up.

"Yes," said Linda, bouncing on the couch. "Now that we have a family, we'll often need one."

Phoebe smiled at her. She was planning menus and shopping lists.

"You see," said Mary, crowding into the same chair with her mother, "we think—I *want* to use your old room. The one you're using now. But you said it had been yours as a girl. . . ."

"It was," said Phoebe.

"That's why I want it," said Mary. "And I think that you should use *your* mother's room. Now that you are grown up, and she's dead—and all."

Phoebe was shocked at the suggestion. She couldn't—she simply could *not* use Julia's room!

But the girls were enthusiastic and persistent. It was a large room, they pointed out, with that lovely curved bay and the fireplace. The chaise longue— Oh, yes, Phoebe must move into it!

She didn't want to do it. Even less she would want to explain to these wide-eyed, pink-cheeked girls why she did not want to move into her mother's room. "I'm too busy right now," she hedged.

"Oh, we'll move you! We'll move everything, Mother! And be very careful! Please, Mother? *Please!*"

The room was clean—she had no further argument. And the move, once made, turned out to be all right. The room was a pleasant one, with abundant drawer and closet space . . . and no ghosts. Phoebe wondered if she might not have taken Uncle Cecil's first step in her reconciliation with her mother, the first step toward facing facts and accepting them.

She wanted to tell him of that step, but found herself too shy to do it. Or maybe she was too busy caring for her enlarged family during the next four days.

The girls enjoyed every minute of the visit. And so did the Lewis children. Kirk took over the third-floor playroom and informed his parents that he thought he would move into the city. "I can put up my trains and leave 'em, and have a workbench, and—"

"Apparently you have more to offer, Phoebe, than suburbia," laughed Uncle Bob.

"We do have a lot," Mary assured him. "Our big house and— Of course we don't have a dad, the way most kids do."

Phoebe, watching them, listening to them, ventured to ask the girls if they really felt the lack of a father.

"It would be nice to have one," Linda told her. "At school, sometimes, the teacher says to ask our dad, or to bring our dad to a hockey game—things like that. But—well—we wish our own dad had lived, and we don't want you bringing in somebody else like that Jesse."

"Definitely not! " said Mary. "He's a creep."

Phoebe rebuked the child. Dr. Holland was not a creep. . . .

"We think he is," Mary insisted.

Phoebe could not, really, have explained in words just why she had defied her Uncle Howard and made the effort she did to keep track of the junkie whom she had seen admitted to the hospital. Except for her pity of him, the boy was not appealing, and he used the foulest language Phoebe had ever heard.

But she still made it a practice to go past his room several times a day, finding some reason to look at his chart at the desk, listening alertly to any talk about him.

There were forty other patients on that same corridor, but for some reason Phoebe kept track of this one. He was listed as seriously ill, over and beyond the effects of the withdrawal routine. No visitors were allowed and so far as Phoebe knew, none attempted to see him.

One morning Jesse Holland caught her slowing her step so that she might get a look into the junkie's room. "You still feeling sorry for that punk, Phoebe?" he asked her.

She faced him. "Oh, Jesse . . ."

He shrugged. "It's all right with me if you are curious about a patient. I just wish I could raise as much attention."

"But he—he's so *alone,* Jesse! He came in here with everyone against him; he has no company . . ."

"Look, girl. That guy's a hophead. And he has TB, besides. That's a very bad combination. We got him, we have to handle him, but this is no time for us to coddle the guy. I can tell you this isn't the first rough time for him on the withdrawal circuit. He knows he has tuberculosis. So—he just plain isn't smart, or he wouldn't be back there in that high bed, with almost every chance against his ever getting out of it on his two feet."

"But," said Phoebe, almost standing on tiptoe to reach Jessue with her argument, "aren't you sorry for him? Don't you wish he could get well? It seems such a waste! He's young and—"

Jesse put his hand on her arm. "You're wonderful, Phoebe," he said. "I only wish I could count on your being sorry for me when I need it."

"Oh, Jesse—"

She supposed it was just about then that her Uncle Doc saw them together. Jesse could be extreme in his manner, overexpressive—and the corridor was a pretty public place with a steady traffic of nurses, doctors, personnel of all sorts going along it. Even Dr. Howard Lewis traveled it.

He must have seen her talking to Jesse, because that afternoon when she went out to the parking lot to her car, Uncle Doc cut across to speak to her and to ask her if Holland was bothering her.

"Holland?" she asked. Then she flushed. "Everybody calls him Jesse on the floor," she explained to her uncle. "But, of course— No, Uncle Howard, Dr. Holland doesn't bother me. He's a little extreme sometimes in things he says or does—but—I think he really wants to help me; he's only friendly, and—" She finished tying her blue scarf around her head.

Uncle Doc's face was stern. "I believe you could do without his friendship and help, Phoebe," said the surgeon crisply. "In fact, I would like to tell you to cut off any efforts he might make in that direction." His tone was sharp, and Phoebe looked at him in surprise.

"I am serious," he answered her expression. "And I've taken on the right to be. You're young yourself, and you have two young daughters."

"But Jesse isn't like *that!*" Phoebe protested. "I know he's what the girls call kooky . . ."

"Er—yes!" said Dr. Lewis. He began to put on his gloves. "I'd like to think you would take my advice, Phoebe," he said.

"It isn't that I like Jesse. But I can't start out being rude to the doctors . . ."

"You're right, when it comes to behavior in the hospital. I hope I have exaggerated your contact with Dr. Holland."

He had. Phoebe knew that he had. But even if he had not, what right had Uncle Howard to pass out orders to her? And why? Jesse was a kook, and she didn't really like him, but he wasn't all that bad.

She was even more puzzled when, the next day, Dr. Kinnamore asked her if she had become friends with Dr. Holland.

What was going on? What kind of reputation did Jesse

have in this hospital center? Had he a police record? Her eyes flashed with anger.

"Do you see much of Dr. Holland?" Dr. Kinnamore was asking her. "Outside of the hospital, I mean."

"Well—not much, Dr. Kinnamore. He's been friendly. . . ."

"Do you like the young man?"

She laughed. "I like to have friends."

"Of course you do. You're a young woman, and you need friends. But do you really enjoy a fellow like Holland?"

Phoebe sat shaking her head. She could *not* understand. . . . Then her head snapped up. "Did Dr. Lewis speak to you about me and Jesse Holland?" she asked sharply.

Instantly she regretted asking, and when Dr. Kinnamore denied that Uncle Howard had approached him, she believed him—or tried to.

But she still wondered . . .

She was ready to believe the worst of Uncle Howard. She did not like the man. She had not warmed to him, nor he to her, as had been the case with the rest of the family. He had been her father's friend; he blamed her mother for what he considered to be her mistreatment of Phoebe's father—and he probably carried over that feeling to Phoebe.

Phoebe listened to what Dr. Kinnamore said, she had listened to Uncle Howard, but of course she did continue to see Jesse around the hospital. He would come into Dr.

Kinnamore's office on legitimate business. He would exchange a few sentences with the secretary there. He would be in the personnel lounge when Phoebe took a coffee break; there were other doctors there, too, and nurses. Phoebe talked to all of them if they wanted to talk to her. Jesse wanted to.

One noontime Phoebe made a quick run to the bookstore on the avenue to buy a copy of *A Tale of Two Cities* for Mary. As she passed its entrance, Jesse came out of the hotel—he'd been to the barber's. They were surprised to see each other, and it would have been plain silly not to walk back to the hospital together!

One rainy evening she gave him a lift in her car; she didn't care who saw her do it! She was too busy, and could honestly say so, when he asked her for a date. "Another time?" he asked her.

"We'll see," she agreed.

One of these times Dr. Kinnamore saw them together, and he mentioned the fact to Phoebe, plainly showing that he did not like her to have dates with Jesse.

"You can do better than Holland," he assured the young woman who sat at the side of his desk.

Had he called her in for dictation just to tell her this? She drew a deep breath. "Dr. Kinnamore," she asked, "what's wrong with Jesse?"

"Do you really like him, Phoebe?"

She shrugged. Not *like*. Not remembering the money she had seen him take, not remembering the odd things he could say, and do—She leaned forward, her eyes bright. "If *you* don't like him, Dr. Kinnamore," she said, "why is he here working for you?"

He laughed. "He's working for the hospital, my dear girl, not for me."

"Oh, but—"

"Yes, I know. He is responsible to me, as Chief of Medical Services. And I am responsible for him. He is a resident in urology—last year he was an intern in medicine. But interns and residents are not chosen, not assigned, according to my personal liking for the men. As a matter of truth, Holland is a good doctor. His medical performance is good. Has been to date. It is on that basis he was placed here, and the system keeps him here. Still—" The big man leaned back in his chair, and his very blue eyes studied his secretary. "Well, I'll say this much. If I were a young woman, I would not marry the man. If I were a girl like you, Phoebe."

"If you were a girl like me," said Phoebe spiritedly, "you would be thirty-two years old, and you would have two daughters."

The doctor chuckled. "You look like a catch to me," he assured her.

So Phoebe laughed, too. She probably was taking the whole situation entirely too seriously. She made the notes of all the things Dr. Kinnamore wanted done, and then she busied herself in doing them.

She typed the duty schedules, the meeting notices—the schedule of ward walks and conferences. She answered the telephone a dozen times, and sorted the mail . . .

The doctor was in contact with his office; he phoned her from some corner of the complex—he came flying in at eleven-thirty, he talked on his phone; he came out, dressed in street clothes.

"I'll be back by three," he told Phoebe. "You can, at risk of life and limb, reach me at the Noonday Club."

"Yes, Dr. Kinnamore." He was to make a speech. She handed him his notes bound in a small leather book.

"And, Phoebe—" He turned back from the door.

"Yes, sir?"

"I thought I'd remind you that a new resident is coming in very soon now and will be on this floor. Well, he'll be on various medical floors. . . . He has a rather special assignment."

Phoebe waited. Mary acted the same way when she made conversation leading up to some particular point.

"He's an Englishman," said Dr. Kinnamore. "Name's Newbern. He is on a research grant."

"Medical research?" asked Phoebe politely.

"Yes. Of course it's medical. He's to do research on the matter of drugs. Narcotics, that is. The grant was made to our university, and this young man is being taken on to direct the study, or to do it, actually."

"Why is he coming to the United States? You said he was English."

"Oh, that. Well, the medical situation in England is such that the government controls give a very low return on a doctor's services. This drives the doctors away from home.

Instead of attempting to stem the tide at the top, the authorities are ready to let their trained, mature men go, and merely increase the registration of medical students. That practice is profligate, to my way of thinking."

If profligate meant wasteful, he was right. "First you said he was a young man, now you speak of him as mature."

"*Young* is always a relative term, Phoebe. He's a well-trained doctor, so he has maturity. And he will be well-trained, to be certified to practice here. The examinations given to foreigners, you know, are harder. . . . They are what ours should be. Newbern is in his late thirties, I think. Which is young, to me. I want him to do good work here. Will you be nice to him?"

"Me?" The suggestion startled her.

"I meant professionally, of course. There will be many ways you can assist him. I foresee that things may be a little tough for him at first. Our research program—we don't go to England often to bring in a man; perhaps he will be considered as a rival by the local talent. Then, he will be in a strange land, beginning new work in a new place. Since he falls into my service, I'd hope my secretary might be willing to extend professional courtesies as she can . . ."

"But of course, Dr. Kinnamore. If you want me to show him around, help him—"

"I do, but what I am hoping, of course, is that you would extend your professional being nice to other sorts of entertainment, should Newbern be so inclined."

Phoebe relaxed in her chair. Dr. Kinnamore was

matchmaking! He actually was suggesting that this Englishman be a substitute for Jesse Holland!

She looked up, laughing, at the Chief. "Oh, come now!" she cried. "Your Dr. Newbern probably has a girl of his own. Or even a wife. What are you trying to stir up here?"

"He's not married," Dr. Kinnamore assured her.

Phoebe could feel the pertness in her; the Chief had permitted this change. "I'll bet he won't like my type," she challenged.

Dr. Kinnamore smiled and felt of his necktie. "What I am hoping is that *you* will like *him!*"

"And you think I should let him divert me from Dr. Holland."

Dr. Kinnamore grinned wryly. "You don't like that fellow, do you?"

Phoebe shrugged and fingered the papers on her desk. "As I say, Dr. Kinnamore, I am thirty-two. I have two preteen daughters—men are not too plentiful for women in my fix. But, don't worry. . . ."

"Dr. Lewis is watching Holland, too, you know. In your behalf." The doctor spoke gravely.

"Yes," said Phoebe, equally grave. "He's shown that he is. But surely my uncle doesn't take responsibility for me."

Dr. Kinnamore opened the door. "You'd be a lucky girl if he would," he said, going out.

Well, thought Phoebe. Well . . .

SEVEN

WHEN Dr. Talley Newbern reached the hospital, he appeared in the halls quietly and unobtrusively; his name appeared on the duty roster; he was *there*. . . .

Perhaps his very quietness increased the stir he made. "Have you seen him?" The questions rustled like leaves from floor desk to diet kitchen, from the personnel lounge to Phoebe's office.

"I think he touches up his hair," said the Floor Head to her.

Phoebe laughed. "Why would he?"

"Oh, he must. He does look young—but his hair is the color of platinum."

"Nice hair line, too," said Phoebe. She was not ready to decide if Dr. Newbern was handsome.

Attractive, certainly. Tall, slender, quick-moving. His

smooth, silvery hair was combed severely back from the peak on his forehead. His skin looked weathered; his eyes were hazel and bright. There was a cleft in his chin. But the impression of strength was too great for anyone—for Phoebe, at least—immediately to label him as handsome.

Others thought he was. Even some of the men showed that they thought him good-looking by their disparagement of him. And the women—aide girls, nurses, patients— Phoebe heard enough of the talk about Dr. Newbern to have it register, but she was very busy just then in the office. Dr. Kinnamore had begun to ask her to "bring her book" and accompany him on his ward walks so that she could take down in notes, and later transcribe fully, his observations.

Since her office duties did not diminish, she must concentrate her busyness. Dr. Newbern came into the office, she spoke to him, and he to her—but that was all of it. There at first.

Even if she had not been busy at her desk, her mind would have been occupied. Dick, her brother, had written asking if he might have some money from his mother's estate. Not a lot—a thousand dollars was all—but getting it required attention from Phoebe as executor, from Uncle Bob as her attorney, from a garage man should they decide to sell her mother's car. . . .

These business conferences took time and had to be fitted in after she left the hospital, or on Saturday; this let her home duties pile up.

"Don't you want Uncle Dick to have any money?"

Mary asked when Phoebe tried to explain to the girls why she was so busy—too busy to make a Hallowe'en costume —not to mention two of them.

"Why does Uncle Dick want so much money?" asked Linda, the direct one.

"It really isn't so much . . ."

"A thousand *dollars?*"

Phoebe laughed. "Well, of course, that is a lot of money. But it is his—or will be, when the estate is settled. He wants to buy a car."

"For a thousand dollars?"

"They cost much more, dear. If Dick were in this country, he could borrow the money. Over in Arabia . . ."

"O.K.," said the girl. "What will we wear for Hallowe'en? Mrs. Haines says the older girls are supposed to take the little trick-and-treaters around. And there's to be a party at school."

"Then we must have costumes," Phoebe decided.

These were arranged. A pirate's costume for Linda— jeans, a white blouse, a bandanna and eye patch. For Mary, a long, ruffled dress and a floppy hat—old things of Phoebe's. "She looks like a floozy," Phoebe giggled to Aunt Dorothy when she finished putting make-up on the pretty blonde child and sent her off to the school party.

But the girls had fun, and that evening, when Uncle Bob came to the house with papers for Phoebe to sign, he found things indeed hectic, as Phoebe claimed. "I didn't know Armand Heights ran to so many children," he confessed.

"They are taking advantage of me," Phoebe told him. "Mary and Linda have declared this headquarters. If the trick-and-treaters need anything from bathroom to a depository for filled bags, our house is available."

He looked down at his papers. "Maybe I should come back . . ."

"We could go up to the third floor."

"It seems that you're needed on the field of battle. I'll come back. Tomorrow."

Tomorrow would be fine. And it would have been, except that when Uncle Bob came, he found Jesse Holland there before him. Jesse told Phoebe to go on and talk to her lawyer-uncle; he would amuse himself.

Jesse didn't often come to the house; until Uncle Doc had interfered, Phoebe had begun to discourage his coming at all. It was just bad luck that he should be there that evening. It was even more bad luck that Eugene Rotan should also decide to pay a call on Phoebe at that time. He had discovered that the holograph will was being presented for probate; his name, he reminded Phoebe and her uncle, was mentioned on the document. "Personally, I don't think that scribbled note is testamentary," he assured Robert Lewis.

Uncle Bob was firm; he suggested that they all let the Probate Court decide things like the validity of the will and the qualifications of the executor.

And while he talked, Jesse Holland strolled in from the kitchen where he had gone to get a cup of coffee, and he was introduced to Eugene Rotan, who made some comment on the fact that Dr. Holland seemed quite at home "around here."

Uncle Bob's eyebrow went up, and Phoebe flushed. "We have business to take care of," she told the two unwanted callers. "If you will excuse us—"

"I told you, sweetie . . ." Jesse began.

"I am asking you to leave," said Phoebe firmly.

And they did leave, laughing at her, but also planning to go on to a "place" which Rotan knew. "We'll be welcome there," he said. "I'll talk to you again, Lewis."

"In my office," said Uncle Bob. He stood at the door until they got into Rotan's car and drove off.

"Now," he said, turning to Phoebe, "we'll get things taken care of before something else pops up. You know? Those two scared me more than the girls' goblins and ghosties."

"Yes, I know," mourned Phoebe. "And I am sorry. I don't like them. . . ."

"They seem to hit it off together," Uncle Bob commented mildly.

They did, they had—which disturbed Phoebe more, she thought, than the warnings which Uncle Howard and the Chief has issued about Jesse. She would listen to those warnings now, and she would have nothing more to do with Dr. Holland! Anyone who could like Rotan . . .

This bothered her.

It bothered her, too, when Mary became ill.

Phoebe had to speak to Dr. Kinnamore about that. "My child seems to be sick—a cold and a temperature— I am afraid I'll have to cut my time a little, come in later, leave earlier, if she doesn't improve at once. I may even have to stay at home for a few days—"

"Why don't you bring her here to the hospital, admit her?"

"Oh, I couldn't do that!" She looked at Dr. Kinnamore "Could I?"

He laughed. "Others do. You have hospitalization on the girls?"

"Yes, of course."

"All right, then. You bring her in—I'll tell Dr. Newbern to look after her. She'll be my admission, of course, but he— Do you think Mary will be able to understand him?"

Phoebe bristled at once. "I don't know Dr. Newbern," she said crisply, "but he speaks beautifully."

Dr. Kinnamore smiled and nodded. "You're right. And he's a good doctor, too."

"Why on earth would England let him go?"

"Unless they'd change their whole system of socialized medicine, Phoebe, they couldn't hope to hold dynamic young doctors like Newbern; these men know they are wasting their productive years on long lines of patients who come to their offices primarily because they want someone to talk to; for the really sick the doctors can't get hospital beds; their hospitals are old, and there are not enough of them. Committees, not trained administrators, run the hospitals. I think the situation must be very bad, or a chap like Newbern would not risk the charge of disloyalty and depart for America. He is very well-trained, you see, and in a special field. At his age, he wants to work and to do things."

"Is the money better here?" asked Phoebe, thinking of Mary more intently than she was attending to Dr. Newbern's problems.

"If Newbern is as good as I think, the money will come," said Dr. Kinnamore. "Just now, he probably is not earning more. He is here on a grant, and I'd hope he could do some good work for us."

"Starting with Mary," said Phoebe, smiling.

"Yes! Though she will be out of his line. But since you think she could understand him—a few of his patients give him a little trouble, I'm afraid. As well as some of our doctors."

Yes. Phoebe had heard them. They mimicked the Englishman's crisp accent. They made a thing of saying "veddy" for very, and, "Nurse, could I have the rec-*ord* of Mrs. Smith?" The other residents made fun of the way he said *ag-ile*, and atti*tude*, their manner mincing.

"I was afraid Newbern might have some troubles," Dr. Kinnamore was saying to her. "But our men really should give him a chance. What difference does it make if he asks an orderly to 'brush' the floor, when we'd say 'sweep' it? Or if he calls a Gurney cart a trolley?"

Phoebe laughed. "I've already said that I think he speaks beautifully."

"My colleagues miss the American twang," said Dr. Kinnamore sourly. "Newbern is a good doctor, too. He is trained in psychiatry—"

"Psychiatry?"

"That's his specialty. Now he is going to do research in this business of narcotic addiction and rehabilitation, which is a big and living problem. He is anxious to explore the American approach to it."

"It's different from the English one, isn't it?"

"Yes. Up to just recently they seemed to be getting good results by allowing the hard stuff—heroin and morphine, codeine—to be bought by a certified addict. That probably has cut down on the crime caused here because addicts are ready, or forced, to use any means to get money to pay for the illicit stuff. In England there is no especial stigma to the use of narcotics."

Stigma. Hmmmn. Phoebe thought about that. Then she looked up. The use of drugs did put a mark upon one. "But," she said, "there is some mark, some shame, upon other diseases, too. There certainly is if we call alcoholism a disease."

"You're right," said Dr. Kinnamore.

"Is it bad to make it shameful? I mean, if a person has pride—"

"Pride seems to be the first thing lost to your drug addict or to your alcoholic. But enough remains that the public attitude drives the sufferers underground. Medically that is bad, because there the victim can't easily ask for and get help."

"I see," said Phoebe. "And is that where Dr. Newbern's research comes in?"

Dr. Kinnamore smiled at her. "You'd better go home and

get your daughter. I can use a smart secretary like you full time around here."

She flushed. "Thank you, Dr. Kinnamore," she said shyly.

Mary Flowers was a beautiful child. She had exquisite, fair skin, dark-lashed eyes, set beautifully; her hair was pale gold, worn long and well-brushed. She looked like an angel, people were always telling Phoebe. And she did, especially in her choir robe and velvet beanie at church. In the school chorus, Mary was put in the front row.

"She needn't be able to sing a note," Linda had told Phoebe. Linda could sing. She was slender, dark, wiry, and not especially jealous of her sister. Phoebe once had said that Mary's doll-like prettiness perhaps made up for her spine.

In the hospital, of course, much was made of the lovely child. After a day or two of being feverish and miserable, Mary enjoyed the whole experience.

"I've fallen in love with Dr. Newbern," she told Phoebe.

"Oh, now, Mary! Really!"

"Well, I have. He calls me 'Ducky,' and his first name is Talley. Did you know that?"

Phoebe did know.

"He used to live in England. Did you know *that?*"

"Mary—"

"I didn't pry. He told me. He lived in an old brick house, not in the city, but somewhat close to it. He says 'somewhat.' He talks the way our math teacher writes numbers, real neatly."

Phoebe smiled, where Mary could not see her.

"He has a mother and a father," Mary told. "And a dog named Cornwall. It's a black dog. He also has a brother, and a niece and a nephew. He says 'nev-you.' Do you think we'll ever go to England, Mother?"

"I don't have any such plans now, Mary."

"Oh, I know that! But Dr. Newbern thinks I would like it."

Phoebe gave in to temptation. "Does your Dr. Newbern have a girl?" she asked, as casually as she could.

Mary gave a little bounce in the high bed. "Oh, I hope not!" she cried.

Phoebe laughed at the child. But the next day she made a special point of thanking Dr. Newbern. She had heard him say, out in the corridor, that he was going downstairs for a late breakfast. She decided it was time for a cup of coffee for herself. She found him seated at a small table in the cafeteria.

"I am Phoebe Flowers . . ." she began.

He was on his feet, holding the second chair. "Of course!" he said.

"Well, I never know if people will remember me in this big hospital." She sat down and took a napkin. "And I wanted especially to thank you for being nice to my daughter."

"She is a delightful child, and of course it is my job. . . . She is doing very well, you know."

"Yes. That's why I am thanking you. Perhaps it was your special skill and ability that got her well so quickly."

"Bed rest, fluids—that takes little skill."

Phoebe leaned forward. "I understand you are a psychiatrist."

His eyes were keenly on her face. "Primarily, here, I am a doctor. An M.D. But, yes, I was especially trained in psychiatry. And now drug addiction—all phases of that situation—has come to be my fancy."

"Oh," said Phoebe, "are you trying to help the man in three fifty-four? He's spoken of as a junkie."

Dr. Newbern touched his lips with his napkin. "He's on my list," he agreed. "But as for helping him—I am afraid his dependence on drugs is probably too great. That happens, you know, in any case of drug use. A psychological dependence adds to the physical problem. I should like very much to help your young man."

Phoebe finished her coffee. "He's not my young man," she pointed out. "I just happened to see him admitted. It was pretty awful." She stood up. "I must get back to work, but I did want to thank you."

Dr. Newbern stood, too. "I only wish," he said earnestly, "that we could find a way to help Mary's bones."

Phoebe turned back to face him. "Oh, *could* we?" she asked intently. Her hands were clasped tightly. "That is the *one* dream of my life!"

He smiled at her. "Of course it is," he said warmly. "I

think you might realize it, too. Through Dr. Lewis. He is a fine surgeon, and I understand he is your uncle."

Phoebe shook her head. "Mary talks entirely too much."

"No," said the Englishman, "I don't believe she was the one who told me that."

Phoebe turned away again. "It doesn't make any difference," she said. "I don't have a toehold with Dr. Lewis." She held out her hand. "Thank you again," she said stiffly. And stiffly she walked away, a pretty, golden-haired young woman in a light brown knitted suit.

Talley Newbern watched her appreciatively.

Other eyes followed her. Particularly the intent black eyes of Dr. Jesse Holland. Phoebe had seen him at the counter. She knew that he watched her, and it made her uncomfortable. He would speak about her sitting with Newbern—and she would have an answer for him.

She was relieved that the day could pass without an encounter; but she was not surprised at all to have him come to the house that evening, and then make a ridiculous scene about her ten minutes with Dr. Newbern.

He was in one of his keyed-up moods; she had become accustomed to them. He strode in and faced her accusingly; his face was darkly flushed, his mouth was a grim slit, his dark eyes burned. All over a cup of coffee? Phoebe would give him the scene he wanted, and put him out in the process. She asked Linda please to finish wiping the supper dishes. The child gone, she faced Jesse.

"I don't know what this is all about," she said. "You have

133

no privilege to censor my choice of companions."

"It was your choice?" cried Jesse.

"It was my choice. I joined him where he was eating his breakfast. I wanted to thank him for being good to Mary."

"It makes a pretty story," said Jesse bitterly.

Phoebe nodded. "I am glad you like it. Now you had better leave, Jesse." She moved to the door and opened it.

"I didn't come clear down here," he shouted, "to be thrown out of your house."

"I don't know what you came for. Evidently to make a scene. Well, you've made it. So—" She opened the door still more widely. A cold wind rustled dry leaves along the porch floor.

And even as she stared at Jesse, his mood changed. He relaxed, a smile softened his mouth; the rasp melted from his voice.

"Oh, Phoebe," he said, stretching his hand toward her. "I'm sorry."

"You should be!"

"I know it, I know it." He came toward her, to take the door and close it. He put his hand on her shoulder. "Forgive me?" he asked softly.

She tried to step free, but his hold tightened. He turned her and drew her toward him; he would have bent and kissed her, but she pushed hard against his chest. "Let me go!" she cried. "What's got into you, Jesse?"

"You girl, me man."

"Yes, sir! And the game stops right there!"

"Aren't you going to ask me to sit down?"

"No. I want you to leave."

"Still? I told you I was sorry I'd kicked up dust."

She waited, standing stiffly. He stood regarding her; she felt itchy, and shamed somehow, under his gaze.

He took out a cigarette and lit it, his eyes still upon her throat, her bosom. "You know, Phoebe," he said, "the trouble with you is that you don't trust people. You go at everybody with a chip on your shoulder."

"That just is not true!"

He argued the point, but she made him leave without letting him into the sitting room. And when he had left, Phoebe kept thinking resentfully of all that Jesse had said and done. The scene he had made, with Linda right there in the house!

She was doing some ironing, and she thumped the iron so vigorously that Linda heard her and commented on it.

"Oh, I'm just thinking hard," Phoebe told the child.

"About Dr. Holland?"

"Not any more than I can help," said Phoebe, thumping the iron again.

Linda laughed. "I don't like him either," she said.

"But there are lots of people we do like, aren't there?"

"Oh, sure," said the child, going back to her homework. Linda was a good student.

There were people whom Phoebe trusted, too. Of course

there were. Not Jesse! But she trusted Dr. Sam. And Dr. Kinnamore. And—and she could trust Dr. Newbern, too. She was sure she could.

In the next days, an incident or two occurred that made Phoebe wonder if Jesse had, really, said anything—or even made a scene with Dr. Newbern about her. He had no right! She did not want Dr. Newbern to think he had a right! She considered speaking to Jesse about it. She even considered saying something to Dr. Newbern.

She did neither, and later she was glad. It was always better, she thought, to wait a little, not act on anger or through fear.

But Jesse was not being kind to the new man. Phoebe saw an incident or two, she heard of others. The nurses were indignant. Dr. Holland, they said, had no room to criticize the way another man talked.

Dr. Kinnamore laughed about the situation. "Nothing reveals an inferiority complex so fast as mockery meant to be disparaging." Phoebe overheard him saying that to another staff doctor. "Holland knows that Newbern is better-educated than he is."

"He's a better doctor, probably," agreed the other man.

"He's very good," Dr. Kinnamore agreed. Phoebe glowed.

"Are you having trouble with Holland?"

"Not trouble, really. But he does seem to be riding Newbern."

Phoebe thought it disgusting of Jesse. He was jealous of Dr. Newbern's manners, ability—a good many things.

And that afternoon, passing the Englishman in the hall, he asked her about Mary, as he always did—Phoebe impulsively suggested that he come to the house—say, on Sunday afternoon?—to see Mary.

Dr. Newbern bowed. "I would very much like to come to your house," he said gravely, "to see Mary."

He did come, in the latter part of the afternoon on Sunday, which was a cold day, with gusts of snow occasionally whirling before a brisk northwesterly wind. The girls were watching for him, and when he stopped to pick up a red-star maple leaf from the ground, and to gaze at the tree from which it had fallen, Linda opened the door enough to call out to him.

"Mary wants to know what you are doing, Dr. Newbern!"

He looked around, laughed, and came up to the porch, then into the garden room. "I was picking up one of your jewels," he told Linda. "Hello, Mary! You look blooming."

She smiled and held his arm. "Dr. Newbern calls our maple leaves jewels," she told Phoebe.

"They are, you know," said the tall doctor. He was slowly turning about to examine the garden room. "How are you, Mrs. Flowers? Oh, but this room is *grand!*"

He carefully laid the leaf on a low table and began to unwind his scarf. "Handle it carefully, Mary," he told the child. "It's a tatty old muffler, but it's all I have."

Mary, giggling, carefully folded the length of wool. Linda took his topcoat into the hall. Talley Newbern now walked about the room, having again picked up the scarlet leaf. "We don't have tree colors in the fall, you know," he instructed the Flowers. "This area where you live—all the tremendous houses, and the lawns, and the colored trees and shrubbery—it must be fairyland in the early autumn."

"Don't your trees turn in the fall?" Phoebe asked him. "I know you have oaks. Sherwood Forest, and all—"

"We have the trees. And even the same bushes. But our climate—I think it may be too wet. At any rate, we don't have the color. Nor does Europe. America is particularly blessed."

He touched the tufted velvet chair, gazed up at the chandelier, saying, "My *word!*" His hand fell on the brass shield of the fireplace. "Does it work?" he asked.

"I don't know. We haven't opened it. But when I was a child we sometimes had a fire in here. It's a coal grate."

With an exclamation of pleasure, Talley hitched up his trouser-knees, squatted on the hearth, and lifted the cover from the small, arched opening. "It surely is a coal grate," he confirmed. "Could we have a fire?"

"There's a wood fireplace in the sitting room—"

He went to see. The wood fireplace was very nice, he said without enthusiasm, but he confessed to being homesick for coal.

"There's the gas, you know," he pointed out. "The

ineffable smell—"

Phoebe chuckled. "Especially when it smokes."

"There's some coal in the basement," said Linda. "In one of those rooms, Mother. . . ."

"Linda would know," she said. "She's explored every inch of this house."

Dr. Newbern smiled at the child. "Do you think we could talk Mums into a coal fire?" he asked the children conspiratorially.

It was great fun. "I think I'll let you work on me," said Phoebe.

"There's a coal bucket," Mary pointed out.

"Scuttle," Dr. Newbern corrected her. "Anything so brass and shiny has to be a scuttle."

They got the coal, they kindled the fire—it finally burned with the desired smell and the proper popping of sparks. They all settled down before it and talked about the Heights and the house. The girls said he must stay for supper—they would bring it in on trays. Could they? "*Mums?*" asked Linda mischievously.

It was a very fine evening. Phoebe prepared the bowls of oyster stew, and let the girls toast cheese sandwiches. She heaped a green bowl with fresh fruit. Everything went in to the low tables in the garden room, with the night pressing against the long windows and the firelight twinkling from every prism of the great chandelier.

"I like him *much* better than Jesse," Phoebe told herself contentedly.

When the girls offered to clear their supper away and

wash the dishes, she talked to the doctor about the work he was doing at their hospital. "Dr. Kinnamore told me you were, among other things, comparing the drug-addiction situation here with that in England."

"Yes. I am."

"We don't handle it as well, I understand."

"That opinion was established," he agreed. "But lately we have been forced to second thoughts on the matter."

"Oh?"

"Yes. Because the figures for this year"—he said *figgers*—"have mounted rapidly. From four hundred seventy-one known addicts, we now have thirteen hundred. And for those under twenty, the count has risen from two to two hundred."

"Why should that happen?"

He took a pipe from the pocket of his tweed jacket and held it up, his eyes inquiring.

Phoebe smiled and nodded. "Of course."

He filled the pipe from a worn leather pouch, tamped the tobacco with a precise finger, put the stem between his teeth, and, taking the tongs, lifted a coal from the fire to light it.

"You'll burn your nose!" cried Phoebe.

His light brown eyes twinkled at her. "Been doing that since I was nineteen," he boasted. "Haven't yet burned my nose."

"You could."

He shrugged and nodded. "I could," he agreed. "If it is hard on your nerves, have the girls make me some spills."

"Spills?"

"I'll show them. Now! What were we talking about? Oh, yes. Permissiveness. That was our system of handling drug addiction, you know. England's system. And I've decided that the fault is not, was not, with the system of permissiveness, but with permissiveness itself. The addicts began giving the drug to others to 'try,' and that of course made the rolls increase."

"Is there a solution?" asked Phoebe. He plans to come again, she told herself. To use his *spills*.

"The solution that seems the most hopeful," Talley was saying, "is to register all addicts. But *not*," he added quickly, "to treat them as criminals. Then, only registered doctors should be allowed to prescribe heroin or morphine. I should also want addicts to be steered to treatment in a psychiatric hospital."

"And that's *your* field!"

"It is. But it does seem plain that there is a psychotic element in addiction. A reason for beginning, and a larger one still for continuing."

It was good talk. The whole visit was good. Phoebe saw the doctor depart into the night, and turned back to her warm hearthside, thinking about the new friend whom she had found. Perhaps Dr. Newbern was not a man to *stir* a woman—to stir Phoebe—as Jesse sometimes could do. . . .

She put her cool hand to her cheek, suddenly gone hot. But that was a shameful thought, she reproved herself. She did not like Jesse! Nothing would ever come of the stirrings which the man could arouse. Though there was nothing wrong in a woman's feeling, there was nothing wrong with her liking a man . . .

Liking one as much as she did Talley Newbern. Phoebe had lived alone for too many years. Too many young years—and they got no less lonely.

Thanksgiving was to be spent at Uncle Bob's house. The whole family went to church in the morning, and they returned to the house to the heavenly smell of roasting turkey, pumpkin pie—bowls of yellow chrysanthemums.

Everyone ate enormously, of course, and the whole affair was friendly, relaxed, loving. Afterwards, Phoebe found the courage to talk to Uncle Doc, and to ask him if he thought anything could be done for Mary's spine.

"Is she getting worse?" he asked.

"That's what I wanted to ask you."

"We'd need to make careful examinations. I've been waiting for you to ask me to get things started."

Phoebe looked at him in surprise; facing him, she was seated on the wide hassock beside his chair. "Why?" she asked. "I mean, why did you wait for me to ask?"

Howard Lewis tented his fingers and regarded his niece through the triangle which they made. "I know," he said slowly, "that you don't trust me, Phoebe."

"Oh—" Jesse had said she didn't trust people. It must show.

"No," said Uncle Doc, "you don't. You have not. Therefore, as a doctor, and part of this consultation is on that basis, isn't it?"

She nodded and swept a lock of hair out of her eyes.

"Therefore," he continued, "I waited for you to approach me on the subject."

"Well—" she said. Then she looked up at him, her eyes shining. "I don't think you have always trusted me. Maybe you still don't?"

Dr. Lewis's eyebrows went up, and he nodded. "Perhaps," he said, "it is good to wait a little. Always. To be sure of one's self." Then he leaned toward Phoebe and took her hand in his. She was surprised, and touched, at the gesture. "Next summer," he said, "unless she has trouble, as soon as school is out, we'll see what we have to work with for Mary."

Phoebe felt like crying—and laughing, too. She immediately told Uncle Cecil of the promise, and the next day she told Jesse Holland. Now, Uncle Cecil, and Dr. Kinnamore —everyone she had told—had been sympathetic and glad that she had this great promise of help.

But not Jesse. He acted very oddly.

Phoebe had gone into the lounge to post a resident and intern duty roster. Jesse was in the room nursing, he said, a hangover. He did look miserable.

She said that he did, and he told her that she looked very happy herself.

"I am happy." And she told him about Mary.

And Jesse—he sounded angry. He actually did.

"Old Lewis isn't an orthopod," he said crossly.

"Well," Phoebe agreed, "I know he isn't. But he is a surgical chief, and he would know the proper man, the proper place— It is very important that she have some help, and quite soon. At her age, appearance means everything. We want her straight and able to move easily, quickly. Then, there's another thing. If we can help with the pain, and avoid her having more pain . . ."

Jesse sat up. "Does she have pain?" he asked, rubbing his head.

"Sometimes, yes, she does."

"Well, I can give you a prescription for that."

Phoebe had opened the door. "Thank you," she said ironically. "I happen to know you can't do anything of the sort."

Jesse got to his feet. "Why can't I?" he demanded. "I'm an M.D."

Phoebe smiled at him and went out into the hall. Yes, Jesse was an M.D. But he was also a resident and not privileged to practice as a doctor outside of the hospital. Phoebe was pretty sure she was right on that point. And at her first opportunity, she would verify her opinion.

Later that same morning, Dr. Kinnamore asked her to locate Dr. Newbern for him. "Mrs. Gardner on Six thinks she should have special nursing. He knows the case . . ."

"Do you want to talk to him, doctor?"

"No. I have a consultation at Mercy. If he thinks she does need the nurses, you can tell the Chief of Services. If he doesn't, pass the buck directly to him and let *him* argue with Mrs. Gardner."

Phoebe laughed and nodded. Dr. Kinnamore went out of the office.

Phoebe could have done that errand by telephone, but she wanted to tell Dr. Newbern about Mary, if there would be a minute. . . . She went out into the hall, asked the Floor Head if she had any idea where Dr. Newbern might be. . . .

"He had a couple of seminars up on Four this morning," said the nurse. "He should be just about through."

"Thank you," said Phoebe, starting for the elevator. She was on her way down the corridor of the fourth floor when he came out of the classroom, a small stack of chart boards in his arms and three interns at his side, still talking to him.

"Hello, Phoebe!" he said, spying her. "What brings you up here?"

"A message from Dr. Kinnamore."

"Oh. Then we had better get at it, hadn't we?"

The interns dispersed. Dr. Newbern straightened his chart boards, and Phoebe told him her message. He would attend to it, he promised. Mrs. Gardner did not, really, need special nursing. She liked to be babied, of course.

"But with specials so scarce . . ."

"Precisely! Are you going back to Three?"

"Yes, sir. And I have something else to tell you."

"Good. We'll walk along then."

So she told him, as they threaded their way through the busy corridor, that her uncle—Dr. Howard Lewis, he knew? This with an inquiring lift of her blue-gray eyes. "Uncle Howard has agreed to help me get care for Mary's spinal troubles. This next summer!"

Talley was delighted. "That dear girl!" he said enthusiastically. His hand drew her to the wall to let a cart go through.

"I don't know," said Phoebe, "if this is a disgusting reaction in a mother, but I find myself jealous of my daughter."

"Oh, now . . ."

"You call her a dear girl—which she is, of course—and she knows so much more about you than I do! And—"

Dr. Newbern bent toward her. "Do you want to know about me?" he asked. His eyes were very intent.

Phoebe could feel herself retreat. Not that she especially wanted to. But there she was, saying something silly. "It's very important," she said, hurrying the words, "to take care of things quite soon for Mary. She's at the age—she wants to be well and pretty. And of course without pain."

Dr. Newbern was nodding. "Some pain," he said, "is inevitable as things now are for her."

This was Phoebe's chance. "Tell me," she said tensely, "*can* a resident doctor give prescriptions to people outside of the hospital?"

Dr. Newbern's face was as tight as Uncle Howard's. "*I* can't," he said quietly.

Phoebe's face flamed. "I'm not asking you to!" she cried. "That was a—a *hypothetical* question!"

Talley Newbern touched her shoulder. "And I'll answer it," he said. "Some residents do prescribe, Phoebe . . ." His left eyebrow asked her permission. "I think here in the States the practice is called moonlighting."

Well, that could be. "Should they do it?" she asked earnestly.

Dr. Newbern shrugged as he pressed the elevator button for her. "I don't think I should say . . ." he told her.

Then, as if on impulse, he followed her into the elevator. "I daresay it is a matter of necessity," he said crisply. But he was looking angry. Talley Newbern could look so. He could *be* angry. She had heard about this; she had herself seen flashes of it.

She shivered and walked out of the elevator at the third floor. He followed her. At he door of the office, he touched her shoulder again. "Let me say this," he said. "I may be mistaken. I am not too expert with hypothetical questions. But I shall venture to say this much. If Dr. Holland should again offer you medicine—a prescription—you might tell him that you can get his license for doing it. I think he will believe you."

She was still staring at him when he turned on his heel and went back to the elevator. He had left it on HOLD.

Well! She thought he did quite well with hypothetical questions.

EIGHT

AFTER THANKSGIVING, of course, came the usual whirl of December and Christmas. This year, with a big family to share the holiday, things were very busy in Phoebe's home. There would be church services, the school activities. . . . "I could just quit work," Phoebe said in dismay, "and keep busy chauffeuring my girls around!"

"How do you manage?" asked her next-door neighbor. "Can I help?"

"Well, you could hold down my job . . ." Phoebe's eyes flashed. "No, you couldn't, either," she cried. "It's too exciting these days."

"Ah-ha!" said Mrs. Spires. "A man!"

Phoebe laughed. "No," she said. Then she reconsidered. "Well, yes, a man. But not as you think. You see, we have this new doctor—and the things he does—"

She would not have believed that one man, doing his work so smoothly, could have such an impact on everyone!

But Talley Newbern did. He moved along the halls, he went to the bedsides, he led a group of students, or nurses, or interns from patient to patient. Dope addicts, most of them. Derelicts, a lot of them. He was attentive, and always kind. Phoebe saw enough of this, she heard enough comment. . . .

And one day she frankly lingered at the hall side of the half-doors of the ward to listen to him.

"You are here studying medicine," he was saying to his students. "But I should point out to you that, in the consideration of the use of narcotics, cause, effect, cure—detection even—one must consider many aspects other than the medical. *You* must consider them. The moral reasons for addiction, the moral results. The financial problems involved, and the criminal side of the situation. Because that can be a tremendous part of addiction, you know. We acknowledge this by putting our patients into rooms and wards which can be guarded. To a great degree, they are quarantined.

"These addicts will stop at little in their effort, their *need*, to purchase drugs. We have housewives come to the clinic; they have been playing the numbers to finance the purchases which they feel they need to make. When the gamble fails them, we get them in a disastrous condition. They need the drug, they beg for the drug—and they are even so desperate they will ask an impoverished resident doctor for a dollar so that they may play the numbers again. You must watch for that."

Someone's voice murmured.

"Oh, yes!" said Talley. "Definitely there are pushers. The men—or women—or boys—who provide the drug. They certainly are a problem, and the law-enforcement people work valiantly to identify and apprehend them. That isn't a medical problem, either, except that a pusher who comes into a schoolyard with Maryjane, with pot— who corrupts the kids—that pusher eventually is going to crowd our wards here, and we shall have medical problems in abundance. Now! Let us examine these patients, and see how many problems we have."

Phoebe was not experienced enough to know if she was right in thinking that this doctor took an unusually broad view of his medical problems. But she did want to learn more about the man and his work.

She listened when Talley came into the office to discuss the "junkie" with Dr. Kinnamore. By then, Phoebe knew that they had many drug-addiction cases going through the hospital and clinic. But this one boy still held a particular place in her interest.

Talley did attend him, she knew. He hoped he could help him; she knew that, too. It was to that purpose that, one morning, he asked for a chance to talk to Dr. Kinnamore. Phoebe arranged the interview in the Chief's busy schedule and hoped, hoped, *hoped* she could overhear.

She would of course have to sit at her desk; she could

and did forget to close the door into Dr. Kinnamore's office—but Talley closed it as he went in. So—she could not hear.

And then, to her amazement, Dr. Kinnamore buzzed for her to come in. Happily she grabbed her pad, her pencils, and went through the door.

Dr. Kinnamore looked at her a bit quizzically. She usually was prompt, but such speed. . . . "Sit down, Mrs. Flowers," he said in a preoccupied tone. "I want to know if I am right— Is Dr. Paule a relative of yours?"

Phoebe gaped. Dr. Paule . . . ? Well, that would be Uncle Cecil, but what— She jumped. "Oh, yes," she cried. "He's my uncle."

"Do you have any influence with him?"

Now she did stare. "I think," she said, "that everyone has influence with Uncle Cecil. He is very kind, and—well—an interested man." What could they want of *him?*

"You think then that he would be kind to us?" asked the Chief, who also was smiling, deep in his eyes. "Without your intercession?"

Were these doctors teasing her? A little, perhaps. "Maybe I could help," she suggested primly.

"All right, Phoebe," laughed Dr. Kinnamore. "Here's our problem. First, tell me. Do you know anything about his rehabilitation center?"

Phoebe wrinkled her pretty forehead in thought. "Ye-es," she said slowly. "Aunt Dorothy—his wife—says that he exhausts himself trying to take care of that and of his church, too."

"He's had some excellent results from his alcoholics," said Dr. Kinnamore.

Phoebe looked up. "But I thought you meant drug addicts."

"We do mean them, my dear. Your uncle has begun caring for the rehabilitation of such people, too. We have this one case. Young Fazio in room three hundred fifty-four."

"Phoebe knows about him," said Talley. "She told me that she hoped I could help him."

Phoebe flushed. "Well, Dr. Kinnamore may remember— he was admitted when I first came here, and I made something of a fool of myself . . ."

"I don't remember any such thing," declared Dr. Kinnamore.

Phoebe smiled at him ruefully.

"I hope you can help Fazio," she said meekly to Dr. Newbern.

"I should like to. I had started him on Methadone . . ."

"Oh, that's the medicine . . ."

"Yes. It works for some heroin addicts. It substitutes another addiction, but, yes, it does help. However, we have found that Fazio has a psychosis which interferes with this substitution. So we must seek help elsewhere. My hope for Fazio—we have him about dried out—is rehabilitation. If I could talk to your uncle—"

"You can," said Phoebe. "I'd mention you to him, but the very work you do would be enough with him. I've never been to his center—"

"Of course not!" said Talley quickly.

"But someone must work there. Nurses—people—"

"They do, Phoebe," said Dr. Kinnamore. "But you would not be the type. Your arm isn't strong enough, and you are too impressionable."

She sighed and looked down at her tablet. "I try very hard," she murmured.

Both men chuckled. "You try very hard to stay exactly as you are," advised Dr. Kinnamore. "And now get back to your typewriter. Newbern and I will work things out for Fazio."

Dr. Newbern, at least, must have gone at once to see Uncle Cecil, for on Saturday he spoke of "her young man" to Phoebe. Her cheeks pink, her eyes shining, she disclaimed any ownership of Talley Newbern.

"You could go far and fare worse," said the clergyman.

"I didn't mean that! Did you like him? I mean, can you work with him?"

"I'd like to try. I was most interested in meeting him. He says that a generation ago our typical addict was a forty-year-old Southerner who took morphine. Today, he is twenty-seven, lives in New York, and uses heroin."

Phoebe looked askance at this man. "Are you teasing me?" she asked.

He shook his head. "Not at all, my dear. Those figures are most important. And I thank you if you had anything at all to do with my knowing Dr. Newbern."

Phoebe sighed. "I do think he is wonderful," she said. "I wish you could see him with the patients, Uncle Cecil. We get some pretty awful ones, sometimes. But whoever they are, he is kind, firm, and thoughtful about them. He says this city is not a drug-user center, but that we get a good cross section of patients, and that we are trying to do something is unique."

"The hospital is . . ."

"And you are."

"My church is," Dr. Paule amended. "But, Phoebe, I don't especially like to think of you—"

"I'm not going to be hurt," she cried, "by seeing what is happening in the world! I have girls to raise. I should know the sort of things that surround them."

Her uncle nodded. "Yes," he agreed, "you should know."

"Talley says I'd be of no use at your center." Her uncle nodded agreement. "But I do wish you could see him when he admits a new patient to the hospital. We had a woman this week—she seemed to have taken an overdose of sleeping pills. She looked awful, and her family was hysterical. And there was Talley with his quiet voice—he soon had everyone calmed down." She laughed a little. "Including me."

It was a different picture, as she might have told Uncle Cecil, when Jesse Holland dealt with a "junkie." He used the term. He had used it for Fazio when he had admitted him last September. He again used it on the gray, chill December day when a boy of fifteen was brought in. Dr. Holland received the case when it was sent up from

Emergency.

The boy was "high." He talked wildly; he was suffering from hallucinations—he made an awful racket in the corridor. Phoebe saw him and was sorry for the youth. He was such a *kid*.

She hurried down the hall to her office. Dr. Newbern was coming along from the other end of the building.

"Dr. Holland has a glue sniffer," she murmured to him.

Talley slowed his step. "Did he tell you that?"

"He's telling everyone."

Jesse was. And not choosing his words delicately. The boy's parents had come with their son. The father had found him "acting strangely." "He got rough when I tried to talk to him. We thought he belonged in the hospital. I think he's been poisoned."

These looked to be nice, decent people. Phoebe was sorry for them. But not Jesse. He spoke roughly to them; he spoke roughly to the boy.

And Dr. Newbern spoke roughly to Jesse—in Talley's own way of being rough, which was to speak icily, to speak precisely—

Phoebe knew what he did and said, because, afterward, Jesse mercilessly mocked the Englishman. She protested when he spoke of the matter directly to her.

"He regards these drug cases as sick people, Jesse," she attempted.

"Who is he to *regard* anything?" cried Jesse, angry that she had done anything but laugh at his mimicry. "He's not

155

in authority over me! I'm a resident, same as he is." His face hardened into cruel lines. "Hey!" he cried. "That's *right!* I can put him on report for passin' out orders to me. And, by God, I believe I'll do it!"

"I wouldn't," said Phoebe. She herself had typed orders that all drug-addiction cases, even suspect, were to be referred to Dr. Newbern, in consultation or for treatment.

But of course Jesse did make his complaint, and Phoebe was in a position to see the results, to hear them.

Because when Dr. Kinnamore called a meeting to discuss the matter, his secretary was asked to sit in on it. The residents on medical duty were present, the interns, and such staff attendings as could manage the hour such a meeting required.

It was held early in the day. At seven-thirty, to be exact, and Dr. Kinnamore apologized for bringing her out that early. "This won't take too long. I have to make use of the pre-duty time. . . ."

"It's all right." And it was. Phoebe in her blue skirt and white blouse sat at the end of the table beside Dr. Kinnamore. There were a dozen men in the room, some looking tired and rumpled after a night's work, some fresh from bed and as slick as new pennies. Dr. Newbern looked as always, his hair burnished, a fresh white jacket pulled on over a white knitted shirt.

Jesse was excited. His dark eyes flew about the room, checking on everyone there. He smiled widely at Phoebe, who did not respond. She was there for only one reason. Dr. Kinnamore dislike taped records.

To begin, Dr. Kinnamore said a few things about Dr. Newbern's being at the Center on a research grant. His work had to do with the psychological aspects of drug addiction. "He has chosen to work on the floor and in the clinics. One of his inquiries has to do with the medical management of such cases."

"How much authority does that give him over the other residents?" asked Dr. Holland brashly.

The interruption annoyed Dr. Kinnamore, Phoebe felt sure.

"It isn't a matter of authority," said the Chief coldly. "We are allowing Dr. Newbern extensive opportunities to direct the treatment of these patients. Through consultation, of course. . . ."

Phoebe heard Jesse say *"di-*rect" under his breath. So did Dr. Kinnamore.

"You brought a complaint against Dr. Newbern, Dr. Holland," said the Chief, "and asked that his authority be defined."

"Yes, sir, I did," said Jesse, lifting his chin.

"I believe your differences with Dr. Newbern had to do with the manner in which you admitted a specific patient," said Dr. Kinnamore.

"Yes, sir. You see, we got this glue sniffer . . ."
"How old was the patient?"
"Oh—fifteen, as I remember."

Dr. Kinnamore consulted the papers before him. "Your report states that this boy was suffering from hallucinations. Was his behavior violent?"

"I didn't let it get that way."

"You restrained the boy."

"Yes, sir."

"In what way did Dr. Newbern interfere with your treatment of the patient?"

"Agggh . . . He objected to my roughing the kid up a little."

"*Did* you rough him up?"

Jesse shrugged.

"I have here, Dr. Holland, another report which says—and indicates—that you not only roughed up the boy, but that you used some of the same tactics on his parents."

"When I admit a case, I've got to be free to examine," said Jesse truculently.

"Yes, Dr. Holland, you do. And when you admit a violent case, I'll agree that restraint can be necessary."

"Well, that's all I wanted to hear you say, doctor," said Jesse triumphantly.

Dr. Kinnamore's eyes were like ice. "It is not all I have to say, however!" he snapped. "When it is brought to my attention that a patient has been roughly treated, that his parents have been manhandled, when the admitting doctor agrees that such treatment has been used, I want at least a chance to remind that same admitting doctor, Holland, that we deal here with sick people."

"If they'll give us a chance, yes, doctor," said Jesse silkily.

"I have been told that you struck this boy."

Jesse shrugged.

"And that you forcibly ejected the father and the mother from the room."

"I didn't coddle them, if that's what you mean. And if Dr. Newbern thinks they should be coddled—" Jesse himself was talking wildly. "These characters come in here, the boy fighting everything, everyone, being sick all over the place, screaming . . . Yes! I restrained him. And when the father objected to that restraint, yes, I put him out!"

"May I ask a question?" asked one of the attendings.

Dr. Kinnamore nodded to him and murmured his name to Phoebe.

"I just wanted to ask Dr. Newbern," said the neat, eyeglassed man, "if he does feel that these dope addicts should be coddled."

Dr. Newbern took a minute to think about the question. He objected, he said, to the overall term "dope addicts." "As for coddling—if you mean easing the way for these disturbed people—I say that, at times, yes, they should be coddled. At times, no, they should not."

"And in this particular case?"

"I would say that in all juvenile addiction cases a bit of coddling is preferable to the roughing-up measures sometimes employed." He did not look at Jesse. "I feel that the initial approach to these misguided people is all-important."

"Psychologically?"

"Yes, sir, but that amounts to the physical, as well. You see, these youngsters, who begin with sniffing airplane kit glue, and develop the unappetizing habit of repeating the experience, increasing the amount of acetone, butyl alcohol and toluene which they inhale, can develop some really serious physical injuries—to the lungs, the liver— This boy we have in hand has a critical anemia, which is typical."

"Just from smelling *glue?*" asked an intern.

"This particular kind of glue, yes. One would think—when it first began, one *did* think—that the practice was unappetizing, and no more than that. But we have discovered, over the years, that the practice can lead to the serious illnesses I mentioned.

"I know of one case, a boy of nineteen, who had begun to sniff glue when he was fourteen. This led to the use of pills; eventually he and a companion beat a third boy into unconsciousness, drove him fifty miles, dumped him at a hospital door—and he was sent to prison on a kidnaping charge. When I talked to that boy—then only nineteen, remember—he was not sure that he could stay away from drugs."

"And you consider the initial approach important."

"I consider it essential, sir."

Jesse stirred in his chair. "Don't put me on hopheads," he said angrily, "and expect me to cushy-coddle them."

"I shall expect you to obey orders on any case to which you are assigned," Dr. Kinnamore told him sharply.

"Would you say the parents are to blame for this sort of juvenile case?" asked the senior medical resident.

Talley was expected to answer, and did. "It may be true that this boy's parents are the underlying cause for his sickness. For his wanting to sniff glue."

"An unappetizing habit," murmured Jesse.

"Dr. *Holland!*" cried Dr. Kinnamore.

Talley Newbern threw off the interruption. "A dangerous habit," he said. "I may spend some time determining the cause of his addiction but not nearly so much time as I shall spend on a hoped-for cure."

"*Agggh!*" cried Dr. Holland. "You can't cure 'em."

"If that is true at this stage," said Dr. Newbern in his clean, crisp manner of speaking, "then I am afraid you and I are bankrupt as physicians."

One of the staff doctors said that he felt the expression was extreme. Another leaned forward to look more closely at Dr. Newbern. "You say you interned in New York?" he asked. "Is the problem as great here in the Midwest?"

Dr. Newbern nodded. "About one half of the total known addicts live in New York, about evenly divided, white and nonwhite. Here—my inquiries indicate that this metropolitan area could show a thousand hard-core addicts," he told. "In addition there would be about twenty-six hundred who use or deal with drugs like amphetamine or the barbiturates."

"Not so serious, hmmmmn?"

"They foster psychological dependence, sir. This is what an enlarged treatment and rehabilitation center might handle. And I believe several institutions might underwrite such a project, as they underwrite the thriving alcoholic establishment. The law-enforcement people and the National Institute for Mental Health would be interested, I am sure."

"Would *you* be interested in working in such a place?"

asked the attending.

"I'd work with it. I am primarily a psychiatrist. But, yes, I would work with such a center."

"I don't believe addiction here is as serious a problem as it is in England."

"In numbers, perhaps not. But your users are younger, and the results can be more terrifying."

"If we could control the pushers . . ."

Talley stood up. "It is a bad approach to put the blame on the pusher," he said firmly. "We should put it where it belongs, on the user. Handle him, and you've started to handle the whole situation."

"But handle him softly and sweetly," said Jesse Holland, laughing at his own wit, expecting others to smile.

"I believe, Dr. Holland," said one of the older men in the room, "that you would do well to listen to Dr. Newbern."

Jesse didn't like his saying that. Phoebe saw the ugly way he looked at Talley. She hoped there need be no more trouble.

Talley, of course, seemed unperturbed by the whole thing. Later she saw him on the floor, even talking to Jesse Holland, as if nothing at all had happened, as if people had not shown their dislike for him. Even the parents of the glue-sniffing boy . . .

"I wish you wouldn't keep talking about addiction," Phoebe heard the mother say to Dr. Newbern. "It's very bad psychologically to assume any such thing. One of the doctors told me Gene was anemic. I wish you would just give him iron and stuff for *that!*"

"How can Dr. Newbern take it?" Phoebe asked Dr.

Kinnamore. "When even the doctors seem to oppose what he is doing."

"It is right to question any treatment or diagnosis, Phoebe," said the Chief. "There need be no personal implication of the doctor."

"Oh, but there is!" cried Phoebe, then she flushed and apologized. "I shouldn't speak to you like that," she said. "But at the meeting this morning, some of the doctors didn't want to listen to him. And even the patients—the ones he wants to help. That boy just *hates* Dr. Newbern. And his mother—"

"Reflected feeling, my dear. Gene dislikes the doctor who has to use stern measures to help him. His mama thinks the measures must be too severe. Doctors in Newbern's specialty don't enter any popularity contest, ever."

"I suppose not. But he *is* trying to help them. Then—there's that Mrs. Heddiger down at the end of the hall. Everyone says Dr. Newbern saved her life when she was brought in, that he worked with her for a whole night—"

"Yes," agreed Dr. Kinnamore. "He did save her. She had taken an overdose and hoped it would kill her. But Dr. Newbern saved her from that violent death. Not expecting gratitude, I can assure you."

Phoebe heard the term. *Violent death.* It struck a chord. But the ringing telephone kept her from asking the Chief about it. However, the phrase stuck in her mind, and she took a special interest in the woman whose life Talley had saved.

This Mrs. Heddiger was not an endearing patient. In any

163

way. She was depressed, she did not want company, she was entirely uncooperative.

In her early forties, she was a successful copywriter for a large advertising company, and many people were interested in her recovery. She would see no one. One man in particular came faithfully. "Beau or boss?" the nurses asked each other.

"He says he can't believe she wanted to commit suicide."

"Dr. Newbern told him that she wanted to be saved."

"Yes, and Berda overheard him say that. She threw *such* a tantrum!"

"I heard it. She has a rich vocabulary."

Talley had not seemed to mind the tantrum or the vocabulary. He worked hard with the woman, went into her room a dozen times a day, talked to her, coaxed her to get out of bed, and to allow the beauty operator to attend her.

One day he came down the hall with a small Christmas tree in his hand. He parried all the questions and teasing—it was a very pretty and glittery tree. And he took it into Berda Heddiger's room.

"She'll pitch it out, and him with it," predicted the Floor Head.

"No—he's got her interested in things again," said the intern.

"Interested in *him*, you mean," said the Head.

Talley had achieved that. Phoebe could see that he had. And she must wonder. . . .

Were any means justified? How deeply involved did the doctor get in such a case? Personally, she meant. And should she be jealous?

She should attend to her own business, she told herself sternly. Which strictly was to be a secretary. But as a secretary she could not help seeing things and hearing them.

Especially with a broadcaster like Jesse on the service. But one need not believe Jesse!

He *said* he had gone into Heddiger's room one day and found the woman making out "with our Dr. Lord Chumley, no less! You wouldn't think the bloomin' Englishman had so much heat."

Phoebe heard him. And she heard of the scene staged downstairs at the check-in desk. It seemed that Jesse came upon Talley there and chose that time and place to taunt him about what went on in "la Heddiger's" room. He got a little broad in his insinuations, and Dr. Newbern told him to shut up!

"Why should I?" asked Jesse. "I mean, from my point of view. Of course I can guess yours— You're afraid Phoebe will find out."

Everyone thought Talley Newbern would knock the man down right there and then.

He did not. He turned on his heel, his fists still clenched, his face very white, and he walked away, down the corridor to the elevators.

Dr. Kinnamore had witnessed the whole scene, and he called Dr. Newbern into his office to say that he was glad

Talley had remembered where he was, and what he was.

Talley just stood there, his face tight. "One can't strike a man like *him!*" he said coldly.

The Chief nodded. "Sit down, Newbern," he said quietly.

Phoebe prayed that the door could be left open. It was. She rattled the typewriter keys, she answered the telephone —and she listened to the talk going on across Dr. Kinnamore's desk. The Chief seemed to be reviewing the work which Talley had done in the two months he had been at the hospital. He especially commended the resident for his work with teen-age addicts.

"Working with Dr. Paule," said Talley, "we have managed to secure employment for a couple of the lads. And in at least one case we have set an older man, a former user, to team with a boy. I keep close contact—for my records, you know. Just at the moment, my chief task seems to be to keep the kids from knowing that I've specialized in psychology."

"You feel you can help them better without their knowing?"

"I can't always help them," said Talley soberly.

Phoebe was interested in his work. Uncle Cecil's contact with the doctor—Talley's own personality—he had a strong appeal to the young. Phoebe's own daughters were testimony to that. He came occasionally to their house, walking the five miles from the hospital to the Heights as if it were of no consequence.

166

Phoebe cherished each encounter with Talley in the hospital. She watched him, and read articles and books on his interests, thinking that she could then talk intelligently to him. She learned the language of the narcotics user. She knew that marijuana worked in a certain way; the user became excited and held about his person the dry smell of old rope. Barbiturates and tranquilizers, on the other hand, made a user sleepy. While the amphetamines—the Bennys —those patients showed a dilation of the eyes, they talked a lot, their lips were dry, and their breath was bad. . . .

"What about Berda Heddiger?" Dr. Kinnamore was asking Talley now.

Phoebe all but leaned over to listen, to hear.

She could not see him, but she knew the way Talley shrugged, the wry, deprecating expression on his face. "I have tried to do what I could for Mrs. Heddiger," he said slowly. "I think she is about ready to dismiss from hospital." But he did not sound sure.

"She's been—difficult?"

"My problem doesn't begin to approach hers."

Dr. Kinnamore chuckled. "I'll tell her how much you have helped her."

Dr. Newbern was on his feet. "Please don't," he said quickly. "Such a speech would make her think she is cured. And she is not. For one thing, the same situation exists, the same reasons that made her attempt suicide. Those circumstances made her lean on pills in the first place."

"Do you know what those circumstances are?"

"To a degree, yes. The important thing will be to make

Berda know what they are."

"You can't tell her?"

"Not just now. She is in the rather familiar stage of thinking, and hoping, that I admire her."

"An occupational hazard," agreed Dr. Kinnamore, his tone dry.

"I am, nevertheless, going to advise Mrs. Heddiger to secure psychological care."

The men had reached the door to the outer office, and Phoebe saw the Chief shrug.

NINE

TALLEY WAITED until after Christmas, then he went into Mrs. Heddiger's room one morning to tell Berda that she should, perhaps while still in the hospital, allow a psychiatrist to see what he could do for her.

Mrs. Heddiger occupied a private room, a beautiful room. There were flowers about, and Berda wore a handsome robe; she sat in an upholstered armchair.

When he had finished speaking, she sat there and stared at Dr. Newbern. She tried to speak, she choked, and he turned to pour water into a glass. When he offered it, she knocked it from his hand.

"Mrs. Heddiger . . ." he attempted.

"What did you *say* to me?" she cried, her voice shrill.

"I said that I felt you needed more care, that—"

"You said I was crazy!" she screamed. "That's what you said."

Talley took a step toward her. "Now, Berda . . ." he attempted.

"Don't touch me!" she screamed. "Don't you dare touch me! If you come one step closer, I'll jump out of the window."

The window was a wide one; it looked down and across the avenue and the snow-frosted park. It was tightly closed.

Talley stepped to the bed and pressed a button which would summon a nurse. He turned back to Mrs. Heddiger. "Now, Berda," he said firmly, "you have no cause to become excited—"

"I'm crazy," she shrieked at him. "And you are ready to take advantage of me. But don't you touch me! Don't *touch* me!"

"I shall not touch you," said Talley. "I have not."

"You have, you have, you *have!*" Her voice rose higher. "And I'm not crazy. I just plain don't want any man—"

Behind Talley, the door opened and Jesse Holland came into the room. "What's all the row?" he asked. "Do you have a problem, doctor?"

Talley had rung for a nurse. . . . "No problem," he began.

But Berda was screaming again. "No *problem?*" she shrieked. "I'll say there is a problem! This man makes a pass at me—and when I won't play his game, you know what he said? *He* said—" Her shaking finger pointed at

Talley. "*He* said I was crazy. He— He—" Berda collapsed into the armchair, sobbing hysterically.

"Now, now," said Jesse. "We'll take care of you, Berda."

She clung to his hand, she sobbed—and Jesse was comforting.

The nurse came, and Dr. Holland sent her for a syringe and what he called "a little medicine."

"I say!" Talley protested. "You are not to give her any sedative."

"Now, look, Newbern— Oh, Berda, don't get all excited again. . . ."

But Berda was excited. She screamed, and screamed, and screamed.

This time Jesse could not quiet her, and the Chief came in with the nurse.

He surveyed the situation. The hysterical woman in the armchair, the concerned doctor standing against the wall, the other doctor kneeling beside the patient's chair, trying to quiet her with promises. Not seeing the Chief, Jesse kept asking for the nurse and "that damned syringe."

Berda peered over his shoulder at Talley. "Don't let him touch me," she pleaded, sobbing.

Talley looked at the Chief and shook his head. "You'd better leave, Newbern," said Dr. Kinnamore. "I'll talk to you later."

He did see Talley later. "This is a ticklish situation we find ourselves in, Newbern," he said crisply.

Talley looked shocked. "You can't think I did any of the

things that woman said or suggested!"

"The situation is ticklish, doctor, because Berda Heddiger is the niece of a board member."

Talley took a deep breath. "Then I am finished," he said.

"No," said Dr. Kinnamore. "Not until after we have a hearing."

"Meanwhile I am suspended?"

"I would say, rather," said the Chief, "that you should change duty, perhaps do your turn on Emergency."

"Yes, sir." But one could tell he thought, still, that he was "finished."

By noon of that day, gossip was sweeping in tidal waves throughout the hospital complex. Jesse talked constantly, while Dr. Newbern said absolutely nothing.

To have such a thing happen!

These quiet English types were Casanovas, for sure.

Oh, a crazy hophead would take advantage of his good manners.

He's too good a doctor to take out of service. Get Holland before you get Newbern.

The guy's too good a teacher. "D'you ever hear him lecture on drug use? Man, oh, man! You don't even want to open a package of the stuff!"

"What does he have to say about LSD?" asked a third man lazily.

"Not the usual things," declared Dr. Newbern's admirer. "But does he ever outline the side effects of a trip! Paranoia being the most attractive of the results."

"He doesn't believe a trip can be altered?"

"By chlorpromazine, you mean? Yes, he discussed that. There isn't much he doesn't know about the stuff."

"Well, I think it's a damn shame," cried the first intern. "He should never have saved that dame's life. When you think of his being in trouble, and Holland— You ever work under Holland, my friend?"

So then they talked about Jesse Holland.

Of course Phoebe overheard a fair sampling of the talk. Dr. Kinnamore had somewhat warned her. "Dr. Newbern works in an area where emotions get out of hand," had been his comment.

Phoebe decided not to believe a word that was said. She did not believe that Talley had made a pass at his patient. She would not believe that Dr. Kinnamore had banished him to the Siberia of emergency duty. Jesse told her that, and she did not answer the man.

Then of course she had to type the duty rosters, and it was true. Dr. Newbern was assigned to emergency room duty, three to eleven, on call four nights a week. After thirty-six hours, he would have a free night. . . .

"What happens to his research?" she went in to ask Dr. Kinnamore.

The Chief was not ready to discuss the matter, but he did point out that emergency duty came up regularly, and was a prime place to see the patients coming in as a result of drug use. Then he added, curtly, that there would be a hearing.

Phoebe decided that she would *not* believe that, after the hearing, Talley Newbern would be out. All the stories were lies. And the morning after the enormous scene which Berda Heddiger had made, Phoebe began to say that everything was a lie.

She said it frequently, and she said it excitedly. Since she was the Chief's secretary, what she said was added to the fulminating gossip.

At noon, Dr. Howard Lewis came across from the surgical building and up to the third floor to Dr. Kinnamore's office.

"Phoebe," he said, "I came for a word with you. I won't need to bother Dr. Kinnamore."

Phoebe was uncertain as to what she should do. "Well . . ." she began.

Her Uncle Doc closed the door into the corridor. He wore a long lab coat over his scrub suit, so he was interrupting his day's work for this errand. He agreed that he had made a special effort to see her. "I didn't want to use the switchboard," he said. "It is, you know, the largest in the city."

Phoebe stood, flushed and confused.

"Of course I've heard of the trouble there was over here yesterday concerning a Mrs. Heddiger, who is the niece of Clyde Boland, a member of the hospital board. The whole matter is regrettable, and subject to inquiry."

"Well, I should think so!" said Phoebe hotly.

Dr. Lewis put up a very clean, long-fingered hand.

"That is what I came to say to you, my dear," he said. "To remind you of the position you hold here in the hospital, and to advise you not to express yourself in any way that would indicate you are taking sides, or perhaps quoting Dr. Kinnamore's position in this affair."

"But, Uncle Howard—"

He glanced at the clock. "I have a full schedule," he said. "I'll repeat my advice and leave. But I do say, as impressively as I can, Phoebe, do not discuss this matter. Let Dr. Kinnamore and the hearing he will set up decide what has happened, and what will happen." He turned on the heel of his white shoe and left.

Phoebe, of course, was furious. She told Talley that she was when she phoned him that afternoon, ignoring all of Uncle Doc's hints about the switchboard. He listened to her impassioned account of what her uncle had done. "My mother," she cried, "was right to dislike that man!"

And—"Don't be a fool!" cried Talley roughly.

Phoebe gasped.

"You should do precisely as he said," Talley told her.

Now Phoebe was indeed confused—utterly and completely. In her book, one showed loyalty to a friend. One—

She went home, stopping to shop on the way. She wondered what Talley was doing, what he was thinking. Well, of course, just now he would be seeing patients in the busy emergency room. As for what he was thinking—of course, he would be indignant. As indignant as was Phoebe.

Only he was being tight-mouthed about it. Uncle Howard would admire *him*. But Talley must be hurt and angry.

If she could only *do* something for him. This was Friday, so the hearing would not be held until the first of the week. And she so wanted things settled, Talley exonerated, that Heddiger woman shown to be—

At home, Phoebe worked hard and late that evening, cleaning, doing a washing, keeping herself too busy to think.

Next morning the girls reminded her that she had promised to take them out to Uncle Bob's, if the weather were cold enough to keep the ice frozen on the rink made by flooding the tennis court.

She had promised, and her interest in the trip increased when it occurred to her that she could talk to Uncle Bob about Talley. He would want to help her friend, and would know how. . . .

So, with the girls tumbling, skating, screeching out on the icy tennis court, Phoebe sat with Uncle Bob in the pleasant breakfast room, drank coffee with him, and told him what had happened at the hospital that week.

"This week things did happen," she assured him. "One really awful thing—and the worst part of it could be the gossip that has arisen about it."

Uncle Bob refilled her cup. "I'm all ears," he told her.

"So is everybody at the hospital," said Phoebe wryly. "All tongues and ears."

"Suppose you tell me."

She took a deep breath. "I hardly know where to begin," she said. "But there is this patient . . ."

She told about Berda, the way she had entered the hospital, the way Talley had worked with her. She told about the little Christmas tree. . . .

"But Thursday," she said, leaning across the table toward Uncle Bob, her eyes big and dark, "he went into her room—as he's done dozens of times. But this time that awful woman says he made a pass at her. She screeched so loudly about it that everyone knew what she was saying. Of course nurses and another doctor went in. Even Dr. Kinnamore did. Though all *he* did was to send Dr. Newbern out of the patient's room, which made it seem that he *had* done something!"

"Your interpretation, Phoebe?" asked Uncle Bob.

"Well— Oh, yes, it is, but he did put him out. And others interpret it that way, too. Besides, Dr. Holland has done some really nasty talking about it."

"Who is Dr. Holland?"

Phoebe told him, again with her own interpretation.

"You don't like him," said Uncle Bob.

"No, I don't," said Phoebe vigorously. "And I do not think it is fair for Dr. Kinnamore to send Talley Newbern down to emergency duty and leave Jesse Holland—"

"Beyond your opinions on the matter, are you involved in this, Phoebe?"

"Well—" She knew she was blushing. Then she lifted her chin. "I thought I'd ask you what chance you thought Talley had in the hearing there will be. This woman happens to be the niece of a board member, and—"

Uncle Bob whistled soundlessly.

"I can't talk to anyone at the hospital about it. I don't know what these hearings are like. But Uncle Doc passed out orders to me that I should keep still. And— Oh!" she cried. "Now I really know that Mother was right to dislike him so much!"

Uncle Bob sat smiling at her and shaking his head. "Poor Julia," he said mournfully.

"But she *didn't* like him, Uncle Bob!"

"I know it, my dear. And yet Howard was the only one ever able to help your mother."

Phoebe could not believe her ears. "You don't mean that," she said anxiously.

"Of course I mean it."

Phoebe sat, devastated. She could not speak—she tried to drink some coffee, and her shaking hand spilled it. Uncle Bob handed her a napkin, otherwise letting her recover as she could.

She leaned toward him. "*Why?*" she asked. "Why does he . . . ? Why is he the way he is?"

Uncle Bob smiled faintly. "Why was your mother her way?" he asked.

Phoebe sat back. "Mother . . ." she began. "My mother had her—problems."

"Yes," said Uncle Bob, "she did. Howard knew that. And he was—always—very kind to Julia."

Phoebe sighed. "And now, I suppose, he is being kind to me."

Uncle Bob's smile widened. "Can't you take that?" he asked.

Phoebe stiffened. "I won't take it!" she cried. "I don't want people being *kind* to me!" She broke off. Too clearly, she could hear the echo of her mother's voice in her own. She twisted the napkin between her fingers. "I'm sorry," she murmured.

"And you have some thinking to do?"

She stood up, looking shamed, confused.

"If you want to go home," her uncle said, "I'll bring the girls in later. They are having such a good time. . . ."

Phoebe bit her lip and nodded. She went to get her coat, her knitted cap, and her mittens. At the door, with Uncle Bob following her, she turned impulsively and hugged him.

He did not speak, but stood and watched her back the station wagon and drive away.

TEN

THAT EVENING, Jesse Holland called Phoebe and asked for a date. "Oh, no," she said at once. Then she thought. "Not tonight, Jesse. I have other things—"

Doing some sewing which she had put off since before Christmas—doing some thinking. But, maybe—

"Could you make it tomorrow?" she asked.

"In the evening. Could we go somewhere for dinner? In your car?"

"No," said Phoebe. "Unless you'd want just to come here—"

"O.K., Phoebe," he conceded. "O.K. How early? How late?"

"Make it seven."

"Dinner will be over, eh?" he asked.

"On Sunday we eat a light supper. Yes, it will be over."

He could take that or leave it.

"I'll be there," he promised, and hung up.

He would be, too, Phoebe thought grimly.

She wouldn't want to have to put into words why she was letting him come. In the back of her mind was some vague idea of straightening things out with him about Talley. It was only an idea, not really a hope. If Jesse had wanted to clear things up in that area, he could have spoken to Dr. Kinnamore. He could have told him—

She didn't sleep very well, thinking about so many things. She was tempted to break the date with Jesse—but she did not.

She and the girls went to church on Sunday morning, ate their dinner, and afterward Phoebe went down the street to sit with Mrs. Haines' mother, to let that useful, good woman get out of the house for a little. The girls took their homework with them and studied. Phoebe watched TV with the invalid and talked to her about the programs.

At five they went home, ate soup and apple salad for their supper. She told the girls that she was expecting company, and when she said it would be Dr. Holland, they made pert faces.

"You're getting old enough to conceal your feelings with good manners," she instructed her daughters.

"May we stay in the kitchen or upstairs?" they asked.

"Well—I think so."

"Can we make brownies?" asked Mary.

"Yes, if you'll clean up after yourselves. And then go to

181

bed without any trouble."

Jesse arrived five minutes before seven. Phoebe managed not to let him kiss her. He laughed and threw his topcoat on a chair. "Where's the family?" he asked, warming his hands at the fire in the grate.

One could hear the girls from the kitchen, but Phoebe told him, and he went out to talk to them; Phoebe sat in her chair and picked up her sewing.

Jesse came back, laughing, and sat down. "They're great kids," he said affably.

Phoebe's eyebrow went up. She decided that the girls' manners must have sufficed to conceal their feelings.

Jesse threw his cigarette into the fire and leaned back, crossing his legs. "Did you have a good date last night?"

She frowned.

"You said you'd be busy."

She laughed. "I was busy," she said mischievously, "and if I told you what I did, you wouldn't believe it."

He got up and roamed about the room. Jesse never could sit quiet. Tonight he was a little more restless than usual. Phoebe continued to sew, and tried to think of something to say about Talley, something that wouldn't make Jesse mad, or—

The front door bell rang, and she looked up quickly.

"I'll get it," Linda called from the kitchen.

"No, Linda," said Phoebe, setting her sewing to one side.

By then Jesse was out into the hall, and she let him go. A

visitor, at night—someone who didn't know that the Flowers used the side door. . . .

Her frown of puzzlement deepened into one of annoyance when Eugene Rotan followed Jesse back to the garden room. She did not like the man; she—

He greeted her and took off his light-colored gloves, put them into his hat—black felt. His topcoat was black, too, and his scarf was pale yellow. Wool. Jesse took his things and put them on top of his coat on the chair. Rotan sat down across from Phoebe and asked her how she had been. His black hair gleamed. So did his black eyes.

"I've been very well, thank you," said Phoebe primly.

"That's good. Well, doctor? What was it you wanted?"

Phoebe's jaw dropped. She saw Jesse glance at her, and she could feel her cheeks getting red-hot. If he thought she would be mad, he was right! Jesse had arranged to meet Rotan here!

Her hands shook too much for her to sew. She held them, one in the other, and felt like crying. If Jesse thought she was such a fool . . .

She was shocked. Really shocked.

Jesse knew that she was, and he talked very fast to Rotan, not to let her get a word in—

Phoebe could only sit and look at these two men. Rotan in his too sharp suit—he looked like a gangster, she told herself. Or near enough not to be pleasant. While Jesse—she didn't like his sideburns. His skin was sallow, unhealthy-looking, and his hands moved all the time.

He was telling Rotan about the "really nasty case" they

183

had at the hospital. Phoebe stared at him, unbelieving. She could smell chocolate from the kitchen, and hear Mary's voice. . . .

"It involves one of our patients," Jesse was saying, "And a doctor."

"You, Jesse?" asked Rotan. He wore a diamond ring on his right hand.

"Not directly," said Jesse. "I'll be a witness, but I am not accused of anything."

"But you wanted to talk to me," said Rotan delicately.

"Yes, I did," said Jesse. "I didn't think I should talk to a lawyer at the hospital."

Phoebe sat stunned. He had arranged for Rotan to meet him at *her* house. He had *used* her! And now it seemed—

"I don't know if you have met this doctor in question," Jesse was saying. "He comes around here sometimes, so you may have."

"Mr. Rotan does not come around here!" said Phoebe icily.

Rotan looked at her, but Jesse did not. He was still intent on laying out his case. "The point I want cleared up for me," he said, "is this: Newbern—he's the doctor directly involved in all this trouble—he's an Englishman, and I've found out that he left England to come over here and work because of a scandal he'd been involved in. A round, red, bouncy scandal!" He spoke with relish, and now he looked at Phoebe.

"I don't believe it," she said flatly.

"It's true," said Jesse. He leaned toward Rotan. "What I want from you," he said, "is to know, if I tell about this information, can I be protected?"

Rotan twisted the big ring. "You mean, you want to blackmail this man," he said equably, "but not get into trouble from doing it."

Phoebe jumped to her feet. "I want you both to stop this kind of talk!" she protested. "If it is your only reason for coming here, why, you can leave, and right now!"

Jesse reached out his hand and tried to pull her toward him; she jerked away from his touch. "Don't be like that, Phoebe," he told her, laughing. His dark eyes glittered, and a muscle beside his mouth twitched rhythmically. His hand felt hot. . . .

Phoebe stepped away. He was so—so excited—so keyed-up! She was almost afraid of him.

"You're a big girl now," Jesse was telling her. "You know what two things add up to two other things to make four."

She could not speak. She really could not.

"Phoebe doesn't like the words you use, Rotan," Jesse said. "And blackmail may not exactly fit into the picture, because, you see, this man has no money."

"Then what's your problem?" asked the lawyer.

"Well, I still want to know if I can be protected. You may call it blackmail if you insist, and the guy could maybe come through with a little money. He's on a grant. But he has something that I would be ready to bargain about. . . ."

"Provided you can be protected," drawled Rotan.

"Yeah! You see, I'd ask him to promise to let my girl alone."

Rotan shot a glance at Phoebe, then he drew a cigar from his pocket and rustled the cellophane wrapping.

Now Phoebe really was shocked. She stared at Jesse, and a thought crawled coldly into her mind. Jesse—if she could stop his persecution of Talley— If she could use herself to bargain with Jesse? Could she? Would she?

A shudder seized her, shaking her from head to foot. Yes, she told herself, she might. To save Talley. That quiet man, that dear man, that—

Warmth enfolded her, and a gladness.

She stirred in her chair and shook her head. No! she told herself. No. If she really felt this way about Talley, of course he must never know. But Phoebe—and Jesse—that was unthinkable.

She got to her feet, a small, determined figure in a blue corduroy jumper.

"I think," she said firmly and clearly, "it is time for you men to go. You will, I suppose, find somewhere to talk about your business. I am shocked to know that you would bring it here. And certainly you cannot stay here and make such plans. . . ."

It took a little time. Jesse tried teasing her. But finally the men did leave, and Phoebe automatically set the room to rights. Her hands were cold, she was trembling. She emptied ash trays, she put her sewing into the little mahogany stand, she—

186

"Mother . . . ?" It was Linda, at the door.

Phoebe went quickly to her. "Are you sick, Linda?" she asked.

"No. It's Mary. She's sick. Upstairs . . ."

Phoebe ran up the stairs, she cared for her pale and shaking daughter, tucked her warmly into bed, and then asked what had happened.

"Jesse let her smoke his cigarette," said Linda.

Phoebe whirled on her. Then she whirled back to Mary.

"Just one puff," said Mary weakly. "I didn't like it."

"But why . . . ?"

"Oh, you know, he thinks such things are jokes," said Linda.

"But, Mary—"

"I wouldn't do it," said Linda. "But Mary always wants to show she's older . . ."

Mary moaned and turned her head on the pillow.

"She acted so funny," said Linda. "Scared-like—and she talked silly. And then, I think she was sick to her stomach."

"Were you, Mary?" Phoebe asked.

Mary shook her head. "I tried to be. I thought, if I could throw up I'd stop feeling so queer."

Phoebe bent over and kissed the child. "Don't ever do such a silly thing again," she murmured.

"I won't. But one thing I know. I'll *never* want to smoke cigarettes!"

Phoebe was frightened and angry. Mary was asleep when she went downstairs, holding to the rail, because, inwardly at least, she was still shaking. This evening—that *Jesse!* Uncle Doc had warned her. . . .

He'd been right. Jesse was an awful person. Phoebe hated him. Uncle Doc had been right. . . . Uncle Doc . . . She put coal on the fire and sat huddled before its warmth.

Had Uncle Doc helped her mother?

Not able to sit still, she got up and went out to the kitchen. She prepared orange juice, ready for next morning's breakfast. She moved about, wanting to be busy, not wanting to think. These people—this conflict—

She hated people! She hated the feelings they could arouse. She wished she need not get involved with them. She wished she could live her life in a shell, protected from everyone. *Everyone!*

Oh, the girls, of course. . . .

And—maybe—Uncle Bob. Aunt Katherine. Uncle Cecil —so far, at least, they had done nothing to—to disturb her.

And of course there was Talley. She sat down again by the fire and thought about Talley. He was a really nice person.

But now there were stories being told around the hospital. This Berda Heddiger—and Jesse's tale of scandal back in England. . . .

Surely, those things were not true! Phoebe longed to know they were not true!

188

She could ask the Chief.

But she knew that she would not ask him.

She stared into the fire. A small grotto had formed among the coals, and in its rosiness little blue flames hissed faintly; she could hear them in the quiet room. Could she ask Talley?

Yes. She thought she could. He would, she thought, understand her wish to *know*.

She stood up and rubbed her leg. She had sat with it folded under her and now it ached. Limping, she went into the sitting room and dialed the hospital.

The biggest switchboard in the city.

She waited and was really surprised at how quickly Talley's voice came through to her.

"Hello! Newbern here!"

The girls liked to try to say *he-ah* the way Talley did.

"Oh, Talley!" she breathed.

"Phoebe! Is it you?"

She laughed. He knew that it was. She'd had to give her name to put the call through. "Are you busy?" she asked.

"No. This happens to be my free night. I went off duty at three. I should have asked you to let me come to your house, except for certain unpleasant things. You know?"

In the glass of the framed picture over the desk, Phoebe could see her head nodding up and down. She flushed. Talley couldn't see her!

"Things," Talley said, after the long pause, "that have

occurred recently."

"Oh, Talley!" she cried. "*That* is what I wanted to talk to you about."

Now it was his turn to pause. Perhaps he too had been told not to talk. Phoebe should tell him that he need not come. . . .

Then he spoke quietly. "I'll be over," he said. "Though it is a bit late."

Phoebe glanced at the clock. "Nine-fifteen," she confirmed. "But that's all right. Don't walk!"

"Not tonight," he agreed, and hung up.

Phoebe brushed her hair and freshened her lipstick. She went to the kitchen and made coffee. She put brownies on a plate, and after a minute's thought, she changed the plate for another one, clashing the china together.

Goodness! Was she that excited? Or just nervous? Upcoming was another of those human contacts. Over an hour ago she had decided that she should make no more of them. And what would come of *this* human contact?

She went upstairs to check on the girls. Both were soundly asleep. They would reproach her in the morning if they discovered that Talley had been in the house. He was *their* friend!

He came by ten, calling out as he came up on the porch. Phoebe smoothed her jumper and ran to the door, her hair flying.

"Oh, come in!" she said gladly.

He nodded and stepped inside, already unfastening his coat. "I was lucky with buses," he told her, turning to look at her. His cheeks were red, and he smelled of the cold night air. Impulsively, Phoebe stood on tiptoe and kissed his cheek.

His arm went strongly about her shoulder. "I must have an irresistible appeal," he said, laughing a little.

"Oh, you do!" said Phoebe, leading the way to the lamplit garden room, to the fire's warmth.

Talley stood sniffing the air. "You've had company?" he asked.

"Yes," said Phoebe. "Earlier. Would you like coffee?"

He warmed his hands at the fire, took the tongs and rearranged the coals, then he came to sit in the needlepoint armchair facing Phoebe, who was curled up on the couch.

"Later, perhaps," he said absent-mindedly.

Phoebe felt nervousness creep upon her. "Did you have a busy Saturday night?" she asked.

"And a busy Sunday," he agreed.

Phoebe ran her thumbnail down the wale of her corduroy jumper. How would she begin? Better not to jump into it. She searched for something to talk about.

"You know," she said brightly, her voice sounding like Mary's, "one of the men on our street went pheasant hunting, and at Christmas he gave two of the birds to Mrs. Haines. You know who Mrs. Haines is?"

Talley nodded, looking up at Phoebe from the pipe which he was filling. She clasped her hands together. "Well, Mrs. Haines gave me one of them," she said, "and if I knew how to cook the thing, I'd invite you to dinner."

"That has a pleasant sound," he told her.

"Do *you* know how to cook one?"

"I'm not skilled at all in the kitchen. But I shouldn't think cooking a pheasant would be too difficult. Can you roast a chicken?"

"Yes," said Phoebe. "Of course I can."

"Then," said Talley. "You should treat the bird as a chicken. And I'll help you eat it. If, of course, that condemned hearing leaves me any appetite."

His eyes keenly watched her face. "What is troubling you, Phoebe?" he asked gently.

She started, then clasped her hands together. "Let me get you some coffee?" she urged.

He waited for her to bring in the tray. He waited while she poured his coffee and put the cup on a plate with a napkin and two of the brownies. "Mary and Linda made these," she said breathlessly.

"How are the girls?"

She filled her own cup and sat down with it. "Mary had a little upset before bedtime."

"Oh?" He was waiting, as she should have known he would be.

"Yes!" she said. "Jesse gave her a puff on his cigarette, and—"

Talley moved swiftly. Like a branch breaking, Phoebe thought. He put his cup aside, he snapped his fingers, and his face tightened. "That's *it!*" he cried. "I smelled it when I came in."

"You smelled what?" Phoebe asked him.

"Holland's cigarette. Marijuana."

The room slipped away from her. "Oh, *no!*" she breathed. But she, too, had smelled it. "Oh, *no!*" she said again.

Talley was on his feet, pacing the carpet. "I'll kill him," he said between clenched teeth. "I'll kill the man!"

Phoebe began to tremble. "Mary . . ." she said.

"Of course she was ill!" the doctor told her. "She's a child— Was it only a puff, Phoebe?"

"It had to be," she said, terror sweeping in on her. "Talley, do you think . . . ?"

"I think she was sick," he said coldly. "The first cigarette—if Mary inhaled that first puff— Oh, she would be panicked, perhaps."

"Linda said she talked silly."

"It was only a puff," decided Dr. Newbern. "But I'll get Holland for it." He came back and sat down, took up his coffee cup and drained it.

"Does Jesse smoke marijuana cigarettes?" Phoebe asked, her voice faint.

"Not as a practice, I trust. But to think he would give it to Mary—" Talley shook his head, got up and refilled his cup.

"But this one puff. . . ."

"I mean to see that it is no more," said Talley. "Now!" He leaned back in his chair. "Tell me what else is troubling you."

"Must there be more?" asked Phoebe.

"No, but there is more."

Phoebe nodded and looked hard at Talley. "All right," she said. "I'll tell you. I do not believe that you ever made a pass at any patient!"

He reached for another brownie. "Good!" he said readily.

But—tonight Jesse had said—

Phoebe leaned forward. "Could there," she asked, "be some scandal revealed about you?"

He finished the brownie and touched the napkin to his lips. "Do tell me what Jesse said to you," he urged, his manner quiet.

Phoebe put her cup and plate on the low table. "The idea," she said earnestly, "of blackmailing you is ridiculous. I know that. You couldn't— The story could *not* be true!"

"Hmmmmn," said Talley Newbern. "It appears that a man will go to great lengths to get a girl."

But Phoebe hadn't said one word about that. . . . "If you mean me," she protested, "that's nonsense. I'm no catch."

He smiled at her. "You are a lovely young woman," he said warmly. "And you are inheriting money."

She began to protest. But of course there was her mother's estate. This house—the bank account which her father had left. "Well," she agreed. "But it all will be divided with my brother." Then she flushed bright red. "If that's why—" she cried.

Talley's gaze told her it was why.

194

She got up and went to stand before the fire. "Yes!" she cried. "That would be why Jesse . . . Oh!" Her face crumpled. "He *couldn't*," she said pitiably. "He couldn't hurt you, just to—"

"Come and sit down," said Talley gently. "We'll talk about it."

"Why," Phoebe asked anxiously, "would he think that hurting you would make me like him better?"

"Perhaps he is ready to bargain with you. Or thinks he can shove me out of the picture."

That was what Jesse had had in mind. And Phoebe herself had thought of bargaining. She began to weep helplessly.

Talley made a soft sound of regret and came over to sit beside her, to offer his own clean handkerchief. It was comforting to have him there, his strength, his masculine calm.

"He can't hurt you, can he?" Phoebe asked.

"Yes, if a scandal would hurt me. One could be dug up and displayed. If you think he is ready to do that, perhaps I should immediately call the police."

"The *police!*" Phoebe turned sharply. He put his hand on her arm and left it there.

"A doctor's best friend," he told Phoebe. "Expecially an innocent doctor's. We are prime targets, you know, for blackmailers. Because doctors are quick to panic and pay off to avoid publicity. Instead—or so the law-enforcement chaps tell me—the threatened doctor should call in the police and help set a trap for the blackmailer, be he Jesse

Holland, an extortionist, or whatever."

"How could you set a trap?" asked Phoebe. "If you're right in saying he wants me, not money."

"I'll wager he'd take some money," laughed Talley. "But see here, my dear—let's get this scandal matter into the open."

Phoebe settled back against the couch cushion and against, she found, his arm. Well, it was a nice arm, a safe one. She gazed into the fire and smiled. "You don't have to tell me," she murmured.

"I'll tell you," he said, and, quietly, he did tell her. About the scandal. About the brother who had worked in the Foreign Office. Talley called him a "small clerk."

Phoebe watched him as he talked, there so close beside her. The firelight shone upon his smooth, silvered hair.

"About four years ago," Talley was saying, "Michael began to experiment with lysercenogenics." He glanced at Phoebe.

She nodded. "LSD," she murmured.

"Right. He—Michael—was the extrovert type. That is the sort to get the most from LSD. And then one has to give some thought as to why he felt the need of a drug."

"Curiosity?" suggested Phoebe.

"Perhaps. At first, it could have been that. But to continue—one asks that question about any drug. LSD, pot, whatever. One asks what life has failed to give such a man, or to offer him. And the conclusion inevitably is that the failure lies within the man himself. With any addict, this is primarily true. Though, of course, life has failed him

196

somewhat, society has failed.

"And it is our business, we interested doctors, to know why, and where, that failure lies. In asking those questions about Michael, I have to think, I had to conclude at the time, that my brother never thought that his excursions into a world of vivid colors, fluid light, and nonexistent towers and bridges would in any way affect him and his relation to the work which he did. In that sense, it would be wrong to judge him to be criminal, but it also was just to decide that he was unsafe. In fact, he became such a risk that he was dismissed."

Phoebe sighed.

"There was no great publicity about it. The Foreign Office wanted the whole thing kept quiet. Our father is a clergyman, you see. There was Michael's wife and his two children—"

"And you," breathed Phoebe, feeling so sorry for Talley!

He swept past her interruption. "The trouble was," he said, "the idiot himself made a great fuss about his dismissal. He protested to the press, he secured counsel—a lawyer, you know?—and all this made the situation doubly difficult for all concerned. I did what I could to help the man. Michael himself. It was this development that got me into my specialty, the study of the psychological picture within addiction."

"And you came to America."

"Yes. It seemed best to do that. Though I worked on it for a year in England, then I had to put in two years as an intern here before I could take the board examinations. Now I have the grant, and my research residency—"

"And you like the work, don't you?"

He sat thoughtful. "It is not particularly a subject to *like*, Phoebe," he said. "But there is a great deal to do, to salvage these unhappy people."

Phoebe nodded. She sat sorry, even desolate. This was the scandal which Jesse would hold over Talley's head. It was not a nice story; it could not have been nice happening. But Talley himself had done nothing! She stiffened. "Why would Jesse do such a thing to you?" she asked. "Does he hate you?"

Talley shrugged. "I'm not the reason," he said. "Not personally."

No, she would agree, he was not.

"But let us say," Talley continued, "that I have been put in a position where I could do, where I have done, things for Dr. Holland. Holland smokes pot, you see, and the hospital knows that he does. He thinks that he conceals it, though he should know better. . . ."

"Does he do it on duty?" Phoebe asked anxiously.

"No. Not as yet, we think. But we also think that he has taken a trip or two with LSD."

"On his vacation?"

"On time away from the hospital—it would have to be. He also uses barbiturates sometimes, tranquilizers. . . ."

"But, Talley . . ."

"He is a man, Phoebe, who a year ago took a wrong turn. At that time, and now, he is well-trained, expensively trained, to be a doctor. He's quite good, too, you know. And it is hoped that he can be persuaded, or coerced, to give up this unfortunate habit. In the hospital, he is not given access to narcotics, he may not prescribe them. His judgment in these matters is not considered to be good."

"But a *doctor* . . ."

"A doctor with a bad temper is dangerous too, Phoebe. Or one who holds resentments. But if he can be cured, if he can be trained— That is why Holland has become an object of my research. He knows it, and he resents it. He knows that I keep records. His little experiment—what he would call a joke—with Mary tonight will go on his record. I have a quite complete file on Dr. Holland. I record what I do for, and with, such a person."

Phoebe shook her head. "The whole thing is revolting," she declared.

"Any crippled man is less pleasant than a whole, a healthy one. You see, in Holland's case, his background is such that he needs to find an entity for himself. He studies medicine for that purpose. He plays with drugs to sharpen the picture. No, it is not a nice thing."

"But, as a doctor . . ."

"As a doctor, he cannot always be trusted, perhaps. But in another sense his being a doctor may work for his salvation. It is a profession, you know, where undesirable characteristics can be an embarrassment and a handicap. This can be proven, demonstrated to Jesse. He is essentially a smart person. If he has found the entity he wants through the M.D. behind his name, perhaps he will discard the bad to keep the good. I truly think he is trying to do that.

"But occasionally he is swept by a need, by impatience—and to escape this course on which he has entered will take patience."

"But if you are trying to help him . . ."

Talley took his arm from the back of the couch; he leaned forward, clasping his hands between his knees. "Often," he said slowly, "where gratitude is difficult to express, or to acknowledge, hatred is manifested."

"Oh," said Phoebe. Yes, that would explain Jesse. It would also explain why her mother had hated Uncle Doc. If he really had helped Julia. She sat shaking her head mournfully.

Talley glanced around at her, then straightened and put his hand on her arm. He leaned toward her and spoke earnestly. "Do not let yourself be troubled," he said. "Do not worry . . ."

"But what about the hearing?" she cried. "Aren't *you* worried?"

"Not worried," he said. "It will be a rough time. I'd prefer it had not happened. But I repeat, don't *you* worry."

"I think it will be just awful," said Phoebe, still mournfully.

"Oh, no," said Talley. He got to his feet, took the last brownie and ate it. He set the screen before the fire. "Could I," he asked Phoebe, "as a doctor, go up to see Mary?"

"She's asleep."

He smiled and waited. Phoebe turned and led the way upstairs and to Mary's room. By the light from the hall, he put his finger to the child's throat, feeling her pulse. Mary stirred a little, and he went silently out of the room. "All in good shape," he told Phoebe.

Downstairs, he put on his coat and made a ceremony of wrapping his throat in the new muffler which the girls had given him for Christmas. He bent over and kissed Phoebe's cheek, then let himself out into the cold night.

She watched him run down the walk and down the terrace steps to the street.

ELEVEN

When phoebe went to work the next day, Monday, she found that the hearing on Talley's case had been set for late that afternoon. She knew that she would not be willing to leave the hospital until it was over, so she called Mrs. Haines and told her of her probable delay. Could she feed the girls if it was necessary?

"Yes, my dear. And we'll study."

Phoebe supposed Talley was at work—with the hearing set for that afternoon, he probably had been reassigned. She tried all morning to think of ways to go down to Emergency—just to see. . . .

As four o'clock approached, Phoebe became even more apprehensive. She had thought that Talley, perhaps, going off duty at three, would come upstairs to talk to the Chief.

He did not. Dr. Kinnamore was in and out of his office—he could have seen Dr. Newbern elsewhere.

Berda Heddiger had gone home, incidentally. Without the psychologic evaluation Dr. Newbern had wanted for her. Phoebe had heard some talk about that. Berda was not popular on the floor. But, in places, Talley wasn't either. Oh, she *wished* the thing were over!

Phoebe was going to stay around until it was.

At three-thirty, Dr. Kinnamore came bustling in and said he would need a clean coat— Oh, good! He had one. And, Phoebe . . . ?

"Yes, Dr. Kinnamore?"

He smiled down at her. "Could you possibly arrange to stay late this evening? There's this hearing— Could you be there?"

She gasped. She didn't know . . .

"I realize you have the girls to consider."

She had already arranged for the girls. But—

"I want a complete record," said the Chief.

"You could set up to have it put on tape."

"Never!" said Dr. Kinnamore, who was changing his white coat.

Phoebe removed the name tab from the used coat and went to pin it on the fresh one.

"Will you stay and do it, Phoebe?" asked the doctor. "You'd be late, of course, and I suppose I could get a girl from the pool."

Phoebe looked up at him, smiling. *"Never!"* she said.

She sounded pert, she sounded confident, but she was none of those things. When she went out to pick up her notebook, she was trembling. She was afraid. She knew that she was going to see Talley attacked and probably hurt. This she would not like happening to a person she loved. And she did love Talley. Just as she loved Mary and Linda—though not just that way, really. No. Not that way at all.

She had thought the hearing would be a matter of using the classroom on their floor, with Dr. Kinnamore and a few others present. The medical residents, perhaps.

She was stunned to discover that it was going to be held in one of the big lecture halls over at the medical school, with the whole hospital staff in attendance, or as many as could make the affair.

It was Dr. Lewis who told her who "all the people" were. In a semicircle around the room, their ranks rose to the ceiling. There was a long table down on the floor. . . .

"The board members," said Uncle Howard.

"But why so many?" Phoebe cried, panic rising. "Why should it take so many to— They are making too much of this, aren't they?"

Uncle Doc touched her arm. "Phoebe," he said, "why are *you* here?"

She flushed. "I know. I am Dr. Kinnamore's secretary, asked to take notes."

"Good girl. I imagine the chair beside his is being saved

for you. Suppose you go there and take down the things that are said. As they are said!"

He pointed to the chair she was to use, and she went toward it, holding herself stiffly erect. She did not like Uncle Doc! There was no doubt of the way she felt! She sat down and arranged her book, her pencils. She wished she need not look around the room and see all the eyes, the faces—

It was a very large room; there were no windows. Ordinarily the space on the floor was used for demonstrations, for patients, or for equipment employed for the instruction of medical students. Dr. Kinnamore and Phoebe were seated at one end of the long table there. The hospital Chief of Staff and the Administrator sat at the other end. A dozen men and three women occupied the other chairs. Board members. One of the women was Berda Heddiger, and Phoebe supposed the solicitous man beside her was her uncle. Or a lawyer perhaps? Phoebe shivered.

"Mrs. Heddiger's uncle demanded this full hearing," Dr. Kinnamore told her.

This gave Phoebe courage to look up at the benches. They rose in steps—as many as six—up to the ceiling. In the first rows were staff doctors. Behind them, residents. Talley sat at the near end of the third row. Jesse Holland was separated from him by a dozen other resident doctors. The interns were on the top rows. . . .

She stole a glance at Jesse—dark hair, sallow skin, darting black eyes. He was nervous. His hands moved restlessly, and his glance flew about the room like an imprisoned bird.

He caught her eye and lifted his circled thumb and finger confidently. Phoebe flushed and looked down at the table. She hated Jesse! If only for what he had dared to do to Mary last night.

A gentleman in a beautifully cut gray suit stood up and rapped for order. Dr. Kinnamore murmured his name to Phoebe—Mr. Hendriks, Chairman of the Board. He would preside, he announced, at this meeting called for an investigation into the conduct of a resident doctor of the hospital.

He picked up a sheet of paper and read the charge. Phoebe's pencil flew.

Dr. Talley Newbern—accused of conduct unbefitting a doctor in attendance on a patient committed to his care . . .

He saved her life, thought Phoebe.

. . . Ensuing publicity of his act within the hospital and before its personnel . . .

The purpose of the hearing was to judge the charge, and the proper action should the charge prove to be valid.

Down the table, Berda Heddiger made a commotion, dropping an ash tray and talking loudly, hysterically. She wore a black suit, with a glittery pin on her shoulder. Her hair had been "done" and tinted since she left the hospital. She still looked ill. Her uncle comforted her, seeming to reassure her.

Dr. Bleyer, the Chief of Staff, rose and demanded that the charge be dismissed as not relevant nor open to action by "this assemblage."

"He has a point there," growled Dr. Kinnamore.

Berda's uncle said that a poll of the hospital board had agreed that a hearing should be held.

Phoebe could not tell, from his manner, which side Mr. Hendriks was on. He was one of those suave, controlled men; he was polite to Berda's uncle; he was polite when he asked if Dr. Newbern was present. Talley lifted his hand and half rose from his seat.

"Do you, sir," asked Mr. Hendriks, "wish to make a preliminary statement?"

"Only," said Talley in his clear voice, "to say, sir, that I did nothing which could be interpreted as improper."

Down the table a board member signaled to the Chairman, who said, "Yes, Mr. Allen?"

"Could we be told, Hendriks," said this gentleman, who was on the fat side and spoke breathily, "just who this Dr. Newbern is?"

Mr. Hendricks nodded. "He is Dr. Talley Newbern, Mr. Allen. A resident on a research grant from the Strechem Foundation."

"An Englishman?" asked Mr. Allen.

"I believe so," said the Chairman. He glanced at Talley, who nodded.

"Just why is he in America?" asked Mr. Allen. Phoebe's pencil point dug into the paper. "Instead of doctoring in England?" He didn't actually *say*, "where he belongs."

"I came here," said Talley—

Phoebe could hear, in her memory, the way the girls

tried to say "here" as he did.

"—because I believed one would have more freedom to pursue his medical career than is possible in present-day England. Since my interest is in research, such freedom is essential." He spoke calmly, with great dignity.

"Could I be allowed to elaborate on Dr. Newbern's answer?" asked Dr. Kinnamore.

The chairman glanced at Mr. Allen, who nodded and sat down.

"Dr. Kinnamore?" said the Chairman.

"I would like to say," said the Chief, "that Dr. Newbern is a distinguished physician. His record in England and in this country is excellent. He came here to establish himself as an American citizen and doctor. . . ."

Berda's uncle jumped to his feet. He was a large man, with a shock of graying blond hair. "What we want to know is," he shouted, "why did he leave England in the first place?"

"You are out of order, Mr. Boland," said the Chairman.

Berda's uncle brushed that point aside. "I mean," he cried, "was there some reason to leave? A scandal, or trouble of some kind?"

Phoebe's fingertips went cold.

The Chairman looked at Dr. Kinnamore, who turned to Talley. He stood up. "No, sir," he said. "There was no scandal to cause me to leave."

"Well!" said Mr. Boland. "I've heard stories that say different."

Phoebe sat, as cold as ice. His brother—in England—

"I heard, too," said this Boland, who must be rich and

influential to be on the board, "that Newbern uses drugs. That he is a dope addict. That—"

What he said further was lost in the roar which swept across the room like a quick fire. Everyone had something to say. Protest, shock—it was an animal sound, and frightening.

Beside Phoebe, Dr. Kinnamore stood like a rock. The Chairman waited helplessly.

"I believe I have the floor," said the Chief, before really he could be heard. But he kept saying it until the room quieted. Then he said it again, and the Chairman nodded.

"Will you please wait, Mr. Boland," he said courteously, "until I give you the chance to speak?"

Grumbling, Boland sat down, and Dr. Kinnamore lifted his chin. "I didn't like this hearing when it was first called," he said loudly. "I don't like it any better now. But since we are into this, I feel I must say that the gentleman, Mr. Boland, is probably confusing Dr. Newbern with another doctor on my service who is inclined to use and abuse narcotic drugs."

This time there was silence, broken slowly by a growing ripple of comment. The board members put their heads together; the staff doctors showed their shock, and some voiced their protest.

No one had, really, believed Boland's charge. They had to believe Dr. Kinnamore. And so they were shocked.

Through it all, the Chief remained calm. He stood quietly beside the table, the tips of his fingers resting on it.

Mr. Hendriks said, ruefully, that everyone was shocked

at what he had said.

The Chief nodded. "I myself am shocked to have to say it. If it were not for this hearing—"

"But if you have such a doctor, sir . . ."

"Our effort—the hospital's effort—has been to try to save the man. He is a well-trained doctor, and I think he is worth reclaiming. Dr. Newbern has been helping with this project, one of many on which he works. In fact, he is using a certain ward in the hospital as a laboratory. Or," the Chief smiled, "as he would say, a lab-*or*-a-try."

Mr. Hendriks was not ready to smile. "But what does he do, Dr. Kinnamore?"

"Perhaps Dr. Newbern should tell you."

"I don't mean Newbern. I mean the other doctor—the addict."

"As an addict, I presume you mean?" said Dr. Kinnamore, knowing full well that that was not what the Chairman had meant. Other smiles in the room testified to knowing it, too. "This doctor," said the Chief, "experiments with drugs."

"But why, doctor?"

"Oh, for kicks. I think that is his term. He uses them to cover fatigue—" Carefully Dr. Kinnamore looked only at the Chairman. Phoebe followed his example, though she wished she could see Jesse's face!

A staff doctor waved for attention and asked if he might ask Dr. Kinnamore a question

The Chief nodded to him.

"If this Englishman is doing research," said the physician, "couldn't it be possible that he has experimented on himself?"

"No," said Dr. Kinnamore. "Newbern does not. He has not."

"Does he use his hospital patients for guinea pigs?" asked a board member.

Dr. Kinnamore turned to look directly at Berda Heddiger when he answered. "You know that is not true," he said. "Dr. Newbern does work with the patients, and he uses their records in compiling his data. He tries to help the patients that come to him, he explores the causes for their dependency on drugs, on their addiction, he tries to rehabilitate and cure."

"Does he effect cures?" asked a staff doctor.

"Not always. Of course not. For one thing, some patients refuse to be helped." Again the Chief's blue eyes turned to Berda Heddiger.

Mr. Boland stirred in his chair. "I thought we came here to talk about the improper behavior of a doctor to his woman patient," he said roughly.

"It was you, sir, who brought up the subject of drug use."

"Yes, I did, but there are other important things. . . ."

"Not as important as the idea that a doctor could be an addict," said one of the women board members. "Because —isn't that dangerous?"

"You still have the floor, Dr. Kinnamore," said Mr. Hendriks quietly.

The Chief nodded. "And I'll answer the question, too.

Because of course it is dangerous. But I will first remind you, Mrs. Lucas, that we are a community of our own here in the Medical Center. We care for over two thousand bed patients, regularly, and the personnel runs to something over five thousand. With clinic patients, visitors, auxiliary helpers—we are like a small town, ourselves. And in any community these days, in this hospital community, drug use seems to be a problem which must be faced. Dr. Newbern has come to us to do research in the facing of that problem."

"Well, as far as I am concerned," cried Mr. Boland, "I am ready to demand that any doctor using drugs should be dismissed. Who is the fellow, anyway?"

Every eye went to Dr. Kinnamore, and Phoebe stole a glance at Jesse. He too was watching the Chief, who stood, big, strong, impressive in his long white coat. "I won't tell you," he said pleasantly.

A sigh swept across the room like a small wind rippling grass. Phoebe made some pothooks on her red-lined tablet.

"But—" protested Mrs. Lucas. "If, as you indicate, there are doctors—or even just this one doctor in this hospital who uses drugs, how do you protect the patients?"

Dr. Kinnamore nodded. "You have every right to ask that," he told the woman. She was middle-aged, pleasant-faced, well-dressed. "I shan't go into technical details," said the Chief, "but we do protect the patients."

"Would you give this doctor's name to the board if there were not others present?"

"Not willingly, ma'am. Because once his identity is revealed, we should have to dismiss him."

"But shouldn't you? Goodness, I didn't suppose that a doctor . . ."

Dr. Kinnamore looked at Talley. "Will you take over with the answers, doctor?" he asked pleasantly. "Dr. Newbern makes this sort of thing his specialty. Come down here, please?"

The Chief sat down, the Chairman of the Board seemed in agreement. Talley stepped down to the floor and thrust his hands into his trouser pockets, then took them out again. "The question, I believe," he said quietly, "asked if doctors were addicts. And the answer I am sorry to give is, 'Yes, they are.' In fact, the matter of doctor-addiction is one of the biggest problems health authorities, and other authorities, have presented to them."

"I can't believe it," said Mrs. Lucas, in dismay.

"The image of a physician enslaved by narcotics can be unsettling," said Talley. "I agree."

"Do many . . . ?" asked Mr. Hendriks. The professional men on the benches were looking thoughtful and watchful.

"The latest figures I have," said Talley, completely poised now, "is that, in this country, about two thousand doctors are, or will soon become, drug addicts."

"But, in heaven's name, why?" cried Mrs. Lucas.

"The etiology," said Dr. Newbern, "of the disease is typical human weakness compounded by facile access to drugs. Stresses, the pressure of a doctor's work, are given as causes. A physician, faced with some physical disability, may undertake to treat himself, thinking that he knows how to handle the situation. . . ."

"Do they know?" asked Mr. Hendriks. The interest throughout the room was intense. Dr. Kinnamore put his hand over Phoebe's. She need not record Dr. Newbern's discussion.

"Not really," Talley was saying. "No, they do not know how to control self-administration of narcotic drugs."

"How do you find . . . ?"

Talley smiled. "Here in the hospital, finding a user is not too difficult. Behavior—oh, there are ways. With a doctor working from a private office, the state Narcotics Control Agency investigates any doctor ordering a suspiciously large amount of narcotics—that sort of thing."

"What can be done for such a doctor?" asked one of the staff surgeons. "What, specifically, are you doing for the man Kinnamore mentioned?"

"He is not an isolated case," said Talley slowly. "But of course he is an individual case. And we can use him as an example. Of course the prime objective would be—will be—to rehabilitate this trained man. Certainly one must employ a careful supervision of his activities. We must be extraordinarily careful of our drug supplies. Not to allow access, or use. He is not permitted to prescribe or administer to patients like Mr. Boland's niece, whom he attended."

Mr. Boland jumped. "My niece?" he cried loudly.

"Yes, sir." Talley spoke crisply. "She entered, you

know, suffering from an overdose of barbiturates. This, combined with the poisoning of habitual use, made her condition critical."

Mr. Boland had not known! He became very red in the face. "You're a liar!" he shouted.

Dr. Kinnamore stood up. "Dr. Newbern is telling the truth," he said sternly. "You had better believe him."

Though unwillingly, Mr. Boland did believe him. He had to. He collapsed in his chair, crushed and sorrowing. When Berda would have spoken to him, he turned away from her. "Let me think!" he cried in anguish.

Phoebe looked down at her tablet; though prepared, she too felt shock and apprehension. If the doctor in question was Jesse . . . She made a real effort to attend to her notes, making them factual, setting down each question, giving the answer briefly, directly.

She found herself fascinated by Dr. Newbern's manner, his ability to handle this group of people. The hearing had become Talley's show.

There was nothing special about his white jacket, but he wore it with an air, his shoulders straight. He possessed full knowledge of his subject, and his listeners wanted to share in it. Questions, and Talley's replies, came thick and fast.

"How would you deal with narcotics addiction, doctor?"

"Recognizing that a narcotics addict suffers from an illness, as well as the future probability of lawbreaking, the approach becomes a highly individualized procedure. In my opinion, the individual practitioner can prevent true addiction in most patients if he can manage the susceptible patient through the early stages of drug addiction."

"Good thinking!" said Dr. Howard Lewis at this point.

Talley looked up at him, as did Phoebe.

"Doctors," Talley continued, "have largely abandoned the problem to the lawmakers and the law-enforcement agencies. Mere laws, you know, will not make the problem go away."

Talley answered a dozen questions, dealt with a dozen aspects. Addicts, he said, turned to drugs primarily out of curiosity. He dealt with the types of people who did turn to drugs, the types who could be rehabilitated; he discussed the question of whether withdrawal should be placed on an ambulatory basis—

And always he spoke as an expert. He was asked again about the incidence of doctor-usage of drugs. He repeated that many doctors could be called users. Some were definitely addicted. "I daresay you think of addicts as juveniles, but the percentage of addicts is higher among doctors than it is among high school students."

Even the doctors were surprised, and stunned, at this statement.

"Then . . . ?" said someone.

"Yes!" said Dr. Newbern. "In both cases, it is entirely too high. And the facts behind addiction include difficulties which you would not think an intelligent person would willingly undergo. Take what it involves for a doctor to use and pay for drugs. If he is an intern, as he often is when beginning the use, he must find employment outside of his hospital work to pay for his habit. He must moonlight. He can perhaps resort to blackmail, or he can employ downright theft."

Phoebe sat, head down, thinking of the money she had seen Jesse take from her home.

Talley was still talking, and repeatedly the questions narrowed in on the doctor on Dr. Kinnamore's service.

Talley continued to be pleasantly reserved on the subject. "That particular doctor is a very smart man," he said, "although young. We hope that much can be done for him. I hope so. I would not care to see the tragedy of my brother repeated. He lost his whole career, you know, to this tragic appetite. I do hope we can help this man!"

And, thought Phoebe, that hope was why Jesse hated Talley. Jesse? Yes, of course it was Jesse.

Now the discussion was widening its scope again, the medical men wanted to take up some of the items which Talley had mentioned briefly before.

He said, yes, amphetamines were dangerous in that they led to narcotic addiction.

"How, doctor?"

"Their use may cause extreme nervousness and sleeplessness. Even without narcotics, you can get hallucinations and delusions—both dangerous. In all cases, I believe we should look first for an underlying personality disorder in our approach to any addiction."

"No," he said, "I think restricting a person's use of drugs

to a constant level is only defeatist in principle."

"Drug addiction," he declared firmly, "cannot, and should not, absolve one of responsibility for crime."

"Originally," he said, "the public attitude to drug usage was that of pity. Now, we consider the addict as a sick person capable of committing crime as a secondary effect of his illness."

But he did not believe that curtailing traffic in drugs had any result other than making it more difficult for a desperate man to get the stuff. Efforts directed toward drug addicts should have goals which were both realistic and more likely to be attainable than mere total abstention from drugs.

The question of numbers kept coming up. Talley said the figures in the United States were probably too low, because they were based largely on records of arrest. He agreed that juvenile use of narcotics had risen since the end of the Second World War.

"What about the poor?"

Talley laughed, without humor. "The poor juvenile," he said thoughtfully. "But you are opening a whole Pandora's box of questions there, sir. Is it a matter of the poor taking drugs because of the rigors of poverty, or does one use drugs and become, or stay, poor?

"It is a regrettable fact of life in present-day America," he said quietly, "that addiction is a widespread problem not restricted to persons in particular environments, economic situations, educational levels, age limits, ethnic groups, or religious connection."

Again and again, the question came up of handling the problem, even solving it, through the psychological approach. Finally Talley said, still pleasantly, that he felt this discussion might wait until another session. The hour was getting late.

But still the questions came, and the replies. Some of the doctors were called away. Uncle Howard came over and suggested to Phoebe, and to Dr. Kinnamore, that "the girl might leave."

The Chief glanced at his secretary. "But she also may stay," he told Dr. Lewis.

"There is no need for notes on this."

"I've told her that. However, the notes she has been taking will make interesting reading."

"You have a clever man in Newbern, it would seem."

Phoebe glowed with this praise for Talley. She would remember what her uncle had said, and tell Talley.

Just then, Jesse Holland heaved himself up from the end of the third row and went up the ramp to the door. He disappeared through it. A dozen eyes watched him go, and the expression on the faces . . .

Phoebe sat trembling, shaken with revulsion. A *doctor!* she thought.

She let her pencil fall, but she sat on, listening—and increasingly puzzled. When th hearing was over, and she went back to the office, she asked Dr. Kinnamore,

". . . but wasn't the important thing that Dr. Newbern tried to kiss a patient?"

Dr. Kinnamore looked at her. "No, Mrs. Flowers," he said dryly. "No, it was not."

TWELVE

THAT NIGHT Phoebe went home, completely exhausted. She picked up the girls at Mrs. Haines' and managed to thank the woman, but the chatter about Mrs. Haines' letting *them* cook dinner—"Minute steaks, Mother, and baked sweet potatoes. It was good."

"Could we have less talk?" she asked crossly, opening the door into the dark house.

"Sure," said Linda cheerfully, going ahead to turn on lamps.

Mary took Phoebe's coat and hung it away.

They didn't seem to mind her being cross, and she was ashamed of herself. She would not let her working be hard on the girls.

"I had a long day," she explained by way of apology. "There was a meeting. . . ."

"I'll fix you something to eat, if you'll go up and change into a robe," Linda offered.

Phoebe began to say that she was not hungry. "Just something quick," she told the child.

"Soup? Milk toast?"

"Just—anything," said Phoebe, dragging herself up the stairs. She went to her room and changed her tired blouse and plaid skirt for her tailored blue robe. She smoothed her hair and went downstairs. "I hope my supper is ready," she forced herself to say. "I am so hungry I have a headache."

There was some mail from "home," there were a couple of new magazines—Phoebe and the girls managed a pleasant enough hour before their bedtime. But Phoebe was still very tired. She would go upstairs herself as soon as the girls had finished with their baths and talking back and forth.

She tried to read, to keep from thinking, and she was getting drowsy when she heard Talley's step on the porch and heard his voice, warning her who he was.

She sighed and went to unlock the door.

"I didn't expect you," she said stupidly.

"I should have telephoned." He had a brown paper sack in his hands. He bent to press his cold cheek against Phoebe's, and he set the sack on the table while he took off his topcoat.

"I brought some ground nuts," he told Phoebe. "I daresay the girls have gone to bed. . . ."

"They're going. You can hear them."

"So I can," he agreed, smiling. The girls' voices rang like distant bells.

"Why, they're peanuts!" Phoebe cried, watching him divide the contents of his sack into four heaps.

He looked up. "Yes!" he agreed. "You do call them that. Don't you like them?"

"Well—of course I do. Thank you, Talley. The girls will like theirs, too."

He asked for permission to light the fire; he spread a sheet of newspaper on Phoebe's lap to catch the peanut shells. He sat in the chair across from the couch, ate peanuts, and talked about going back to "his patients" on the third floor the next day.

Phoebe said almost nothing. Now and then he would glance at her in concern. And finally he said, "I expected you to be confused. But are you all right?"

She sighed and laughed. "How about you? Are *you* all right?"

He brushed his nutshells into a small heap and spoke thoughtfully. "I seem to be," he said. "The board took no action—"

"No. They became too interested in the discussion of drug addiction. I felt a little sorry for Berda's uncle. He evidently did not know—"

"Or wished not to know," said Talley.

A coal snapped into a shower of sparks, and Talley kicked away those that popped out upon the hearth. When he sat down again, Phoebe asked him, "What is going to happen to Jesse Holland?"

"I still hope the man can be salvaged."

"Do you like him?"

Talley looked up, surprised. "He's a kinky sort of chap," he said good-naturedly. "A man with a problem, Phoebe."

There was something about the phrase. . . . Phoebe turned it over in her mind, but she could not connect it with anything specific. She tried to rouse herself, to show an interest in the things which Talley was talking about—peanuts, and his sister-in-law Rhoda—

"I find that to be an uncommon name in America," he said.

He was being kind to Phoebe, and she felt that she was failing him somehow, somewhere. She had been so frightened by the charges made against him—her very fear had failed him. She had even considered offering a bribe to Jesse. . . . Wouldn't Talley be shocked to know that! And probably so disgusted he would never care to see her again. Oh, dear! She just really was not good at personal relationships. She had always known that Jesse was not her kind, she had been warned that he was not—

But, for that matter, this reserved, clever English doctor was not "her kind" either. And she did have difficulty adjusting herself to these people.

"It seems," she said aloud, breaking into something Talley was saying—she didn't know what, "that I have no ability to read people."

He smiled at her. "What makes you decide that?" he asked.

"Because I've had it proven to me. I let Jesse come here

to the house—I endangered the girls . . ."

He made a low sound of protest.

"Yes, I did!" she insisted. "And I should not have worried about you for one minute! That's how I know I should attend strictly to my own business. Take care of my house, and the girls."

"You are at the hospital every day."

"For five days a week, eight hours a day, yes, I am. And that's another thing! For those forty hours, I should be—I *plan* to be—purely a secretary. Because you see, Talley, I just have to protect myself from hurt—and shame—and being upset."

"It doesn't sound like too much of a life for a young woman as warm and sincere as you are, Phoebe."

"I can make do. My mother did that way, and for those same reasons. She had been hurt, and she didn't want any more of it. . . ."

Talley pursed his lips and nodded. "To wrap oneself in cotton wool," he mused. He glanced up at Phoebe. "Cotton!" he explained. "Yes, one would be protected. Unless you think the means of protection is no better, really, than the thing you would avoid."

Phoebe said nothing, a bit stubbornly she would have had to admit.

Talley got up and stood before the fire, his elbow resting on the mantel. "You know, Phoebe . . ." he began. Then he looked at her keenly. "D'you know anything at all about flying?"

"Flying?" she asked stupidly.

"Yes. Airplanes—all that. Do you know enough . . . ? Look! " He came to sit on the couch beside her, turned to face her. He was so close she could have put her hand into his or touched his cheek. . . . "Do you know what I mean when I talk about an airplane taking off into or against the wind?" He gestured with his hands.

Phoebe nodded.

"Well, then! Because aircraft, you see, to function best, should take off against the wind."

Phoebe looked up, puzzled.

"It really should, my dear. Look!" Again he gestured. "Because if you go the other way, downwind, or with the wind, the length of run required will increase in direct proportion to the square of said wind. That is, if the aircraft will fly at sixty miles per hour, and it takes twelve hundred feet of runway to get to sixty miles per hour no wind, then with a fifteen-mile-per-hour tailwind, the aircraft must go seventy-five miles an hour, and to do so would require eighteen hundred feet of runway. This is all right for some planes. But what about those fifteen-hundred-feet runways? If a pilot would go into the same fifteen-mile-per-hour wind, he would need only nine hundred feet of runway, and not— D'you see?"

Phoebe frowned. "He'd be making trouble for himself —or someone—by going downwind? Though to an ignorant person like me, that does sound the better way."

He laughed and hugged her close to his side. "Don't call Phoebe ignorant," he told her.

Phoebe sniffed. "I know, first-hand, what I am talking about. And I know, too, how very smart you are!"

He shook his head. "But you don't want to sail any airplanes into the wind," he said sadly.

"Oh, Talley, it's only—"

He patted her knee. "I understand." He leaned toward her. "May I kiss you, Phoebe?"

She did not move, but she sighed, ever so lightly. Instantly he was on his feet. "Right!" he said briskly. "You are tired." He put her peanut shells into the fire; he picked up his coat.

Phoebe followed him to the door. "Thank you, Talley," she said uncertainly. "Will you come back? When the girls are here—to see you?"

He smiled at her, nodded, and let himself out.

She had not handled that well, either, Phoebe told herself drearily.

Though believing that Talley was smart, and liking Talley, Phoebe, through January and February, stuck with her determination not to become involved with "people." She was the one who had to live with the results of the emotional winds which had knocked her about those days after Christmas. Her shocked need to believe the revelations about Jesse—and her shame to think she had ever liked or trusted him. Her shock and fear for Talley—and her realization that she loved the man. She didn't want to love any man! To upset her life, and upset the girls—

She was just asking to be hurt. And she would do no

more of it. No. She would go with Talley's wind, long runway or no.

As time passed, of course, the intensity of her resolve relaxed. The girls and their interests, the simple pleasures she knew with her family, and the good work she was doing at the hospital, all helped her to adjust her position to one of quiet friendliness.

Talley was no longer working on the third floor. He had been taken over by the psychoneurology department, and an enlarged space for his patients had been made for him on the tenth floor.

Phoebe saw him, and often, but it was not quite the same as having him go up and down the hall outside her office door each day. Talley knew that it was not, and he complained about the change. He was the first one to look her up and show her the article in the Medical Center's newspaper which cited her for the suggestion she had made the month before, and which had been accepted and put to use—to keep an informed volunteer worker on special duty near the recovery room to answer questions and reassure relatives. This measure had proved popular, and "Mrs. Flowers is to be commended for her interest in the hospital and its patients."

Of course it was exciting, the praise, the talk, the pleasure she had to feel in the various comments. Her cousin Patrick brought the matter to the family's attention.

In this rosy glow, Phoebe forgot all about keeping herself aloof. People seemed to like her, and so she could like them.

During spring vacation, she agreed that the girls could invite their two special friends from home to spend a week end. This was a busy, happy interlude, and on Monday it seemed restful and quiet to go back to the busy hospital and the stack of work on her desk.

Dr. Kinnamore wanted her to accompany him on a ward walk; there was the usual heap of Monday morning mail. . . .

Her telephone rang, and Phoebe's hand went out to it even as her other hand finished typing a word.

"Mrs. Flowers," said the voice of some girl down in the main office, "there is a Mr. Timpone here. He wants to see you."

Phoebe frowned. "Timpone?" she repeated. The name was vaguely familiar, but— Then her face brightened. Oh, yes!

"Would it be Gig?" she asked. "A big man, colored . . ."

"That's right," said the voice. "Shall I send him up?"

"Yes, of course," said Phoebe. "Tell him how to go." Smarter people than Gig had got lost in the mazes of the Center.

But what on earth was Gig doing here? The man was a nurse—a licensed practical nurse. He had worked in their little hospital at home. He was huge—and willing. He could give medicines, and he specialized in caring for men who were in casts, or who were incapacitated by strokes, spine injuries. . . .

229

Phoebe went into the hall to intercept him when and if he reached the third floor. Which he did, rather more quickly than she would have expected.

She led the big smiling man back to her office. She asked him about home, his family—he had married a girl from Virginia while serving as a corpsman in the Navy—she asked about Dr. Green.

"And what brings you here, Gig?" she finally asked.

He shifted his bulk on the small chair. Almost any chair would be small for Gig.

"I need a job," he said, pulling at the edges of his light blue sports coat.

"*You* need a job?" Phoebe repeated.

"Well, yes, ma'am, I do. You see, there ain't nobody broke his hip this past winter, and there's a new supervisor at the hospital who thinks there isn't call for a male nurse full time. She said they ain't sech a big hospital. And somebody said you was working here, which *is* a big hospital. . . ."

Phoebe laughed. "Yes, Gig," she agreed. "It certainly is big."

"Yes, ma'am."

"Well, now let's see. About a job . . ."

She went right to work on it. She talked to the floor supervisor, she talked ot the Chief of Nursing Services, she talked to the hospital manager. She said to each one of these people that Gig was a good worker, strong, pleasant to work with. The patients always liked him.

Within a day or two, he started to work, and everyone

said that he was doing fine.

He was assigned to emergency room duty, because his evident bulk and strength lent him authority, and Phoebe made a practice, each morning, of coming to work through that section of the hospital. Gig was grateful to her, and said so. "Yes, ma'am, everything is going just fine!"

Evidently he was doing well.

Easter came and went, with new clothes for the girls and a new hat for Phoebe. Uncle Bob said that her mother's estate would be settled before long. Bulbs were flowering in every yard in the Heights, in the round beds of the hospital grounds, in the park. . . .

And, all of a sudden, Phoebe realized that she was not seeing Gig any more. Was he on a different hours-schedule? Had he been assigned to ward work? She asked about him at the emergency room desk.

"He's left," said the nurse on duty there.

"You mean, he's working somewhere else?"

"I wouldn't know," said the nurse. "A guy like him—Excuse me. There's an ambulance coming in."

There was an ambulance coming in, but later that morning Phoebe went directly to the manager's office. And after some red tape, she finally was admitted to the presence of that busy man's assistant.

The assistant was courteous and brief. Oh, yes, he said, he knew about Timpone. "We regretted the way things turned out."

"He's a good nurse," said Phoebe belligerently.

"I think you are right," said the smooth man in the brown worsted suit. "But, regrettably, a narcotics agent bought some drugs from him. You see, Mrs. Flowers, your man Gig was selling junk—amphetamines and barbiturates —to young people around the hospital. To an intern, to an aide—students and teen-age volunteers."

Phoebe sat astounded. "But how . . . ?" she asked.

The smooth young man across the desk was trying to tell her how. "He took patients to the various wards and offices," he said. "He got some of the stuff from the doctors' wastebaskets. Pharmaceutical samples, you know —the stuff was available. I suppose we are to blame for what happened; we put temptation in his way."

Phoebe did some fast and furious thinking. "I understand," she said. "But Gig had been trained. He knew . . ."

"Yes, Mrs. Flowers," said the assistant manager. "Yes, he did know."

Phoebe went back to her desk and tried to absorb what she had learned. Gig would be in real trouble—with the federal agents, she supposed. Could Dr. Green help him? Could Phoebe? Uncle Bob? Oh, what could she do? Not only for the big and stupid man, but for herself. This matter of drugs . . . It kept coming up again and again! What *was* this horror which seemed to pursue her?

Perhaps, she thought afterward, someone told Talley about her and Gig. Perhaps he knew for himself—or even, perhaps, he just happened to come to see them that evening. At the time, Phoebe thought it just happened, and she was glad to see him.

He came early; dinner was over, but she and the girls were planting geraniums in a couple of ornamental urns set beside the front steps.

Talley came up the street; Mary spied him and went flying to greet him. Phoebe thought she must have a talk with Mary about the decorum desirable in girls about to enter their teens.

But, then, Mary was also about to enter the hospital—in a month or two. Phoebe began to gather her gardening gear—trowel, clay pots, and her gloves.

"Hello, Talley," she said when he came up on the terrace.

By now, Linda was hanging to his other hand.

"You have potting soil on your cheek," he told Phoebe.

She wiped her face against her sleeve.

"It doesn't look bad," he assured her. "May I help?"

"The girls will put things away. You and I will sit on the porch like proper old-folk."

The girls chattered to Talley for a few minutes while Phoebe went inside to clean her face, to get a sweater, and turn on lamps. Since he was here, she would talk to Talley about Gig. He would know if something could be done for the man.

Mary made some lemonade and brought it out. Talley pronounced it "not bad," and the girls showed their disappointment.

"Oh, now, see here!" he cried. "For an Englishman, 'not bad' means beautiful and delicious." He drank from his glass. "And very good!"

The girls giggled merrily and would have stayed on and on, talking to Talley. But Phoebe watched the time and sent them packing firmly.

"It isn't polite to leave company," Linda attempted.

Her mother's face answered that one, and the girls, though slowly, finally departed. Talley moved to sit beside Phoebe on the swing. She was young, and pretty, and clean, this Phoebe Flowers.

Listening to her, her voice, with an occasional tremor in it, could twang a string inside a man. Watching her eyes, with a hidden terror in them, charged a man's batteries.

"Could we take a walk?" Talley asked. "Just here in the neighborhood?"

She stood up, nodding. "I'll tell the girls. . . ."

She came back, and they went down the steps together, down again to the sidewalk that led along the street. The trees were full-leaved, the hedges lush, the fragrance of lilacs and early roses filled the evening air. The sun lay close to the horizon; in the east, darkness began to tint the blue sky with lavender shadows.

"I'm glad you came this evening," said Phoebe. She told him about Gig, and he listened—as if he had no knowledge at all of the matter.

And she asked him tensely, "What is this horror which lately seems to be all around me?"

Talley was gazing up at a rooftop; the architect had used

an easy mixture of Italian, French, and American style—volutes, mansard, and sash window. "That is not the question," he told Phoebe.

She turned sharply to look at him.

"You know," he said easily, "we all know what the horror is." He took his pipe from his pocket. "But the question is," he said, "what can we do about it?"

Phoebe spoke to the neighbor who, on top of a thirty-foot ladder, was attempting to do something to the roof gutter. He would watch her walking along with a man and later tell his wife—she would tell her neighbor. . . . . "What do you mean, *we?*" she asked Talley. "You can't mean *me.*"

He put the pipe stem between his teeth, then took it out again. "Well, yes, I do mean you," he said. "All of us. Doctors, lawyers, church people—all the individuals, any individual who is socially conscious. . . ."

"What on earth could I do?"

"Someone is doing something. Your narcotics agent—the one who nabbed your boy—" He glanced at Phoebe. "He told me that here in the city addicts were being forced to turn to amphetamines and paregoric. . . ."

"*Paregoric!*"

"Oh, yes," said Talley. "When heroin gets scarce, or even disappears, your addict will buy amphetamines—which is illegal—and paregoric, which, in this state he can buy in two-ounce bottles at any drugstore."

"But—"

"No, it isn't as good. But use of such things prevents the

narcotics user from getting sick through withdrawal symptoms."

"And Gig—"

"We think he'd been tipped to the rise in the market for amphetamines. He probably had done a small business in the little town where he lived—"

"Where *I* used to live," said Phoebe, her distress making her sound cross.

"That's it," said Talley serenely. "Down here, in the city, he could pick up the amphetamines—more of them, and more easily—and sell them. Our city has done a lot to make heroin scarce, expensive, and of poor quality—"

"Have *you* done it, Talley?"

He laughed. "No. I am just a doctor, trying to care for the results of not stopping the traffic completely." He paused to look up at a large red brick house. "Italian," he murmured. "The irregular spacing of the eave supports balances the wings of the house with its ornate entrance. . . ."

"The man who lives there is a banker," said Phoebe.

Talley nodded and resumed their walk. He would have then put his arm about Phoebe's shoulder, but she drew away from him.

"I don't think you are so much concerned about the neighbors," he said quietly, "as that you are indulging your naturally suspicious instincts."

That was what Jesse had said! That she was suspicious, that she didn't trust people.

Her chin lifted. She had not agreed to take a walk with

Talley Newbern to hear him criticize her and accuse her—

But was he right? Was it true that she was suspicious of people? Yes. She supposed she was. That was why she made few close friendships, and had no intimates. She liked people, but she always drew a line. She thought of poor Charles Reid back home. And Talley, here beside her. Ready to be friendly, and more—

But she felt, she acted—she behaved as her mother had taught her to behave! Oh. indeed Julia had left her mark! She— Without warning, tears filled Phoebe's eyes and began to trickle down her cheeks.

Talley had stopped again, gazing at what he called "his kind of house"—steep-roofed, half-timbered, the windows leaded. . . . "Pure England!" he cried happily. "Elizabethan, at that! Oh, Phoebe . . ." He broke off, astounded. "But you are weeping," he cried in concern. "What did I do? What did I say?"

Phoebe put out her hand and sniffled. "I don't have a handkerchief," she gasped. "And you didn't say anything." She tried to laugh, and accepted the handkerchief which he gave her. "I'm just being a silly woman," she told him, blinking her lashes.

"Oh, well, then!" he said, relieved. "I like my women foolish."

She shook her head. "The reason I got weepy," she said, "I was realizing that the shadow of my mother still was upon me. And I don't want it to be. But living in her house—maybe it was wrong for us to come here and live in her house."

Talley's face showed his interest. "I understand your mother had a problem . . ." he said. Now, there was that phrase again!

"Oh, I don't know about any *problem!*" Phoebe said sharply. "Mother complained that Dick and I deserted her. We did do things on our own—but even as children, she made no attempt to live *with* us. Or to share her life with us. We knew nothing about her work, her friends—and she knew nothing about us. She didn't want to know. And she didn't want us to know about her."

"That," said Talley softly, "may have been her greatest gift to you, my darling."

Phoebe stopped walking; she turned to face Talley, there under a wide-spreading maple tree. Its seed wings floated down, their fall whispering ever so softly against the ground. "What do you mean?" she asked tensely.

"Because," he said, speaking gently, his eyes holding hers, "your mother finally died the violent death of a drug addict, my darling."

Phoebe heard him. But she repeated the words silently, her lips moving. She stared at Talley; her eyes got wider and wider. Then she turned and walked swiftly down the street, away from him. He followed her and caught at her arm, holding her there beneath the lamppost. Shining new metal signs, lacy and pretty, had lately been put up on the old wrought-iron gaslight standards. In the pink light, Phoebe leaned forward to stare at Talley. "That's not true!" she said roughly.

"Yes," said Talley, "it is true. You asked me, and I answered you—"

She stamped her foot noiselessly upon the ground. Frightened, angry, protesting, she cried out at him. "Don't say *awnswer*," she said. "And *awsk*. Don't talk—" Her face crumpled. "Oh, Talley, Talley!" she cried. "I'm sorry—"

"Shhhh." He took her hand, and together they walked toward her home. Talley did not speak. Phoebe was thinking. Her thoughts darted through her memory, opening one door, slamming it, going on to another, like a child hunting for something it feared to find. There were things and places—where she should have known. . . . Her mother's withdrawal—she would be "tired" in the evening and go to her room. She didn't want to talk. . . .

She was a woman of strange moods, stranger ideas and opinions. . . .

After Phoebe left home—in recent years especially, her mother would make strange telephone calls. She would say, "I don't know what to do. Phoebe. I'm *desperate!*"

And she had been—desperate.

Phoebe looked up at Talley, her eyes like Mary's, young, trusting, pleading. "If I had only known," she said woefully.

"Yes," he agreed. "Such a life is a lonely one."

"She could have told me," said Phoebe. "The times we were together. I did come to see her—but she didn't tell me!"

"No. And that is too bad because you must meet the horror of it now, when you will feel helplessly that you should have done something about it. Of course this sort of thing is a horror. Until just lately, I supposed you knew about her problem."

"I didn't," said Phoebe. "Oh, I *didn't!* I would have done something—"

"What would you have done?"

Phoebe walked slowly along, thinking hard—about the medicines which she had found in the bathroom cabinet, and the syringe which had puzzled her. She had thrown it all out in that first week of sorting and finding things—the notes. They had been incoherent, a lot of them. Or resentful. There had been the books, with marked pages. Edgar Allan Poe. Havelock Ellis. "I would see thick, glorious fields of jewels, solitary and clustered. . . ." Phoebe remembered that sentence, because she had thought it beautiful. Her mother had heavily underlined it. And there was one from Thomas De Quincey that she remembered. ". . . a fearful enemy for months. I have been every night, through his means, transported into Asiatic scenes . . ."

Phoebe stopped and again turned to face Talley.

"Who told you all this?" she asked. "Uncle Howard?" Her tone was bitterly accusing.

Talley shook his head. "Not a word of it," he said. "No. But someone you like and trust."

Phoebe nodded. "Uncle Cecil," she said.

"Yes. But not as gossip, Phoebe, darling. Only because

he hoped I might help you, should you need that help."

"But Uncle Doc—" She was remembering that someone —Uncle Bob—had told her that Uncle Doc had helped Julia. "Poor Julia," he had said.

Again she leaned toward Talley. "*How* did he help my mother?" she demanded.

"In many ways, Phoebe. He helped her to live with her appetite, and to control it."

"He didn't *cure* her!"

"No. But with his help she was able to hold a job. He made her keep up the house for you and the children."

"Where she lived alone with her problem! Where she was *alone!*"

"No. Not in that sense. Dr. Lewis worked with her, and for her, to the end."

"Did she always have it? Your precious 'problem'?"

"Gradually increasing, yes, I believe she did. Your uncle discovered it in full effect—oh, that was ten years ago. She had to have a small operation, she had to enter the hospital. . . ."

That was the year Linda was born. And Phoebe could not go to her mother. Her mother did not come to her when David had been killed six months later.

"I didn't know," said Phoebe again mournfully.

"As I told you, it was one thing she did for you."

"I didn't know," Phoebe repeated.

"But you know now."

"Yes. Oh, yes!"

"You're older now, and more able to know."

"Is that where Jesse knew her?" she asked. "In the hospital? No, not when she was a patient—"

"She came regularly to the hospital for the medicines your uncle let her have. That probably was where he knew her, if he did."

"But she didn't stay with the things Uncle Doc tried to do for her? She couldn't have. . . ."

"No, she didn't. Because Rotan told her she need not."

"*Rotan*." Phoebe screamed the name.

Talley took her arm and led her on toward the house. "Yes," he said. "We're watching that man."

Phoebe was still pushing her way through folds and folds of thick, smothering curtains. "Was her—her dependency on drugs so great . . . ?" she asked fearfully.

"It was too great, finally, for her to handle."

"Yes. Yes, it must have been. Oh, Talley, I didn't know."

"What would have been your reaction?" he asked in a calm and businesslike tone. "Had you known?"

Phoebe began to reply quickly, but before a sound could escape her lips, she stopped, thinking. "Yes," she said then faintly. "Yes. My feeling would have been a mixture of revulsion, shame, anger—a withdrawal from her—"

She took a deep breath, then she said mournfully, "These past months, I have been thinking that my mother's worst—well—*sin* was her interest in Rotan, in her letting him have such a hold on her." She broke off, shaking her head. "I'm sorry," she said, her tone that of a hurt, bewildered child.

"Oh, my dearest," said Talley, "those people have little interest in sex. No. Rotan's relationship—he got pills for her. I don't know what, of course. But obviously more than she should have had. I am sure he was the one to procure them, though he was never caught."

And he had feared the notes which Julia had written and left behind, lest they implicate him. He had wanted them, and the will, destroyed.

Phoebe was weeping again drearily. "Poor woman," she murmured. Then her shoulders stiffened, and her head lifted. "Talley!" she said sharply. "What about heredity? Me—the girls—"

"Through environment, perhaps you could have followed her path. Your uncle protected you by not telling you of this thing. It was better that you should just misunderstand your mother's ways, and not see too much of her." He spoke calmly. "She was a weak woman, Phoebe. Just as my brother was a weak man. Life was too much for their amount of strength. You could have 'inherited' this weakness if your mother had been where she could set a personal example to you. Or have persuaded you. Hers was not, I will confess, the expected environment, the respectable old house in which you now live. . . ."

Phoebe thought about that. Her "respectable old house" was now a half-block away; its lights could be seen through the blowing trees. "It was better—for us, at least—that we didn't spend too much time with Mother?"

"Oh, yes. But of course I will say that a *problem* in itself can be inherited."

"That word again!" cried Phoebe. "What *problem* are you talking about?"

His smile was indulgent. "A tendency to cut corners," he suggested. "To seek an easy solution. Do you do that?" Immediately he answered his own question. "No," he decided, "you do not."

They walked slowly along. Phoebe stopped at the foot of the terrace steps. The lights upstairs bloomed rosy pink; the girls were going to bed, with their familiar, usual rituals.

"In talking to Uncle Cecil," Phoebe said, speaking reluctantly, "did he say that my father knew about this—this habit of my mother's?"

"We discussed that, Phoebe," said Talley, again using his calm and forthright tone. "And we decided that he probably did not know. She may have begun the journey, but it is always difficult, you know, to acknowledge weakness or failure in someone you love."

"And you think he did love her?"

"Didn't he?" His voice was deep.

Phoebe began to tremble. She put her two hands on the bronze railing and bent her head to them. She was trying to remember how she had felt about her mother—concern, yes. And a sense of guilt about her. . . . "Where did life fail her?" she turned to ask Talley. "My father?"

"No," said Talley. "She hurt him deeply."

"She always *said* he failed her."

"She said that about her daughter, too. Didn't she?"

"Yes. Yes, she did. And I didn't think I—I didn't *mean* to fail her. Though, perhaps, as a child . . ."

"Of course you didn't," said Talley. "A child, like Mary or Linda, would not fail a grown woman in the sense you mean."

Phoebe nodded.

"She may have thought her family failed her. I mean her brothers and her sister—"

"She may have tried to tell herself that, Phoebe. One hunts for crutches with which to support one's conscience. No, if there was failure behind your mother's—er—trouble—" His golden eyes glinted in the faint light. "I think we could put the blame only upon life itself. Not upon her family. You withdrew, all of you. But things might have been worse for her if you had not withdrawn. Conflict is not good, you know. . . ."

Phoebe put her foot on the first step. "How," she asked, "did you find out all this? Why did you try to find out?"

His hand fell warmly upon her forearm. "I became interested in all that concerned you," he said. "I knew that there was a block in you about your mother. When I came to know your Uncle Cecil, through his rehabilitation work, you see? he let me talk about this, and then he and his wife talked to me. They would talk to you. So would Dr. Lewis.

"I then looked up Julia Edwards' medical records. This

was a sickness which she had, my dear. And not a pretty one, either. The scars are lasting."

"Oh, Talley—" She went up the steps. "I thought," she said, turning to look at him—as he came up his face was on a level with hers—"I thought my mother just didn't love us. That she couldn't love us."

"That may have been true. In her later years."

"I have watched for those symptoms in me," she said. "When the girls do something, and I scold them."

"You don't, you won't ever, push them aside, my dear. Phoebe, please, now that we have talked about this, please put it out of your mind. It would be unbearable—"

"Don't feel sorry for me," she told him. "Like my mother, I am what my life has made me."

She walked to the steps of the porch, but there she turned and held out her hand. "I am tired," she said, "and I have to do so much thinking. I—I'm sorry that you had to find out all this about me. . . . But don't be *kind*. I know you are sorry for me, but—"

She would not let him persuade her. He had to leave her, knowing that she thought he had been kind as a doctor, but that, as a man, she felt he must be revolted at the whole situation.

She did feel that way. She felt that Talley must hate all connections with drug use. He saw so much of that, sordid, hateful. And her mother had cast such a stain upon her! Through his brother, his life had been changed, he already had been too hurt by it ever to want to be anything more than kind to Phoebe.

246

And she wanted more than that from him! She would never have more. She knew that now. Her mother—she always had spoiled things for Phoebe. And now—now—

If Talley loved her, he might say . . . But she didn't *know* that he loved her. He had never said—and now he would not.

THIRTEEN

FOR TWO DAYS, Phoebe went about her routine tasks in a cloud of misery, in a daze of unhappiness. Everything was going wrong. She tried to control this feeling, but she was so shocked, so hurt— Yes! That was the word. What she had learned about her mother was in itself a shock, but the implications of her mother's tragedy spread like ooze which penetrated every corner of her life and being.

It changed Phoebe's whole relationship with Talley.

It changed the way she felt, or could act, with her uncles. They had known—and had watched her with that knowledge in mind. . . .

It could affect the girls. What if the Institute should come to know . . . ?

Oh, of course she was being extreme! But the ideas, the speculations would not depart. She had lost all ability to reason or the trust which would let her accept another's advice and reason.

If things could just break off for a time. She needed to *think*. She needed perspective. That was exactly what she needed—to stand away—

On Friday evening she asked the girls how they would like to go up "home" for Saturday and Sunday and see their friends . . . ?

They were delighted. And Phoebe herself found some peace come into her mind at the thought of returning to the small town, to her small house— If she could just stay there and live again in that house, do her job at the little hospital. . . . Perhaps she could!

Oh, perhaps she *could!*

She and the girls took off by ten the next day; they would, Phoebe planned, stay at the motel, but, yes, the girls could go to see their friends—she meant to see Dr. Green.

It was Saturday, and he did not hold afternoon office hours, but he probably would be at the hospital, and when she phoned, he told her to come over. What was she doing in town?

"A little change from the big city."

He was waiting for her in his office. Not in his familiar white clothes. He wore a sports shirt and gray-green slacks. But he was his familiar, quiet self, big, wise—

He listened, almost without comment, while Phoebe poured out her story. She told of the discoveries which she had made about her mother, she told of her shock, her shamed disbelief. And yet she had to believe—

"And live with what you know," he agreed.

"I don't think I ever can!" she cried. "Not among the people who know! "

"You are in despair," he said quietly. "And you think you can run away from that despair."

She started to agree, then broke off to gaze at him, wide-eyed. "Can't I?" she asked softly.

"I don't think so, Phoebe."

He got up and walked around his office. His desk was a welter of correspondence, forms, medical journals and advertisements—drug samples. Phoebe had kept things tidier for him. She wanted to ask about his present secretary, and she would, once this subject had been dealt with.

Phoebe in her pink skirt, her pink and white striped blouse, and her neat white shoes sat primly in the chair and watched Dr. Sam. He took a book from the shelves, opened it, closed it. He stood for a long minute and gazed out of the window. The grass was very green, and the new leaves of the trees were like lace.

"Ever since I have been in the city," Phoebe told him, "this matter of drug addiction has been like a horror to me. When I first went to work at the Center, I saw a man brought in. A junkie. He was horrible, and the way he was treated was horrible. Everywhere I turned . . ."

"And you think you could run back here and escape all that?" asked the big doctor.

Phoebe had not yet said what she hoped. "Well," she

defended herself, "I was happier here."

"You can be happy in the city."

"Oh, but—"

"Yes, I know. The memory of your mother, the knowledge that other people about you share that memory . . ."

"It's so *terrible*, Dr. Sam!"

He nodded and sat down again at the desk; he leaned forward and looked intently at the pretty young woman. Her smooth hair was like pure gold, her eyes . . .

"Do not be so crushed by what you have just learned, Phoebe," he told her. "You should not despair. This matter of dependency on drugs, this weakness, if you like, or this sickness—city or town, you will find that our numbers are legion."

She leaned forward, and her hand automatically pushed her hair behind her ears. "I don't understand," she said uneasily.

He watched her, his hands clasped together on the desk. "I said that our numbers. *Our*. We. Phoebe, my girl, there are those of us who cannot take, alone, the pressures of life, the tremendous pressures of a professional life, and those of one's home and family life, which can be, which have been anything but—pleasant. Not being able to take these pressures, and to break under them, is the real, perhaps the only, tragedy of life. And often, often, my dear, that tragedy is not acted out before the footlights, but is played alone in a woman's bedroom, or in a little town, in a little hospital, by a small-town doctor like myself."

Phoebe stared at him. Then, her hand clutching her throat, she leaned back and away from him. "No," she said. "No!"

"Yes," he answered her. "Yes. I have used morphine. I did, for years. I began it when I was an intern. I—wanted to be a surgeon. It was the one thing I wanted in my life. And when I was assigned as surgical intern, I would get so excited—I—well—" He laughed a little. "It isn't glamorous —but I would get diarrhea. Bad. It would come on me—I'd be scrubbed, or ready to scrub. And there was an old nurse, well-meaning, sympathetic, who, one day, gave me a quarter-grain of morphine. After that, I would ask for it. It was not good, it was not a good thing to do—but it did let me stand for an hour, or two hours, it stopped the diarrhea, and let me handle the retractors. I was at the beginning of my surgical career, and I thought I had to do something. Then—I kept on doing it.

"When, during the war, while I was in Europe, my wife and child were killed—I couldn't handle that, either. And the habit became—a habit. I still must handle it."

Phoebe sat shaking her head from side to side. "But you're a wonderful doctor," she whispered.

"I am a good doctor, in that I do good, clean surgery. Yes. But I am not a strong man."

"Oh, you are! " Phoebe begged. "I have to believe you are!" She was weeping.

He waited, watching her. Then he said again, "Don't despair, Phoebe. There is no need for you to be so crushed. Your mother sent you away from her, let you go, so there is no danger of her habit enslaving you."

"Talley said," Phoebe spoke dully, "that was the best thing she ever did for me. He's a doctor at the Center who does research on drug addiction."

"He must know what he's talking about. It was a gift."

"Did you know . . . ?" Her head lifted.

"No. I thought she was a selfish woman. And she was, of course."

"Oh—"

"Perhaps she couldn't help herself. But don't let her tragedy overcome you. Your generation has learned to live with the atom bomb—and not supinely, either. You can live with this."

"I hope you are right," she told him. "Though I don't know how I can. I came here, you see, to get you to tell me what to do."

Dr. Sam smiled at her. "First," he said, "you must remember that an addiction to drugs is an illness, not a crime."

"Oh, but—"

"Yes, there must be regulations. We regulate smallpox by requiring vaccination of all school pupils. We try, by law, to confine the tuberculous. We use propaganda, talk. *You* can talk about this. First think, learn, and then talk instructively about your mother and about me. Learn and understand as much as you can about such an affliction."

"I still can't believe . . ." she said again. "How can you be a doctor and . . . Are your patients safe?"

"Oh, I hope so, Phoebe. I think so. I keep them always in mind. I did when I accepted the decision that I would be allowed to practice only under certain conditions. You know, in our state addiction is grounds for the revocation or the suspension of a doctor's license because of unprofessional and dishonorable conduct."

"But you're not dishonorable!" cried Phoebe with some heat.

"That is debatable. I put my appetite before the welfare of my patients, my dear. I also accepted the terms by which I was allowed to continue my practice. I can have no narcotics permit, and I can continue only so long as I myself abstain from the use of narcotics."

"Do you?"

"Yes. But it has not been easy."

"Then you are cured."

He smiled at her.

"I suppose," she said unhappily, almost impatiently, "this is what Talley would call adjusting to the community."

He considered the phrase. "Tell me about this Dr. Talley," he said.

So Phoebe did tell him. She talked with increasing animation.

"The man sounds good," said Dr. Green. "And *you* sound as if you might be ready to share your life with him."

She drew back, startled. 'Oh, no!" she cried. She hunted for an excuse. "I've been living alone for a long time," was the best one she could find. She would not mention her shame again to Dr. Green.

He accepted her excuse. "But," he protested, "you're too young. It's not good to live alone."

Phoebe smiled at him. She could, she thought, ask why Dr. Sam had never married again.

But he was asking her. "Why did you come to see me, Phoebe? Were you running away from things? Or did you really want my advice?"

She started to answer, then stopped to think.

"Did you perhaps come back with the thought of marrying Charles Reid?"

Phoebe flushed. "Chuck?" she asked. "Oh, no!" she said. "No!"

Dr. Green nodded. "Then here's the advice which you may or may not want. I would say for you to stay where you are. Live in your mother's home and try to learn to know her, to understand her and her problems. Not to decide she was right, or even to judge her. Just to know her. Second, you should stay where you are and share your daughters' lives there. Don't shut them out. How about this Talley? Do the girls like him?"

"Oh, yes," she cried. "And he—" She broke off. "We all like him," she continued primly.

Dr. Green chuckled. "Well, I'd say then for you to get to know him better, too. And that brings up perhaps my most important item of advice. Don't follow in your mother's footsteps. I am not talking about narcotics. I want you to make friendships wherever they are offered you. It is, I repeat, not good to live alone. What if you do get hurt?

255

Or are disappointed? Nobody's perfect. You are not. You have certain habits— You run the corner of a heavy sheet of paper, or a book page, under your thumbnail. You sit with one shoe sole across you other foot. It gets your stocking dirty. You—"

Phoebe put up her hand. "Oh, now, Dr. Sam!" she cried, laughing.

He nodded and laughed, too. "Just stay busy, Phoebe," he said kindly. "You'll be happy. Not every minute, perhaps, but even too much sunshine can cloy."

"Yes, I know. But—in the months I've been in the city— Did you know, Dr. Sam, about Gig?"

"That he was pushing drugs? No, I didn't. When the agents asked me, as his former employer, I had to say that I didn't know. He'd not been with us for several months, Phoebe. About the first of the year, we had to discharge him for stealing."

"Did *he* use drugs, Dr. Sam? He was selling them in the city."

"Yes. Pushing. And pushers seldom use the stuff."

"I felt to blame. I vouched for him in order for him to get a job. I thought I could trust him. But I've decided that I know nothing about human relationships. It does seem that *everyone* . . ."

"Now, Phoebe . . ."

"But, Dr. Sam . . ."

"Even if you were anywhere close to the truth, you should not lean so heavily on what may look to be statistics. Do you know about the little boy who passed several crippled peddlers on the street and then asked his mother why it was that selling pencils caused a man to lose his legs? You've just met up with the trouble of many statisticians. But look at your statistics, my girl. Count up. There was your mother. And this Jesse you told me about. Gig, as a pusher, perhaps fits in. And there's me. Now that seems a lot of people whose lives have touched yours. And it is a lot. But, remember, you work in a hospital. In hospitals people like you see a lot of illness. That accounts for your knowledge of Gig and me, and of Jesse. Your mother, however . . ."

"But," Phoebe cried, "even one is too many!"

"Of course it is too many. But suppose you turn your eyes to yourself and your position in this picture. You are in a spot where you can keep your list from growing."

Her head lifted, her eyes flared in question.

"Yes," he said. "There is yourself. And your girls. Who else do you know? Suppose you make that list. In fact, I insist that you make that list. Of anyone whose life touches yours. Neighbors, family—in that huge hospital complex, there must be two thousand patients, and many thousands of employees."

Phoebe nodded. Talley had said something like that at his hearing. She could remember the way he had said it, the way he had looked. Brightly alert, interested, sure of what he said. . . .

She looked up at Dr. Sam, her lips curved into a shy smile. "I have a family now," she told him. "Two uncles, an aunt—another uncle by marriage, and an aunt. Cousins.

They have their homes. We go to church together—the girls go to the same school as their cousin."

"And they have been kind to you," said Dr. Sam.

"Yes! They have. Even Uncle Doc. He isn't easy to know. Mother just despised him. But he— Next month, you know, Mary is to have surgery on her spine."

"Oh, good! Very, very good."

"Yes. I know it will help her. And—" A frown came back to her eyes. "You didn't know about Gig?"

"No," he said. "I suspect, through hindsight, that he started his traffic while here. I could beat him for using you."

"I have to add him to my list," said Phoebe. "And you, yourself. But, oh, I shouldn't question you. . . ."

"Yes, you should. It is exactly the sort of thing you should do."

"Well— Could you stop? Entirely, I mean? Get rid of the need or the want?"

"I have tried," he told her. He spoke gravely. "I have tried in every way. For years, my so-called vacations have been spent in the attempt. But this seems to be a thing with which I have to live. I have learned— It's quite a lot like having a crippled leg; a man must learn to stand on it and work—"

"But you're such a good doctor!" said Phoebe.

"I've done my job," he agreed. "I am sixty years old, Phoebe, and I have done the job there was for me to do." He stood up, and Phoebe rose. Dr. Sam took her hand and walked with her to the door.

"Keep busy, Phoebe," he told her. "And above all else, make yourself available as willing to help those who are trying to clean up this dreadful matter of drugs. This is a young world we have, and you have a choice seat in the grandstand. Your girls, and your experience with responsibility evasion, should let you do a lot in this field. I don't know what triggered your mother— Do you think your father knew?"

"I'm not sure. Something went wrong. Perhaps he suspected it and tried. . . . Uncle Cecil thinks she had a sense of guilt. About sex, you know. And if drugs silenced that—"

"Yes, perhaps. As a child, do you recall anything . . . ?"

"Yes. Looking back. Not then. Then I thought she was always sick, tired . . ."

"Yes," said Dr. Green sadly. "But again I urge you to remember that the most tragic thing about this use-of-drugs business is that the young people are the ones affected. Colleges offer some staggering statistics. But any young person, going for the first time to a party where marijuana is being smoked, may try one of the cigarettes just to be part of the crowd. One cigarette may do nothing but make a girl sick . . . and vow she will never smoke again."

Mary, thought Phoebe, chilled to her bones.

"If she sticks to that, fine. But—many do not. There are those fallacious arguments, you see, that marijuana, pot, hashish—whatever you call it—is not harmful. But it does cause addiction. And it does *not* make a musician play

259

better, nor a writer see things more clearly. He has doped his judgment as well as his blood stream. He is running away from himself, his sexual unfulfillment, his failure to be a topnotch person in almost any way. He buys, or is given, one of the little brown cylinders—marijuana is green and could not be mistaken for tobacco . . ."

Phoebe listened, sick at heart. She had seen—Jesse had dared to smoke those things in her home!

". . . his heart beats rapidly, his speech is hurried, he thinks he is being witty, he thinks he is full of bright ideas—but he can never quite explain the conclusion of those ideas. His eyes are dilated, he may twitch and acquire a puffiness under his eyes. He may fall into a dreamless sleep and awake without any physical or psychological effects. But—if he smokes more and more of the stuff—and he will increase the number to get the desired effect—if he smokes six to eight of the things a day, he is a habitual user. And for a young person to acquire such a habit— Oh, Phoebe, you work on this project! Hope and pray that your girls will work on it. I tremble to think what the next twenty years of middle age are going to be for our present hippies and far-out kids. We are letting a whole segment of our future be destroyed. Where will we find a replacement for that loss?"

He spoke so sincerely, was so truly distressed, that Phoebe knew a new distress of her own, another sort of shock. She could fairly see the gap in the ranks of young people growing to maturity, to what should be their productive years, and not able to—

"Why do they *do* that?" she cried. "Why should there *be* such a problem?"

"You could talk to your Dr. Talley. . . ."

"His name is Newbern. Dr. Talley Newbern. And I will talk to him. I'll offer to help, if I can. But—"

"If you'd ask the users, these college kids," said Dr. Green, "they would come up with excuses. Not reasons, of course. They would mention pressures, as I did. The competition to get into a good college, then into graduate school. The Vietnam situation. But we had the same thing in other wars without resorting to pot, or grass, or tea, or bhang, or boo . . ."

Phoebe laughed. "You know about it!" she cried.

"I know a lot about drugs, and habits, the whole thing," the big doctor admitted. "Our young people go off to college; they come home sick. I get to see them. I know the possibilities of the future. And I do what I can."

"Marijuana is widely advertised as not harmful."

"That's nonsense! Marijuana, in law, is equated with opiates, and should be, though the abuse characteristics of the two are not the same. Marijuana is not marked by physical dependence nor withdrawal symptoms. Pure marijuana. The danger lies in the adulteration of the stuff with hallucinative drugs—to increase the kicks, you see. And the next step—

"Of course the argument is that marijuana is not as dangerous as alcohol, and in itself it is not. Alcohol is legal, pot is not. But the matter of pot not causing physical dependence is immaterial. There are psychological factors which draw a man to the drug and precipitate a pattern of chronic compulsive abuse. There are those who insist that marijuana increases one's sharing in life. They also insist that addiction to it does not lead to addiction to the opiates."

"Does it?"

"Sometimes. Those same people argue against the legal restrictions against pot."

"It didn't work on alcohol," said Phoebe.

"No, it did not. Now! You go back to your young doctor—"

"And talk to him about drug addiction?" asked Phoebe, her eyes round.

Dr. Sam laughed. "Among other things," he said. "Among other things."

Phoebe nodded. "I hope they'll let me help in this matter," she said wistfully.

"They—" said Dr. Sam, grinning. "*He* will let you. In fact, I expect him to be glad to let you."

Phoebe shook her head. "Oh, I don't know . . ."

"You'll find out," said the doctor. "You'll find out."

FOURTEEN

Her interest aroused, Phoebe wanted to return immediately to the city, but she had the girls to consider. She went back to the motel, driving past her little house, which she would now sell. She knew she could trust and follow Dr. Sam's advice. And, really, it was what she wanted to do.

When the girls came in, she suggested inviting a couple of their friends to eat dinner with them; they could go to the movies afterward. . . .

It made for a long and lively evening. The next morning Phoebe took the girls to service at their old church, and afterward visited with the people whom she knew. But she would not go to any of the offered homes for dinner. "We have to start back to the city," she said. "The girls have studying to do."

263

"You would think of that," said Mary pertly.

"That's right," Phoebe agreed. "I would think of it."

By three that afternoon they reached their own street and house. The familiar stretch of lawn, shrubbery and trees welcomed Phoebe. Her lilac bush was in bloom, and the climbing rose at the corner of the garage was a mass of pink. She pulled a blossom free and held it to her nose as she walked back to the house and the side door. The perfume was musky, the petals like velvet.

"Talley's been here!" Linda called from the porch.

Phoebe's heart jumped. He'd come! He had not been disgusted about her mother! And if he had been? Well, Phoebe could have had nothing more to do with such a man. But—he had come!

Automatically, she said that the girls should call him Dr. Newbern. They made no comment to that.

"He brought a bottle of wine!" said Mary. "Look!" She held up a brown paper sack from which protruded—yes, it was wine.

"He left a note," Linda added. "He says the wine is for the peasant."

"For the . . . ?" Phoebe ran up the steps and took the note from the child. "It's *pheasant*, Linda!" she said, laughing. "But, my goodness, I'd forgotten all about it."

"You put it in the freezer," Mary reminded her. "Way last Christmas."

264

"Yes, I did," Phoebe agreed. "Maybe we should cook it now."

"In Talley's wine?"

"I'll see about that. Perhaps we should save that for him to drink." Talley had been here! He'd been here!

She went into the house, set the wine on the table, and urged the girls to take their things upstairs and unpack. Yes, she would have to do the same.

"His note said he would come back," Linda called from her room. "Why don't you cook the peasant?"

"All right," said Phoebe, suddenly happy. "I will. Who's going to help?"

They flew about. Phoebe brought the frozen pheasant. *He's coming back!* her heart sang. She brought up some pickled peaches to go with the bird, which was as stiff and as hard as a rock. She put it into a bowl of hot water. *He's coming back!* She didn't know when to expect Talley— but she would get everything ready so she could serve dinner an hour after his arrival.

Mary peeled potatoes, Linda set the table in the alcove off the sitting room, using good china and crystal, the sterling silver. "It's a party when Talley comes," she sang crooningly. Phoebe decided to give up the struggle to make the girls speak of him as "Dr. Newbern." She went out and cut lilacs and roses for a bowl in the middle of the table. *He's coming back. . . .*

Thawed at last, the bird was stuffed and trussed like a chicken and put into the oven.

"For dessert," said Mary, "we could have some of that

265

fruitcake from Christmas."

"We could!" agreed Phoebe. "There's hard sauce, too."

Linda made a face.

"But Talley will like it," Phoebe assured her.

"You have something yellow on your face," said Linda. "And you're not going to wear shorts, are you?"

Phoebe looked down at her Bermudas. "I suppose not," she agreed. "Not with flowers on the table."

Still singing her silent refrain—*He's coming, he's coming* —she ran upstairs and brushed her hair until it sparkled. She put on her yellow linen shift and white shoes.

From her bedroom window, she saw Talley coming down the street, and she ran down the stairs in time to open the door for him; her face was aglow with welcome.

He looked at her for a second. "You may kiss me now," she said gravely. His arms drew her close; he kissed her. She clung to him. He seemed so solid, so—good!

Behind her the girls made sounds of approval and stood grinning. Talley glanced at them, then he kissed Phoebe again. This time, said Linda, *really*.

Phoebe pulled free, confused, pink-cheeked, her eyes shy.

"We cooked the peasant," said Linda.

Dinner was a great success, with Talley insisting on "washing up" afterward. He made a big thing of donning an apron for this task and rolling up his sleeves. He had the girls in gales of laughter. "I trust they have studying to do later?" he asked Phoebe, in a lull.

"They do."

"Good!"

"I want to talk to you . . ."

"Oh, now, Phoebe . . ."

"Yes, I do."

"But out on that porch swing? In the dark?"

She blushed, but agreed. "Though I do want to talk," she insisted.

He sighed, but his eyes were smiling.

The washing-up was completed with a deal of talk, too. Linda announced that having a tall man was a great help in putting dishes on a high shelf.

"But we ate all the pheasant," said Mary. "There's none left over."

Phoebe laughed helplessly. "Will you two girls please go up now and study?" she asked. "And finish so you can go to bed on time? You have to be tired."

Talley stood with her to watch them go up the stairs, then he took Phoebe's hand and led her out to the swing on the porch.

"I do want to talk," she said again.

"We'll talk." He sat down beside her, put his right arm about her and drew her close to his side. He turned her face toward him, and he kissed her. She let him. It was a comfort and a joy to relax against his warmth and strength, to feel his cheek against hers, to hear his deep voice.

It was Talley who finally brought up the matter of the talking which she wanted to do.

"Oh, yes," she said, sitting erect. "I was told—I want to

know myself—more about your work, what you do, what you plan to do . . ."

"Who told you?" he asked. "Do you object to kissing a man who's been smoking?"

"I've already kissed you."

"There will be more . . ."

She shivered a little and laughed a little. "I went back to my home town yesterday," she said primly. "I went to see the doctor I used to work for, and your name came up."

"How was that?"

"Well, he said he thought you must know a lot about the drug problem, and he said that I was missing a great opportunity—considering Mary and Linda, you know—by not talking to you about the work you do. He thought I should even try to help you."

"My word!" said Dr. Newbern. "My name did come up!"

"Yes, it did. So—"

He laughed, hugged her shoulders, and said he supposed, put that way, he could do little else than talk. "What is it you want to know?"

"Well," said Phoebe, liking the smell of his pipe smoke. "You might start with telling me what—or something about—what you plan to do with your research and work at the Center."

He nodded and sat thinking for a long minute. Somewhere a radio or hi-fi was playing "Stardust." A small dog barked.

268

"In any drug-addiction project," he said, speaking slowly, "the primary purpose is to prevent if we can, cure if we can, and if we can't do either, to adjust the patient to the community, and the community— My work here is to force the community—this community, as a test—but eventually almost any community—to force *society* to accept an addict and not ostracize him. I believe that is most realistic and most important."

"Rehabilitation."

"Er—yes. But in a two-sided way. The addict himself, and the people about him. One must work to prevent, and to correct, addiction. But when we have an addict who must be handled, he should be able to work, to gain employment. He should be able to go to church and to have friends."

"That's what you are trying to do for Jesse," murmured Phoebe. "And I found out yesterday that my own dear Dr. Sam—this man I've worked for and fairly worshiped—also has used drugs. Morphine, he said."

"And this shocked you."

"Of course it shocked me!" She spoke tensely. "He told me about it when I told him how I felt about learning that my mother . . ."

"He wanted to show you that such facts have to be accepted, and lived with, before anything much can be done about the attending problems."

"Yes. I suppose that was what he was showing me. I still think it is awful. . . ."

"Any sickness can be awful, Phoebe. And tragic when

no effort is made toward correction, prevention, eradication. Crippled children and the insane used to be hidden, or worse. Now, we highly civilized people turn our backs in disgust upon the users of narcotics."

She nodded. Revulsion had been her first reaction toward her mother, when she knew. . . . "It seems very bad when a doctor . . ."

"I understand your feeling. And you are right. It goes against a doctor's primary oath and obligation to use narcotics, or alcohol, or engage in any indulgence or activity that would interfere with his steady hand, his skill, and judgment."

"Dr. Sam," murmured Phoebe. "And Jesse—"

"I'll say this about Jesse," said Talley quickly. "I am afraid he is a lost cause. The man does not want to be helped."

"But Dr. Sam—he is allowed to practice by promising not to use narcotics."

"Which is good. Which is what I mean about being allowed to function in the community."

"He says he still has the appetite—when he is tired. And I know he gets tired. I've known times when he seemed gray and stiff—" She sat sad for a minute. Then she said, "I asked him how others found out—the hospital or the medical society. And he said, 'I told them.'"

"Poor devil."

"Yes," said Phoebe. "And then there was my mother. . . ."

"Your uncle helped her. He gave her regular medica-

270

tions, substitute sedatives—he made her able to hold a position in a department store. And not be dependent upon her family."

"Yes, he did do that, but I wish he could have cured her."

"I didn't know her, of course, but her general disposition seemed to have been such that a compromise was the best which could be secured for her. Of course, at the end—"

"I don't want to think that she committed suicide!"

"Then don't think that. She could have forgotten and taken a second dose. Or perhaps she could have drunk some whiskey after taking her usual sleeping pill. Others have made that mistake."

Phoebe put her head against his shoulder and sighed. "She was a strange person," she said.

Talley's hand patted her arm comfortingly. "Psychologists," he said, "have attempted to identify the addict personality. I don't agree that there is any such clearly defined person. My experience tells me that the addict population includes a wide range of personality characteristics and runs the gamut of psychiatric diagnoses from the normal to the psychotic."

"But," said Phoebe, troubled, "you don't condone it?"

"No! We must fight it where we can. If only because of the terrible waste. . . ."

It was a waste. Phoebe could so testify. Her mother's companionship with her daughter, that daughter's need for a mother. And her son's, too, one could suppose. Those things sacrificed and lost.

"We don't condone cancer, either," Talley was saying. "Or diabetes. But until we can cure them, we must handle those things. We must handle the use of drugs. Prevent it if we can, and even someday cure it."

"Can those things ever be done?"

"I hope so. I think so. Though to date, medical treatment has had only dismal results. Relapse is so frequent that one must decide he deals with a chronic disease. Your only good approach is prevention, if elimination of the problem is to be achieved."

"Like smallpox," murmured Phoebe.

Talley lifted his head and turned to look at her in surprise. "Yes," he agreed. "Quite!"

"But what about those already addicted? You said . . ."

"Oh, yes. That would best be called social treatment. I endorse it fully. Our goal should be toward both social and medical rehabilitation, first of those who are not contributing citizens of the community—people like the junkies we get into the ward—and second the rehabilitation of those addicts who are already contributing citizens. People like your mother and your Dr. Sam."

Phoebe nodded. "What about the laws against . . . ?"

"Not at all," said Talley. "The multitude of laws now relating to addiction have done little, if anything, to decrease the number of addicts here in the United States. They do, however, increase the confusion as to whether addiction is a crime or a disease, and reinforce the public idea that addicts are violent, uncontrolled, and dangerous people."

"I don't want Jesse Holland giving my daughter his marijuana cigarettes!" said Phoebe tensely.

"No. Certainly not. There are those who argue that marijuana is not too bad. But it *is* psychologically addictive. That is where I come into the picture, and I must decide that if prevention is not possible, then we must control it and seek means of adjustment, both on the part of the user and the public."

"If you don't believe in legislation against the sale or use of narcotics . . ."

"I should like to think we could enforce such a law, Phoebe. But since we cannot, we should at least modify those laws and adjust the penalties. Your lawmakers are beginning to urge that sort of adjustment. As things are here, the users become criminals and, like criminals, they hide or seek to deceive. Of course, in England our open sale method doesn't seem to be working either. Not too well.

"And if we must have legislation, I should like to see the civil commitment of addicts, not waiting until they commit crimes. Now there is no federal law to force an addict to help himself. We await the crime and conviction. Then we treat about ten per cent, with a one per cent, at the best, cured."

"And you," said Phoebe, "work with the results of use rather than the legislation . . ."

He considered this. "I feel that drug addiction is a disease, and since I am a doctor, I do work with that disease. But I am a firm believer in preventive medicine. And as a psychiatrist, of course, I consider sources and reasons."

Phoebe put her hand on his. "I wish I had known you when you were training to be a doctor."

"Oh, my dear!"

"I would have liked you," she insisted.

"And I should have liked *you*," he told her. "But, then, the possibilities . . . See here! Haven't we had quite enough of your talk about my work? I'd like to make love to you and some plans for us. All right?"

"I promised Dr. Sam I would do something about this drug problem."

"And so you shall. I presume he meant in the realm of young people?"

"Yes, he did."

"What were you like when you were that sort of person, Phoebe? Mary looks somewhat like you."

"Yes, she does."

"You married young . . . Did you like being married?"

She considered his question. "Yes," she said. "I did like it. I was in love with David. But he's been dead for ten years. . . ."

"*I* love you, Phoebe," Talley said earnestly. "I love your wide eyes, your smile. I love your shyness, and your brave forthrightness." He bent to kiss her. "I love you," he said softly, his lips close to hers.

She let him kiss her and hold her. Once she lifted her head to look into his eyes. "Can I trust you, Talley?" she asked.

"Can I trust *you?*"

She nodded. "All right," she said. "It does take two."

"It takes a lot of us."

She sighed. "There will be a lot of us."

"There are now. Your family, and mine. Our daughters—" He could feel the way Phoebe trembled. "Our daughters," he said again. "And, in the kitchen, Linda said she hoped I would marry you so you could have some babies. It seems she likes babies."

"She does," said Phoebe, laughing, confused. "But I don't think she—"

"She didn't put any ideas into my head!"

"What about Mary?" Phoebe asked tartly. "Did *she* have some plans?"

"Oh, yes. She thinks we might open up and use the whole house."

Phoebe laughed helplessly. And Talley joined her. "We'll make it, Phoebe," he said confidently. "Do not be afraid of our future."

"I'm not afraid, but I can be terrified of the past."

"Yes. And I shall try to protect you from that terror."

Phoebe sat erect. "But *how?*" she asked. "I'll remember —and think . . . Then, there are the girls . . ."

His arms about her, he drew her close. "And there will be love," he said softly.

Sighing, she leaned against his shoulder.

He took her hand and put it between the buttons of his shirt. She trembled, feeling the warmth and the strong beat of his heart. "Always," he said. "I shall love you always, Phoebe. Please tell me that you believe me."

She turned and put up her two hands to draw his lips down to hers. "Always," she whispered against them. "Always."

Behind them, there was the rustle of bare feet on the stairs. Mary stood in the upper hall, her hands clasped in awe of her sister's daring. Their mother would be angry—

But Linda moved very, very quietly. She slipped one foot down, then the other—her shadow scarcely seemed to move. Through the window she could see the swing and Talley—and her mother—sometimes they were as one figure. Sometimes . . .

She turned, looked up at Mary, and beckoned, but Mary shook her head. Slowly, Linda went upstairs again.

"Things are going to be all right," she said. "They aren't even talking."